PRAISE FOR

SUZANNE STREMPEK SHEA

AND

LILY OF THE VALLEY

A *Boston Globe* Bestseller!

"[A] satisfying tale of dreams realized in peculiar ways. . . . Shea lovingly renders Lily's family and friends . . . with the same affectionate brush strokes she employs to describe her protagonist's beloved art. . . . Readers may well count themselves lucky to have gained vicarious admission to her colorful circle."

—*Publishers Weekly*

"When Lily Wilk reaches into the red velvet bag, I know I am happily, unmistakably back in Suzanne Strempek Shea country. I love this book and this place."

—Anthony Bukoski, author of *Polonaise*

"Engagingly told. . . . Lily Wilk will probably remind you of someone you know."

—*Times Union* (Albany, NY)

"Shea uses her rich palette to create this heartwarming portrait of Lily Wilk. . . . Filled with impeccable details of small-town life and characters you'd want living in your own neighborhood."

—Leslie Pietrzyk, author of *Pears on a Willow Tree*

"Full of energy and sweetness. . . . A fine, cozy read, the kind that's best appreciated lying on the lawn in summer or by the fire in winter. It makes you look at what's close to you with new eyes."

—*Booklist*

"A refreshingly heartwarming novel, upbeat and unsentimental . . . very funny. . . . Every paragraph is a delight."

—*The Plain Dealer* (Cleveland)

"Told with a freshness and real grace."

—*Kirkus Reviews*

"A charming and captivating writer . . . among the best of fiction writers today. Shea's blend of compassion and tenderness is a natural pleasure to appreciate on the page, and her stories humbly remind us of our own capacity for joy."

—*MetroWest Daily News* (Greater Boston area)

HOOPI SHOOPI DONNA

"Deeply satisfying . . . a bittersweet tale of dreams deferred but not discarded."

—*The Philadelphia Inquirer*

"[A] sometimes rollicking, sometimes heartbreaking, effectively quirky read."

—*Kirkus Reviews*

"A wry, beautifully rendered novel that is touching but never sentimental, a generous-spirited story of the terrible fragility and ultimate redemption of family love."

—New York *Newsday*

"Donna is a Polish-American Dorothy, whose journey to Oz ends when she also realizes there's no place like home."

—*Sunday Republican* (Springfield, MA)

"Shea's voice, channeled through Donna, is simply a delight. . . . Sarcastically funny and poetically moving. . . ."

—*Pittsburgh Post-Gazette*

SELLING THE LITE OF HEAVEN

"Wonderful . . . I can't imagine a single reader who will be disappointed. . . . *Selling the Lite of Heaven* is a charmer."
—*The Washington Post Book World*

"An impressive fiction debut . . . warm, funny, engaging. . . . The magic is that you really get to know—and identify with—the main character and her small world, which—in Shea's capable hands—seems rich and wonderful."
—*The Providence Sunday Journal*

"The author's affection for what are clearly her own roots breaks like winter sun through the deadpan gloom, giving the story its undeniable offbeat charm."
—*Boston Sunday Globe*

"Shea's wry yet warm rendering of a community where strong mothers rule and meek daughters find creative ways to rebel is satisfying on many levels."
—*Glamour*

"Suzanne Strempek Shea masterfully examines the timeless mystery of the heart: What is this thing called love? . . . *Selling the Lite of Heaven* offer[s] us priceless wisdom at unexpected moments."
—*Milwaukee Journal*

"Entertaining, discerning, and witty, *Selling the Lite of Heaven* is a delicious book crowded with the stuff of living and with the trials and triumphs of humanity."
—*Daily Press* (Newport News, VA)

"Shea's comic odyssey, a fairy tale for grown-ups, is . . . overflowing with charm. . . . Irresistible."
—*The Patriot-News* (Harrisburg, PA)

Also by Suzanne Strempek Shea

Hoopi Shoopi Donna
Selling the Lite of Heaven

Published by POCKET BOOKS
and WASHINGTON SQUARE PRESS

LILY OF THE VALLEY

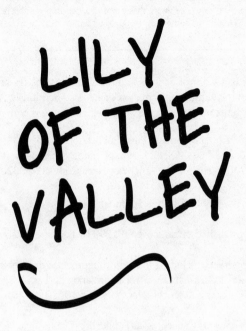

A Novel

Suzanne Strempek Shea

WASHINGTON SQUARE PRESS
PUBLISHED BY POCKET BOOKS

New York   London   Toronto   Sydney   Singapore

A Washington Square Press Publication of
POCKET BOOKS, a division of Simon & Schuster, Inc.
1230 Avenue of the Americas, Nerw York, NY 10020

Copyright © 1999 by Suzanne Strempek Shea

Originally published in hardcover in 1999 by Pocket Books

All rights reserved, including the right to reproduce this book or portions thereof in any form whatsoever. For information address Pocket Books, 1230 Avenue of the Americas, New York, NY 10020

Library of Congress Cataloging-in-Publication Data

Shea, Suzanne Strempek
    Lily of the valley / Suzanne Strempek Shea.
        p. cm.
    ISBN: 0-671-02711-5
    I. Title.
    PS3569.H39126L55   1999
    813'.54—dc21   99-25768
                                             CIP

First Washington Square Press trade paperback printing September 2000

10 9 8 7 6 5 4 3 2 1

WASHINGTON SQUARE PRESS and colophon are registered trademarks of Simon & Schuster, Inc.

Front cover illustration by Nina Berkson

Printed in the U.S.A.

This is for my first art teacher, my mother,
Julia (Milewski) Strempek.

And for those in whose classrooms and studios I learned more
about how to see: The Rev. Charles Jan DiMascola, Scott
Campbell, Tom Hawkins, David Hawkins, John Eide, and the late
Allan Gardiner.

While writing this book, I was fortunate enough to spend time in the company of writers and artists who make full use of the creativity with which they were blessed. I thank Tommy Shea, Elinor Lipman, Tanya Barrientos, Susan Tilton Pecora and The Saw Doctors for fueling me with their joyously wrought words, pictures and music.

I also am grateful for the help from my agent, John Talbot; my editor, Greer Kessel Hendricks; Pocket Books; St. Therese; and my readers.

1

The night of the day I turned ten, we all got to go out to supper at a place that printed a quarter page of half-off coupons every other month in the weekly paper and invited kids to step on this big carnival scale before they ate, then again after they were done, and the only thing their parents would be charged was one dollar if any amount of weight gain over a pound was registered.

Once I finished what I could of the Southern fried chicken, the French fries, cole slaw and decorative sprig of parsley, and after I blew out the white twig of a candle jabbed into the thick-skinned Boston cream pie slice, the waitress held out a red velvet grab bag brought out only for special occasions like mine.

I stuck my right hand in and felt my way around the obvious: the butterfly net, the hairbrush, the alleys in their net sack, some kind of floppy stuffed animal staring through the dark with bulging glass eyes. I considered the plastic hammer, the rolled-up paper kite, the doll's rough yarn braids, and what was either a magnifying glass or a hand mirror. I spent a whole lot more time rifling through that bag than I think anybody expected me to. But that was because nothing in there really caught my great interest.

Until I came to the box.

Slowly, I ran my fingers along its edges and determined that it was not very large. When I gave it a shake, I found it to be not that heavy. But it was a box, and boxes hold the promise of containing many pieces that might connect together to make one big fantastic surprise. Greedy, I pushed aside the coiled-up Chinese jump rope, got tangled in the strap of the tiny binoculars, scraped a knuckle on the lucky horseshoe, then pulled out the unknown.

On the way home I studied the parchment-colored carton in the quick few seconds of light spared by each streetlamp we passed under. I placed my right hand over the delicate one that was sketched to decorate the lid, and I mimicked those fingers that so gracefully held a pencil over a sheet of paper blank except for all your imaginings. I was the first one out of the car, the first one at the door, and the first one inside the house. I ran straight to the kitchen table, yanked on the light string, pulled the cover off the box, and examined the contents: a black fat-leaded pencil already sharpened to a perfect point, a cold and golden metal sharpener for when it wore down, a rectangle of pink rubber eraser, a slim pad of smooth newsprint, and a small white sheet of paper with the title "Instructions."

"Take the pencil in hand," the first sentence told me, "and draw a line."

I took the pencil in hand. I drew a line.

"Draw a circle."

I drew a circle.

"Draw a square."

I drew a square.

"Have you completed all these commands correctly?" the page asked, and it offered a picture of each thing, just in case I needed a reminder of what they were supposed to look like.

I studied my line. I studied my circle. I studied my square.

All appeared to me to be as good as what I saw printed next to the directions, though maybe not as sharp and bold and exact—but I hadn't used a ruler or a compass or anything, so what would you expect?

"Are they just as they appear in the illustrations?"

I checked again. I had done what I was supposed to.

"Then we wish you sincere congratulations!" the words told me. "Now you are an artist."

And from that day, that hour, that minute, that second, with the kitchen light swinging overhead and me still standing at the table in coat and dripping boots, big green mitten forgotten on my left hand, new pencil sharp and ready in my right one, I deep down truly have never thought of myself as anything but.

That is it, the longest and the most detailed version of the reply I give people when they ask me when and why and how I got started in all this. I am out in the world doing my work when the most curious ones stop to peek over my shoulder. They might stare at the placement of my hand, at the wrap of my fingers, at the movements of my brush or my pencil, at what any one of those might be leaving in its wake, while I give them the long or short of it, whatever I feel like relating that particular day. Sometimes our eyes never really meet, and those times, even if you offered me money, I couldn't tell you what these people looked like. I am busy and I have a job to do, and I answer as I continue to make a line or mix a color, my words the soundtrack to the things I am making out of nothing right before their eyes.

I hear them breathing. I feel them inches from me. At some point I realize they are gone—usually right after they say something like how they wish they had some talent. Right after they tell me they couldn't do what I am doing. And just before there is a chance for me to ask them what is it that they are able to do. I'm not just saying I would—if time allowed, I truly would like to find out. Because everybody can do something. It's just that most people don't have that something come right out and tell them what it is, as was the case with me. They might have to fish around a bit. Sometimes it even takes years. Or a whole life.

As for me, life so far has consisted of thirty-nine years. And for twenty-nine of them, I have joined together line and circle and square and have made for you whatever you have wanted. Because I am an artist. That is what the instructions told me. That is the title under the lily of the valley flowers that so fittingly frame the name *Lily Wilk* on the pale green business cards I hand out from the zippered compartment of my pocketbook. It is what that same card, enlarged fifty percent, tells readers who spot the ad I run every other week in the *Pennysaver,* inviting all to contact me for their artistic needs. It is what my friends and relations tell everybody I am. It is what I tell myself, silently in my head, when somebody who sees the ad calls to say it doesn't matter what I paint for them. Just make sure it includes a lighthouse, and that it fits this frame they got on sale, and that the color of whatever I end up with comes as close as possible to matching their wall-to-wall.

I must remind myself of my true occupation when somebody requests a caricature of every kid who'll be at their own kid's birthday party, and I spend an eternity of an afternoon fending off a pointy-hatted shrieking mob of sugar-fueled brats who knock into me and steal my pens and throw up on my drawing board. Or when I am asked to fit on one single glass door the neat capital letters that will spell out how this particular place of business is the best, the newest, the oldest, the biggest, the cheapest, the tastiest, the fastest, the one that can make and deliver your custom order within twenty-four hours. Sundays included.

No, my work is not in any museums. And as for galleries, I don't know if you'd think this counts, but for years I've been bringing paintings down to Mrs. Sloat at the post office, and she so kindly displays them prominently. A couple times a year, somebody falls in love and buys something like Lis' Cafe and its glass-brick front all glowing and ready for twin lobster night. Then I bring down another piece to hang in its place, on the nail pounded into the wall above the stamp-licking table, next to the recyclable-paper bin and the clipboard displaying the Ten Most Wanted.

If I am asked, I tell people I've exhibited widely. But I don't get into the specifics of how that mostly has been at the occasional amateurish local festival, where I must cautiously stand guard as people slosh their beer and point with greasy fried dough at the small display of the paintings I really want to make, and sometimes manage to pull off in my rare spare time. Local subjects: The egg carton factory billowing steam at first light. The dark huddle of buildings that is Main Street. Men, old and young, hunched playing their cards down at the AmVets. A woman reaching to hang her wash while the wind whips the linens around her like a fancy gown. The smoking remains of the vacant mill the day after the sad juvenile delinquents lit a fire in it to keep warm, and then fell asleep until they heard the sirens. Real things I've seen and have felt honored or touched to spot and take in through my eyes, out to my hand, and onto paper the way maybe only I, out of everyone in the entire world, see them. Not all greeting-card pretty, but why do things have to be neat and perfect to earn a place on your wall? Once in a while somebody at one of these festivals agrees with that. And before walking away empty-handed, they'll go on for a bit how that one over there's the painting they'd get if they ever found themselves rich enough to blow good money on junk like art.

Unlike my fellow vendors, who do a brisk business in lace hair accessories or wooden garden ornaments painted to look like the rear view of a wide person bending over, I am rarely able to earn back the rent of my twenty-five or fifty-dollar space. My particular take on beauty has not turned out to be what people want from me and has never gone far in paying for my rent, utilities, health insurance, car, food and sundries. What does bring in the money is something with a function, a purpose, a tangible usefulness that justifies the cost. If I'm going to paint, people want me to do so on simple wooden rectangles that will read "Welcome," "Come Back Soon," "Keep Out" or "Police Take Notice." On bone-shaped signs for dog-houses that shelter Neptune or Itchy or Gus, or just plain old Dog. On boulders at town lines, where a community's official seal looks so, well, official. They want "Detroit Debris" scrolled across tailgates. Circa-whatever on the fronts of homes so old that the vintage deserves to be announced to all. Once, and only once, I was asked to tell the story of a couple's meeting, courtship, engagement and impending marriage, all illustrated on the ten fake nails of the ten lumpy fingers of the one anxious bride-to-be who shook so much the night before the big day that I had to wait until she passed out from her sixth rum and Coke so I could finish the flat left thumb that held the critical scene from the love story: her groom-to-be and his then-soon-to-be-ex signing their divorce papers.

I had a different life envisioned for myself back at age ten, when I grabbed every spare stretch of paper and practiced careful rows and rows of the lines, circles and squares that I saw as the bones of all the landscapes and still lifes and portraits and other masterpieces I surely would go on to create. Fields of them stretching toward the great horizon that was my mysterious destiny, one big rainbow arc of pictures adorned with fancy medals and ribbons, all being admired by people in berets and bow-tied smocks who couldn't help but swoon and gasp in foreign accents as they walked past my easel, where I, the artist, stood with palette and brush and pencil and golden sharpener, and strung together line and circle and square to make the world as no one before had ever viewed it.

Someday, I for years have told myself silently in my head, I will make something that people everywhere will stand in line for hours just to look at and study and be struck by. Then, satisfied beyond belief, they will travel all the way home in stunned silence, reflecting how they have been changed in some vital way by the sight of a thing made by my own right hand.

I have yet to get around to creating that particular piece, and if I have to give you an excuse, the one I offer is that I, for years, have been busy from morning to night—even if it has been on jobs far from what I really want to do. Whatever you want—that has been my mission ever since I turned ten and Valentine's Day was approaching and somebody in the Ladies' Guild complained about the high cost of paper tablecloths with hearts printed on them, as opposed to plain white ones with no such seasonal embellishment. And my mother piped up, "Why don't you go buy the white ones, and why don't I have my daughter decorate them for you—she does things like that for me all the time. She's an artist." So that's what I did, and that's what I am. An artist. Somewhere along the way, though, quotation marks sprouted up on either side of the word.

I always used to say I'm glad not to be as bad off as the many people I know who hate what they do for a living. Like

Billy Doyle, who, back when I was his girlfriend and he started his first real job right out of high school, loathed it so much that he asked me to paint on a big dartboard a picture of the frozen-food warehouse where he would be wearing long johns all seasons of the year, struggling to list inventory with a pencil held in a shaking insulated glove. Or like that woman, Helena, down my street, who drives very slowly to and really fast from her day at the mascara wand factory, her sky blue Plymouth Horizon zooming dangerously through the curvy underpass in Cheneyville each weekday afternoon just after three, that homemade voodoo doll of her lecherous shift supervisor swinging wildly from a small noose tied to her rearview mirror. I'm nowhere near as flattened by my work as they were and are, but I have arrived at understanding some of how it feels to be giving so much of your life and time to what you believe you maybe were not put here to do.

Like how I maybe was not put here to stand on an over-sized potty chair and dodge the dangling row of fake legs being shown off in the sunny window of the surgical supply store on Main Street in Ludlow. But that was me all this morning, stepping around empty oxygen tanks so I could apply the finishing touches to the words "ANNUAL HALF OFF ALMOST EVERY-THING SALE" I'd painted big and backwards across the inside of the glass, each of the letters being snipped in two by a large, steely pair of scissors. Maybe I was not put here to carefully paint the words "Adam" and "Eve" onto the respective restroom doors down at the Parish Center. But that was me at lunchtime, underlining each name with a branch of fig leaves and, finally, adding accents of tiny and irresistible apples. Maybe I was not put here to apply one final coat of Industrial Red #6 to the fire hydrant down near the French school. But that was me just around supper, all because I once again said yes when Frannie from the highway department called and asked me if I, once again, was interested in taking that on.

"Hey, Picasso!"

Somebody yelled this from a car roaring past. I didn't look up. Over the years hundreds of comments have been hurled at me from passersby, so I'm used to it. Usually they are alerting me that I missed a spot. Usually I ignore them, just like I did right then.

"Just tell 'em to shove it."

An older woman in a pale pink windbreaker shouted this from behind me as she raked her front yard with choppy but efficient strokes that left the grass looking like a well-combed head of hair. "They'll be selling postcards of that plug once you get your big break."

"Right—sure—that'll happen someday," I told her.

I heard only more bits of raking; then the woman yelled back:

"Someday's today."

I finished my favorite part of the project, the last link on the silver chain that minds the hydrant's cap once it gets unscrewed in a hurry during a fire. Then I turned to wave away her joke. But when we met eyes, her expression was nothing but totally serious.

I knew maybe four things about this woman: That her first name was Lorraine, which had been written on the badge she used to wear on her blue-and-yellow smock when she worked in the Fotomat booth back when we had one in town. That Chunglo was her last name, the one spelled out in bronze reflective letters on her black plastic mailbox. That she owned all the know-how and equipment to decorate elaborate cakes for your most special occasions. That once a year she was invited to be guest speaker at one of the Brown Bag Lunch meetings out at the old academy in Brimfield, and the following Thursday the paper always ran a couple photos of her demonstrating how you can doll up even the cheapest box mix by squeezing out a gorgeous and edible bouquet of the most exotic frosting flowers.

But there apparently was more to learn about Lorraine Chunglo:

Like that she was a psychic.

She had to be. How else could she have had any idea that this actually was a big someday for me? How, because of a phone call I placed that morning, the next day I would have an appointment at New Directions, where for one full-hour session I would speak in person with the career counselor who, for many years, has run an ad two spaces to the left of mine, just past the one for the dry ice company and right up against the stump-grinding service.

"Together, we will find your true path," reads the line beneath a drawing of a compass and the digits of the big black phone number I'd finally dialed.

"You're good," I said, turning again to compliment Lorraine Chunglo. But she must have gone inside her house.

Probably to laugh at me. Because the someday she had referred to was an entirely different one—this I realized only after I unlocked my back door that late afternoon and heard my answering machine capturing the words "Mary Ziemba calling."

The voice was continuing: "I'll spell that for you . . ."

It had to be a joke, somebody with nothing better to do putting me on. But just in case it wasn't, I jumped at the phone. Whoever was providing them, I didn't need the letters. Around my town, Mary Ziemba's name was as well known as God's.

She was one real bigshot—the owner of the Grand Z chain

of grocery stores that almost exclusively fed our half of the state. You either bought your food there, or you grew your own, or you starved. And it was people's natural need for food, combined with the lack of any real grocery competitors since the death of Food Basket, that long ago had made Grand Z a household word and Mary Ziemba the richest local woman anybody could think of. Her business story was legend, and shoppers entering each of the eleven Grand Zs were greeted by a wall-sized photo of her as a young, skinny immigrant in a long, dumpy dress, sleeves rolled up to reveal the surprising Popeye forearms with which she, all by herself, long ago pushed around town a cart of her homegrown vegetables.

That town was mine. It was where Mary Ziemba first had settled, it was where she since had lived, and it was where she had retired a few years ago, on top of a pine-treed hill edging the valley that, thanks to her great and unbridled generosity, for ages to come would echo her surname. Everybody around here was born in the hospital's Ziemba Wing. Everybody borrowed their reading materials from the Ziemba Public Library or its roving bookmobile. Everybody learned to swim in the tepid little lake at Ziemba Park. The most selfless among us were named Ziemba Volunteers of the Year and got fine cash awards and the chance to be first in the buffet line at an annual recognition breakfast. The hungriest among us grew up strong and healthy on free groceries from the Grand Z Food for All program, founded decades before handing out dented canned goods was something rock stars did for photo opportunities. The neediest among us vied for the Ziemba Grants that propelled winners free of charge through four entire years at the colleges of their choice. The most directionless of all of us learned marketable skills in the fancy carpeted Ziemba Pre-Release Center up at the new jail. When we were kids pestering my mother for some money to go downstreet, she'd complain, "Hey—who do you think I am? Mary Ziemba?" And we'd all crack up at the thought of something that would have been so wonderful, but that unfortunately was not true.

And I haven't even gotten around to the most important fact about Mary Ziemba: She had a thing for art. At least for art made by people that most other people have heard of. I was back in high school when I clipped and saved a newspaper story about her small and cautious but enviable collection of American artists, and it always had thrilled me to know that within only a few miles of my own door hung a Cassatt, a Homer, two works by the first two Wyeths, and, side by side in what the story described as "a reverent alcove," a Stieglitz and an O'Keeffe.

"Yes?" I managed that much into the telephone. "Hello?"

"Hi, this . . ."

"Yes, I heard you; I just came in." I said that every time I picked up on somebody I decided I wanted to talk with after all, but this time it was the truth. To underline that, I added, "I really did."

"Well then, I'm glad I caught you," Mary Ziemba said in a voice that, well, actually could have belonged to any regular person. "You know, I wanted to tell you I've admired your work for a long time."

How could I have known that? What had she seen? I lowered myself onto the arm of the wing chair next to the telephone table. "Really?" I asked this too quickly, I knew. "I mean, thank you."

"No—thank you," she said firmly, putting the emphasis on me. "I've been meaning to speak to you for a while. Now here I am."

Neither of us said anything for a moment, and both of us

could hear the ticking of one big clock somewhere on her end of the line. It was the same sound I figured the Cassatt could hear, and I felt closer to greatness just listening. Then came the big interruption, of that moment, and of my life as it had been rolling along less eventful with each passing year:

"I need you to make me a painting," Mary Ziemba said to me. "I'd like it to be a watercolor. I need it completed by Christmastime. When there will be an exhibition. You may name the fair price."

If I had to take all my thoughts right then and line them up in order of how they rushed onto the big movie screen of my brain, I'd have to be honest and say my first was the image of that Grand Z turning into one Grand S with two big lines running down the middle of it. One enormous dollar sign that could dwarf an entire Grand Z store and parking lot put together. Electrified and visible for hundreds of thousands of miles around. People up in Canada would be able to look down and see it. People in Mexico even. Astronauts orbiting. All would remark, in their respective tongues, how truly fantastic it was that I finally was getting the big break that each and every one of us deserves at some point in our individual lives.

The things the money would make possible were the next to flash. There were obvious benefits, the biggest being the overflowing bank account and the many people I regularly owed being flabbergasted that I was paying my bills without having to be sent another one of those pink warning notices. Then came the parade of splurges, led by an entire rainbow set of egg tempera and some of that watercolor paper I recently had read about an order of silent monks in the Berkshires pressing by hand and selling only one month out of the year.

Then arrived the staggering reality, that I could purchase myself something even better than anything I could ever carry off in my hands. And that was time.

Finally. The time to do nothing but draw and paint the things that I alone wanted to draw and paint. Without a single worry as to would they ever sell or was I just wasting my time. The great desire of anybody who correctly or incorrectly calls themselves an artist: to make something just for the pleasure and the challenge and the heartache of the experience. The idea that this could happen to me made me slide from the arm of my chair to the actual seat.

Then everything suddenly blew away like somebody had opened a window in March, and before me I could see the exhibit. My exhibit. My very own personal one. Of this painting, and nothing else. People in their finery, good wine in two colors and real glasses, strange little snacks on crackers being passed around by waiters in tuxedos who offered helpful descriptions of the ingredients that made up what you were about to eat. Everybody from everywhere coming there to view what I had done, all of them saying they had never seen the beat of it. They would stand in line for hours just to look and study and be struck by my painting, and then would travel all the way home in stunned silence, reflecting how they had been changed in some vital way by the sight of a thing made by my own right hand.

There was one last thought before I got sucked back into reality, and there was no avoiding it: the fact that Jack, if he ever got wind of this, would not be amazed at all. For everything he had lacked as a perfect husband for me, nobody I knew ever came close to topping him in the cheerleading department, in his great and unwavering faith in what I could do with my talent.

He was the one who, even back in high school, always

thought my time would come. I might have to wait a while, he'd say, but one day, because of what I was able to do, things were going to happen that would send my head spinning.

"You are a treasure," is how Jack put it, and he ended every card and note to me with those words. Even from the first one when we were fourteen and my acrylic of a single, stark white eggplant beat out his Dali rip-off melting watch for first place in the freshman art show. Even down to the last thing he wrote me five months and four days before Mary Ziemba's phone call, when I was spending a gorgeous April day painting a seven-foot-long banana split onto the side of Rondeau's Dairy Bar. While Jack was back in our apartment packing all that belonged to him and Little Ted for his big middle-of-the-day coward-sneak back to the first wife he still loved after four and a half years of supposedly feeling that way about me.

"I am nothing," he printed neatly and correctly on the back of an oil bill we'd yet to scrounge up the money for and that, just before I finally did go downstreet to pay, I had to coat on the back with white paint just so Hedda behind the counter wouldn't be able to make out the message. I painted over those three words, just as I painted over the five in the line he added before signing his name: "But you are a treasure."

Now, it appeared, somebody finally had come to dig me up. And for the first time in the five months and four days since Jack ran off, I not only had a genuine full-sentence thought about him, but it actually had nothing to do with wishing him harm. The night was getting stranger by the minute.

There was no big clock in my house to fill up the background as Mary Ziemba awaited my reply. In my home now, there is only me. And, until I put on the radio or TV or I have somebody visit or I make some kind of clatter myself, there is only silence. But right then, faint but getting stronger by the second, came the slow and steady sound of something big and important steaming my way.

When you've never heard the sound of something, you can imagine that it's anything you want it to be. And that's what I did right there—I thought I knew that this was the sound of what was going to happen—that with this one painting I was going to make my mark. That I finally would be doing for a living what I was supposed to. But, unlike Lorraine Chunglo, I know as much about the future as most of the rest of us do—which, I many times have lamented, is absolutely nothing. So I stopped the predictions right there to give my answer, before Mary Ziemba, or I, had any chance for second thoughts.

I said this to her:

"I can make for you whatever you want."

2

My mother wanted to see Jesus in the kitchen.

"I have nothing to pray to while I do the dishes," she had complained soon after my abilities were revealed. "A nice religious drawing, to hang over the sink—could you do that? Please? I would even go out and buy a real picture frame with glass."

"I'd like a painting of Ma," my father whispered to me one night soon after my mother's request. "I'll hang it across from the bed, so she'll be the very first thing I see when I open my eyes."

Jesus I could understand, as he doesn't show up in person that often. But my father's order I found weird because why couldn't he just flip over to his left and get a good, long look at the real thing? I didn't argue, though. I just made them what they wanted.

I watercolored Jesus at a homemade kitchen table, fork in hand, reading a stone tablet by the light of his halo while enjoying a heaping plate of fish that he probably, earlier on, had multiplied from just one. In the background, Blessed Virgin Mary washed the dishes in a sink carved out of the rock wall. Through the window, you could see Saint Joseph doing yard work after a long day in the carpentry shop, like my own father did after he came home from his eight hours of maintenance at the bowling alley. Lawn mowers hadn't been invented yet, so I had Saint Joseph chopping at the grass with a big machete. It was an ancient version of a scene inside and out of my own kitchen, except that we had modern conveniences and up-to-date clothing and, as good and nice as we might try to be on even our best days, none of us ever would come close to being anything like the three people in my painting.

As for the portrait of my mother, I worked at it long and hard, never satisfied with the looks of my efforts—her round head floating there in the middle of the sheet of paper like the big yellow-and-blue hot-air balloon the guy from Brimfield sails slowly and quietly over our hill every once in a while when the wind takes him that way and he has no other choice but to sit and enjoy the ride. I gave my mother the short neck she always has had. I gave her a circle of pearls that she has yet to possess. And I gave her the lacy collar of a fancy evening dress she could only dream of, and even if she did dream that and that dream did come true, she'd be at a loss for a place to wear it. But even with all that stuff, and even with the same odd smile we all knew—left corner of her mouth abruptly up, right corner straight out to the side like she was always unsuccessfully holding back a grin—she looked unhappy. Unnatural. Strange. And then it hit me, one morning in school, as I was walking the aisles of our classroom for my turn at collecting spare change for the faraway missions. My classroom used a Quaker Oats container for this, and I watched the coins drop in, the one Lincoln head joined by a Jefferson, another Lincoln, a Roosevelt, then, from David Midura, who always carried around more money than any kid I knew, the paper face of some president I didn't recognize because what did I know about big bills? The money circled. And I suddenly saw my mother as the quarter, and the rest of my family as the pennies and dimes and nickels falling into our places at the edges of her. That was it—that was the problem. My mother was not herself without the rest of us near her. I couldn't show her without showing everybody who made her the person I knew her to be. It nearly killed me to endure the rest of the day before school ended and the bus dropped us off and I ran straight up to my room and started drawing the answer, the essential wreath of people—my father's head to the right of my mother's, Louise's and Chuckie's above. Mine down below, and, to the right of me and just beneath the knot of my father's abbreviated tie, I drew our house, as genuine a member of the family as I knew there to be.

To capture it, I sat across the street and looked at it there in front of me: the butter-colored square with a triangle on top of it, a rectangle of green grass below, circular trees to the sides and pointing high above, and over everything, a broad sky the color of the purplish-slatey dress Louise had worn the year before in her class photo, the only day of the year except for field day at Mountain Park that we were allowed to come to school wearing anything other than our uniforms. I studied the shade of the light blue edging around the windows that my parents had dreamed up and had specially mixed and shaken in the big, noisy paint machine down at Chudy's. I looked at the filmy white sheers in the first-floor windows—dining room ones on the left, living room ones at the right. My eyes ran up to the half-drawn shade in my parent's bedroom, second floor left, and then, to the baseball-cracked pane in the front window of the room that Chuckie would have all to himself forever, except if God ever gave us another boy, which I had the feeling would have happened by then if it were ever going to. My eyes went up to the witch's hat point of the roof and the tiny circular attic window that on hot days my mother pushed open for ventilation. I followed the peculiar angle of the crooked chimney that grew from the middle of the roof and leaned toward the woods. Next to it, the antenna, a simple metal T-shape that Unc had found tossed out at the dump—still in the box and with all the screws and bolts and flat brown wires and booklet of directions for installation, if you can believe such good fortune—was the finishing touch.

I went on to liven up the rest of us. Hair in our pretty much matching shades of nothing-special brown, eyes all hazelish except for Chuckie's gray ones. The skin pale on our oblong faces. As much clothing as I could fit at the bottom of necks to give the hint that we were proper and wearing something. And there we were in my portrait, the circle of the five of us Wilks and our house—the who we were and the where you could find us, if you ever had the need to come looking. But you didn't have to bother about coming by—here we had all the people we needed. When he awoke, my father would see a portrait not only of my mother but also the rest of us. If he ever complained that this was not what he had ordered, I would have to say that, as the artist, and as one of the people in this family, it was my opinion this is the way it had to be.

Turned out there was no grumbling. Both my parents were thrilled when I showed them the two paintings I had done, and they ushered us all into the car and drove right over to Grant's that evening for the proper-sized frames. At home, my mother got out the Windex to clean the sheets of glass before she set the paintings inside to be sealed in by a gray flat of cardboard and a series of little pins that had to be bent back into place with a screwdriver.

Even though he said he was taking a chance on causing one

big crack in the wall above the sink, my father nonetheless bravely banged a nail into the yellow-painted space. Tiny little chips of plaster fell and sprinkled the red plastic drainboard. My father ran a dishrag across to clean up the mess and gave my mother the honor of hanging up Jesus. She did that, then she took a step back and blessed herself and said, "Now there is nothing else in the world that I want." She pulled me close and directed me to her side so we could both stand and watch Our Lord eat his fish on just one of the regular and probably mostly boring kind of days all of us know and that he had to have lived through, even though mention of them never made it into any Bible I ever read.

Next, we all trooped up to my parents' room, where my father pulled my mother's sewing machine away from the wall so he could climb up on its bench and hit another nail, this one dead in the center of one of the many hibiscus blossoms that crawled up the skinny trellises spaced every foot or so. That wallpaper had been hanging there forever, maybe longer, having been pasted up by the people who built the house and lived in it for ages before my parents saved enough to come along and make it theirs. It had to be a good half century that those same coral blossoms were up there showing off in their prime, and now they all surrounded us as my father set the portrait of my mother in its place across from his side of the bed. And there we were, my mother, my father to her right, Louise and Chuckie above, me down below, the neat part in my hair just about touching the pearls that hung around my mother's neck, my father's tie stopping short of the crooked chimney below which we all lived back in that time when the five of us translated to the two-letter word "us."

• • •

The drawing is now mine. Given to me by my parents when I was twenty-one and moving into my own place. Handed to me wrapped in holly-covered Christmas paper even though it was June. Because that's all my mother could get her hands on with the short notice given by my father, who took her aside and whispered that as much as he loved looking these many years now at all of us first thing in the morning and the last thing after he said his prayers, he thought it would be a good and nice thing for me to take along to my own home.

"To remind you of who you have," is the way he put it just before they all left at the end of that long Saturday of helping me get settled. "To remind you of what makes up your family. Some people are not as lucky as to have even one person who cares. Look what you have here."

That's when he pointed to the painting that was ten years old at that point. I followed the direction of his finger, then took in the real people. My mother, wiping at her eyes, her blue-and-white checkered apron like the one that Dorothy uses as an actual dress in *The Wizard of Oz*. My father wearing his work coveralls despite the day of the week. Chuckie in his ratty blue sweatshirt, leaning against the kitchen doorframe and eating another of the brownies my mother brought over in a tinfoil-lined box. Louise holding a sponge, arms crossed over the big maroon UMass T-shirt she had begged Chuckie to bring when he drove home from his graduate school studies just to help us.

I looked at my family, at what I had there, until they all disappeared into one big teary blur. By the time I came back from hunting up a hanky out of one of the boxes in the bedroom, they were backing out of the driveway and I heard the familiar little eggbeater whir of the car's engine as all of them rolled away from me.

• • •

The drawing now hangs to the right of my doorway, in the same spot it has for the eighteen years since my father took a hammer out of a wooden whiskey crate of old tools and banged a nail that he'd brought out from his pants pocket as if it were just a coin or something else you carried every day. I once saw a TV show on some kind of Indians who kept a special bag next to the doorway of their teepees. In there they'd place the items that were most important to them, those they couldn't really live without. The bag was kept in such a handy space so in case they had to up and leave in a moment due to trouble or some disaster, they could easily grab it and run. Like them, I hung my drawing there, knowing that if I ever had to take off in an instant, there was nothing else that I would have cared about saving or bringing with me.

I've gotten lots better at my art since I made that drawing, and people love to ask me why I display this old thing, and not some recent work that visitors might notice as they were looking around my home and maybe become so impressed that they would want to buy it or hire me to make something similar. And I say that the old drawing hangs there because it reminds me of many things. One of which is how enthusiastic my parents were about the great discovery of my abilities. I'm sure they probably found it refreshing that, unlike my two siblings, I suddenly had what was considered to be some real direction—even though nobody knew where in the world it would lead. At that point in time, Chuckie, even with his four more years of life and sense over me, wanted to grow up to be the guy who did nothing with his day but unlock and later lock the gate at the dump. Depending on what she had for dinner, Louise, only one grade behind me, dreamed of becoming either a holy martyr with her face on a medal, or one of the June Taylor Dancers on *The Jackie Gleason Show.* She practiced often for that latter vocation, rolling all over the living room floor and making choreographed shapes with her arms and legs for an invisible television camera hanging overhead.

My parents weren't alone in being amazed about my own direction: that I suddenly was an artist would have been news to anyone. My mother had hung on our walls nothing more sophisticated than the very same faded prints of the First Noel and the Last Supper that her mother had lifted decades ago from her own mother's walls back in the old country. The only museum we ever went to was the farming one in Hadley, where a long time ago we all stared for a long afternoon at rows of very old potato rakes and hay wagons and then had our picture taken with a heavy leather horse collar slung around all of us. Art in first, and second, and third, and fourth, and as much of fifth grade as I'd been through up to that point had been nothing more than one tedious hour of clock watching every Friday afternoon. Our assignment never varied from making get-well cards for some classmate's ailing relative. I always stuck with thickly crayoned words, never even considered drawing floral bouquets or sailboats or finally-vacant hospital beds to pretty up my message of sincere wishes that God would grant the speediest of recoveries.

I do not come from the kind of people who back then would have been considered to possess any special talents at all—except if you count Chuckie, who could recite from George Washington on up the list of all the U.S. presidents. Then in reverse. Quickly, too, and with the ease you would display if you simply were giving the names of your mother and father. Other than that, the people I share any inherited characteristics with knew only the regular things you need to get yourself through the day: cooking, driving a car, how to perform various errands, and whatever knowledge is necessary for

earning some kind of a living. None of those abilities were anything that came close to being artistic, at least in the way I think
that most people would define the word.

As for me, prior to my tenth birthday, my only true ambition had been to make it to age twelve, when I finally would be
allowed to wear pantyhose and Chap Stick on Sundays, holi-
days and holy days of obligation. I did not, and I felt no need
to, think past that goal. And except for when company who
had nothing else to say to a kid asked me what I wanted to be
when I grew up, I never gave any of that a thought. Even when
the question came around for the fortieth time, I would just
shrug at whoever had posed it and I would give the excuse that
I had to go and help my mother refill the clam dip. Back then,
the future seemed as far away as the other side of the world.
And, much like the nativity-scene Jesus over in Ware, who one
Christmas Eve long ago was said to have cried a little rosary of
frozen tears, it was too much of a mystery for somebody my age
to waste time trying to figure out. But as of my tenth birthday, I
suddenly could see my destiny, as clearly and as vividly as if I
had always needed eyeglasses but never knew it until I tried on
somebody's pair, doing so for no other reason than to see just
how stupid I'd look in them.

"Just so long as it'll make you happy," my mother said
when I told her this. "I'll pray for you."

Lots of people say things like that, but with my mother it
really meant something. She wasn't like a nun or anything, but
she did know her stuff when it came to things religious—at
least that was the impression I and everybody else had because
of her job. From ten A.M. to two P.M. every Tuesday, Wednesday,
and Friday, she sat at a big wooden desk in the front room of
the rectory, fielding telephone calls and tending to the doorbell
while Father Krotki was out visiting the faithful confined to

their houses, nursing homes, and hospitals. If you didn't count the people on the other end of the telephone line, my mother was always the first to know who in our parish had been born and who had died, who was planning on marrying, and who was suffering a breakup, getting the itch to become a Catholic, or carrying such heavy burdens in their hearts that they had to schedule a private appointment for counseling with Father. In the evening if possible, these people would ask her in their dragging voices. Or, at least at an hour when it was dark. And would it be okay if they parked in the back? Behind the bushes next to the barn? Out of sight of the gas station traffic and the rest of the nosy public?

Those three days a week, my mother always came home with some kind of juicy news to whisper behind a cupped hand into nobody's ear but my father's, and after my tenth birthday she never walked in the door without a fat manila envelope of stolen paper for me to practice my artwork on. It was more like salvage work, her setting aside the crumpled copies of bulletins that had gotten stuck in the mimeograph, the church envelopes that never got picked up, the stack of brand-new scratch pads printed with the name and address and telephone number of a wholesaler of liturgical wines.

Even before my calling became clear, my father never had been one to leave his workplace carrying just his empty lunch box. He was such a handy handyman at Rolla-Way Lanes that Mr. Rolla was always rewarding him in some way in addition to what my father never failed to note was a very generous paycheck.

"Take this home to that fine family of yours," was delivered at great volume as Mr. Rolla handed my father a carton of Tootsie Rolls on the verge of rocky staleness, or the pack of lightbulbs that had turned out to be the wrong wattage for the fixture in the men's room. Up until we entered high school and begged for mercy, my sister and my brother and I were forced to slip around in the garish green-and-orange bowling shoes that Mr. Rolla felt were past their prime for the sport but that still could be considered superior footwear for a child. Everybody in the world could see us coming a mile away, and once we passed, everybody in the world knew exactly the size of our swiftly growing feet.

After my tenth birthday, my father regularly began to save even the stubbiest of the originally tiny scoring pencils, and in Mr. Rolla's storeroom he found a dusty water-damaged case of advertising handouts so old that they told how fifty cents could buy both you and your date two free turns on the pinball machine, three strings of bowling, a bag of State Line potato chips, and an ice-cold Moxie to refresh and revive yourself when you were through. The flip sides of the advertisements were blank. Perfect for scrap. Or artwork.

All of this stuff came home, to me.

"Go, draw," my father and my mother would suggest.

So I did.

Once in a while I talk to other people's parents—those newest to the category, the ones who wheel their still-spotless carriages up to the location where I am working for the day— and they tell me how they hope their child will turn out to be blessed with some kind of creativity. Usually the babies look like they were born yesterday, and the parents appear anxious about doing the exact right thing, not only today but all the many tomorrows. Do I remember seeing the decorations hanging in my nursery and did the choices of those shapes and colors have any long-lasting effects on me? Did someone ever encourage me to draw with my left hand rather than the right one that I obviously use? Did I ever really get any benefit from coloring books? They ask me such things, as if I am some kind of expert in that area. I have never had a baby, but all I can say is that I once was one and neither I, nor my parents, ever wasted time worrying about any of that stuff. And just look at me now, this very evening, driving as fast as the law will allow, to the home of my first true and important patron.

On white lined paper and with a red marker I grabbed off my table I had carefully taken down the directions Mary Ziemba dictated to me over the phone—even though there was no need for either of us to make those efforts. Her home—at least the start of the driveway leading to it—was one of those landmarks I never failed to point out to visitors when hauling them around to our few local points of interest. My commentary usually goes something like, "Up there, up to your right, you can't see it, but there's supposed to be this big mansion on like a hundred acres. Home of the richest person around. A supermarket queen. The best thing is, she owns some fantastic art. Right up that driveway."

If that doesn't impress, I then tell how Mary Ziemba last year had her color picture in *USA Today's* business section for giving away to a particularly large and down-and-out local family the entire contents of the Grand Z aisle of their choice (they went and selected Health and Beauty). But even with that kind of extravagant detail, it's hard to get visitors excited about looking up into nothing but trees and hills and imagining something spectacular is hidden from view. All I have to say is, the next time, I can be much more informative.

I can tell them that nothing matched what I'd imagined as I drove east on Route 20 late that day, passed the mountain of old tires neatly corralled by a stockade fence, came up onto the divided highway out of town, took that first turnoff before the state park road, proceeded slowly like the small sign planted next to the beginning of the driveway requested, and spotted the heavy wooden arch over the road. As Mary Ziemba promised, the gate had been left open for me.

The house turned out to be far from the kind of place you might see on a Hollywood gossip show, which was what I always had envisioned—a movie-star place, long and low and space-age, more windows than walls, flat roof despite the tons of snow we usually get. All painted white. Everything white. She would sweep out of it in a flowing caftan, maybe a turban wound around her head, certainly crystals dangling from a cord around her neck.

I watch too much TV. The house turned out to be deep maroon. Clapboards, with black shutters. And it was a colonial. Here was a woman who could live in any kind of house, and she had picked a colonial, just like ninety-nine percent of the rest of the people in town. The difference from the other such houses was that hers was much bigger—three floors that I could count, plus, for somebody like her, I figured that untold wine cellars and rec rooms probably had been dug underground, and numerous additions for the indoor heated pool and insulated garage just had to be tacked onto the back. There indeed were the many windows I had been expecting, but they were of normal size, and the same twelve-over-twelve panes I had in my own little apartment. The setting was what could make you the most jealous, high up on a sloping meadow, forest behind and to the sides, a football field of open space in front that allowed for a spectacular unobstructed view of the compact valley where I lived, the one I'd left minutes before. From up here, the wide bowl of red and yellow and orange foliage was pierced only by one faraway water tower and three tiny steeples, all looking like accessories from somebody's train set.

The leaves were just beginning to fall, and some drifted their gold onto my head as I stepped out of my car. I made the only sound I was aware of, crunching over the pea stone path that snaked up to the big front door. Then I heard something else. Little snippings. Cutting or chopping very nearby. I looked to my right. Between the thick stems of the several rows of faded giant sunflowers that edged the path, I could see a figure in aqua, bending away from me and clipping to the quick then yanking free from the earth some of the many dead, trailing, bushy plants that not too long ago, in warmer weather, had to have made up a vibrant front garden. Whoever it was stood up. Turned. Squinted through the thick stems. Spotted me. Smiled.

"Welcome," Mary Ziemba said.

She wore the same haircut I had in second grade. Short. Straight. Bangs. Like Paul McCartney's head when America first caught sight of it. Only hers was a gray that she, unlike me in the shower every five or six weeks with my carefully mixed squirt bottle of Natural Woman's "Toasted Nutmeg," didn't try to camouflage. Her face was the shade of veal, a white like somebody had just scared her but good, and the only other color that stood out was provided by the brown of her eyes. She was more or less just about level with my full height of five and a half feet, and she consistently stood as straight as I do only in the early stages of trying to make a good impression. She removed a work glove to shake my hand, and did that with vigor.

"Come on in," Mary Ziemba said brightly. I thanked her for the invitation and followed her, feeling greatly overdressed in my heels and long skirt and tunic, half my collection of beaded necklaces clacking against my chest with each step. The artistic gypsy look for that business meeting in the country is what I'd thrown on after she asked me how soon could I come over to talk and, though I knew it probably would make me sound unprofessionally eager, I had answered, "Half an hour?"

Mary Ziemba hadn't bothered to change—unless she'd been dressed in something worse than this pair of sweats that had seen better days. Dead leaves and seed pods dotted the faded fabric and clung to the thick white socks that scrunched down then disappeared into a pair of black rubber garden clogs edged with mud. Her only jewelry was a silver Timex, as flat and no-nonsense as the one the school nurses consult when taking a pulse. She gave it a look before we went inside. I followed and checked the fake Rolex I got for ten dollars from a guy who had shining rows of them laid out on a bath towel in Times Square the December before, when I took a bus trip to view Radio City Music Hall's Christmas pageant.

"I'm late," I realized.

"No," Mary Ziemba corrected. "You're right on time."

We exchanged pleasantries at the little table at the far end of the small and narrow kitchen the side door had allowed us into. White stove and sink and icebox lined up on the right, same color cabinets and counter on the left. At the end of the black-and-white checkerboard floor, next to the windows providing a view of an inground pool covered for winter in kidney-shaped royal blue plastic, Mary Ziemba offered me a seat and a cup of strong Salada from a green teapot that was old and chipped but not unpresentable.

"I didn't make these," she confessed as she slid a plate of muffins over to my side of the table. "Don't get the wrong impression."

"No chance," I told her. "I know these from the bakery—your bakery."

They were Grand Z Squash Blossom Specials, a steal at three for a dollar, available only during harvest season. They were the size of the balls down at RollaWay Lanes, yet they were marvelous and light, even though every crumb was jammed with some sort of ground-up seed or fiber or nut, healthful yet tasty, and leaving you with no guilt about having seconds. A bag of them was my standard hostess gift when visiting somebody at that time of year—only I never brought up where they came from, and if anybody complimented my baking skill I always said, "Oh, it was nothing."

"You know, these are an old-country recipe," Mary Ziemba told me, her pronunciation, decades after leaving her homeland, still bearing hard-edged remnants of the language she'd spoken there. "No blossoms really are used—it's far too late in the season. But I thought it sounded nice for a name. They're big sellers. So you shop at the store?"

I looked at her, surprised. "Of course," I said. "Doesn't everybody?"

"Well, you could choose to spend your money someplace else. Anybody could. So I thank you." She tipped her teacup to my generosity.

I didn't make mention of this, but it was true that I did every once in a while get a kick out of hitting Cornucopia out by UMass, where organic lingonberries are as common as bread and milk are at your corner convenience and, if you have the need, mysterious substances like spelt and arrowroot await in bulk quantities. But I was very much a regular at the traditional American mega-supermarket that was Grand Z, with my name long ago engraved on my own A-to-Z Super Shopper Card and the layout of the labyrinth of shelves as familiar to me as the few cabinets in my own miniature kitchen.

I actually had celebrated my sixth birthday in her store, and this I told Mary Ziemba, figuring she would be interested, and that it might underline my loyalty.

"We read in the paper that Twinkie the Kid was posing for pictures in the snack aisle on the very same day, and my parents drove my uncle and my brother and my sister and me down there to have a snapshot taken with him. When my father told him it was my birthday, Twinkie sang to me—the birthday song—though it was kind of hard to hear him from inside the costume. Then he gave us three twin packs of Twinkies that he told us we didn't have to pay for."

"That must have been one of the better actors," Mary Ziemba said. She shook her head and looked disgusted even these years later. "Companies used to send costumed characters around to the stores every year, and every year without fail there would be a problem. The guy would be an hour late and the children would be out of their minds waiting. Or we'd get a prima donna who demanded to juggle for the crowd at the cash registers, rather than halfway down an aisle, next to his products. One—a similar walking pastry—was caught shoplifting. Bars of soap. We spotted him pushing them into a slit he'd cut in his cream filling. The final straw was the stalker—as they call them these days—a big slice of American cheese that would pick a woman and follow her up and down the aisles for the duration of her whole shopping trip. Not saying a word. Just waddling along in back of her, his individual wrapping of plastic the only sound."

To make the photograph that so long ago was pasted into my family's album, Unc had to stand far away, so he could fit all of us in head to toe. We posed far down the aisle, my parents and Chuckie and Louise lined up on one side, nobody but me to Twinkie's left. My eyes were wide and my smile went on for miles. I was thrilled beyond description to have his buckskin-gloved hand clutching mine.

And, though you couldn't see it in the picture and I didn't know it that day, somewhere nearby, Mary Ziemba was sweating out the afternoon.

"No job is simple, is it?" I asked.

"What fun would that be?" she asked in turn, and I didn't have an answer. "Take another muffin."

I followed her order, mainly because she had put out one of those little tubs of healthy whipped fake margarine. It was a great accompaniment, and this was a special occasion. I have to say that even though I was nervous, the food helped me come close to forgetting the reason I was there: that we had business to discuss.

"So, what exactly would you like me to paint?"

Mary Ziemba poured us both more tea, and replied, "A portrait. I need a portrait."

"Okay," I said. And instantly I knew what to do.

I saw the finished work flash on the white wall behind Mary Ziemba's head, like somebody had just switched on a slide projector. As clearly as if I'd just touched my brush to it for the final time. The whole scene would be quite realistic, but would have a magical quality that people would be stymied to describe and that would make the subject irresistible to view no matter how many times you stood and took it in.

I would have her standing in the garden—but we would have to fake most of this because I'd want everything to be in full bloom, and Mary had said she wanted the painting completed by this Christmas. Also, I'd want her wearing better clothes. But soon I certainly would know her well enough to discuss things like that, to, probably with no embarrassment, urge her up to her closet and help her select something. A dress, maybe, one in good condition, as this is what she would be wearing for all to see.

I would pose her in the gold of a long-armed late-summer sun, surrounded by all the many fragrant blossoms and maturing fruit, and the hopeful buds of things yet to be born. Her left hand would be resting on the back of the somewhat mildewed old wicker chair I'd spotted in the corner of the garden, where I imagined she sat often and admired not only her plants but the yard, the field, the valley, the hills, and the sky beyond. At least I know that's what I would do if I lived there. Her right hand would hang down at her side, holding some kind of freshly picked root vegetable, maybe a beet or something with a rich color that would be fun and interesting to punctuate the scene with, partially hidden by the folds of whatever kind of garment we had selected. Her feet, if I could get her to remove her shoes, would be bare and warm on the neatly tilled earth. Her hair would be combed straight and her face would be forward and her regular brown eyes would look right back at any viewer. I knew to the letter exactly what I was going to do with her. But I thought I'd allow Mary Ziemba some input, as she, after all, was the patron.

"What did you have in mind?" I asked, hoping to genuinely sound like I was open to suggestions. "Any special location? Indoors? Outside?"

"Whatever you think is best," she said. "As long as everybody can fit."

The house had been quiet the entire time. There had been no voices, footsteps, slams, knocks, barks, tweets, scratchings. I knew next to nothing about Mary Ziemba's private life. But, be they human or animal, it would make sense that there would be others involved in it. Most people have somebody attached to them in some way, whether or not it is their choice or to their liking.

"Everybody?"

"Yes. The portrait is to be of me. Me and my family."

"Fine," I said. Several people could fit in a garden. I would have to rethink a bit, but I could handle this. I wondered if they'd be willing to stand in their bare feet—I was starting to like that theme of being connected to the earth.

"When can I meet with them?" I asked. "With all of you? Together. I'd like to talk about what we'll be doing."

"Good idea," Mary Ziemba said, and she reached down and brought up a heavy carton from beneath the table. "Meet my family."

The brown cardboard box was tall and undoubtedly large enough to once have held the two dozen sixteen-ounce cartons of Lucky Charms that the big, happy printing said it was designed for.

"Pink hearts, yellow moons, green clovers," sang the cereal leprechaun decorating one side, flashing to memory the disappointing toughness of the marshmallow shapes my brother and my sister and I long ago had craved and got to sample for the first time only when the Wednesday food pages finally carried the proper coupon. Mary Ziemba removed the cups and plates and pot from the table and wiped the surface down with a sponge. She followed that with a dish towel, to make sure everything was dry. And then she slid the box away from me and tilted it until an avalanche of fading Polaroids, flat sepia tones, dark slides, color enlargements, and glossy black-and-white photographs cascaded out.

From what I could see, these were images of men and women and children from this and other times, a good portion of those other times having long since passed. There had to be half a dozen of the same faces, at varying stages of life, attired in clothing of all types. They wore overalls and evening finery and loose diapers and Bermuda shorts and leisure suits. Soldiers' uniforms and poodle skirts and workout spandex and graduation gowns. Their hair was styled in flattops and braids and shags and beehives, or they had none visible. They posed on horses, in rowboats, in prams, at tanks, on sleds, in Volkswagen Beetles and near one small plane. They stood proudly showing off diplomas and puppies and bouquets, trophies, engagement rings, birthday cakes, and large game fish. They danced with men who looked sweet or dangerous; they draped their arms around women who appeared to be enjoying the experience. They feasted from holiday tables, sang at a baby grand piano and in front of a small young rock band. They swung determinedly at baseballs and made saves just inches from the goal line. All of them were very busy. And the other thing they had in common was that all of them appeared to be very happy.

This was not a coincidence.

"I've done my best to collect the finest shots—the most flattering photos, the best ones I had," Mary Ziemba told me. "Hopefully you can do something with this."

I scanned the heap of people and places. I peered into the box, at the higher mountain that had yet to be poured out. A small girl on a big gray horse waved her prize ribbon at me so excitedly, despite it being colored the gold that translates to nothing better than third place. I thought, and then I said what I was thinking:

"What do you mean—'do something'?"

"You know, make a painting."

I looked down again, and it became clear. "I'm not going to be meeting anybody, am I? In person."

"Everybody is all right here," Mary Ziemba answered matter-of-factly. "Do you have trouble working from photographs?"

"No," I said, because I didn't. It was great to have a live and living subject right there in three dimensions, but for me it was almost as wonderful to have a picture of them so if you wanted to start working no earlier than like when the eleven o'clock news came on, there was nothing to stop you. I could do it both ways. Especially now, if I wanted to find something good about being alone—I could do my work at any hour without worrying about bothering a soul.

"Well, I know you can do faces," Mary Ziemba told me. "I sometimes stop in your post office—I've seen your faces. That boy with his bicycle. He's a big reason why I noticed your work."

She had a good memory, one that included the watercolor of Little Ted and his black mountain bike, just as he had posed at the beginning of the previous summer, leaning against the blue wall out behind the fish market, arms folded across that green tank top, shadow slanted and jagged, his eyes closed and mouth smiling as he lifted his face to the sun with the unspoken joy of having three free months in front of him and not one solitary obligation. By the end of that summer, Little Ted would prefer to be called by the nickname of Bullseye, in celebration of the four perfect scores he made in bow and arrow at camp. But that sunny day out in back of the market he was still Little Ted, just hours away from receiving his regular modeling fee of getting to pick dinner. That painting had taken me two months—which sounds a lot longer than it really was. Per the arrangement, he was able to visit his father and me only one weekend per month, so the painting had taken no more than a handful of days, and a total of ninety-six Chicken McNuggets. A man walked into the post office a few days after I hung it there. He bought a book of ten self-stick postcard stamps and handed Mrs. Sloat $350 in cash—my posted price. He happily left carrying what turned out to be my last and best living-and-in-person painting of Little Ted. The buyer didn't leave a name, so reaching him to ask for it back now that I have no Little Ted to paint or otherwise enjoy is out of the question.

At the time, I was thrilled to have made a sale—the compressor on our Frigidaire had quit the week before and we'd since been storing our milk and cream and previously opened condiments in a beach cooler wrapped in a blanket in the corner behind the phone chair. I remember saying to Jack that as much as I'd loved that painting, I could always make another. I could talk Little Ted into standing out back for me the next time we had him. And Jack had said, "Well, of course you can."

Whatever it is you have missed one time, you always think you'll have that second chance. And nobody—at least nobody that I ever happened to come across in my life—ever argues with you to the contrary.

"Yes," I answered Mary Ziemba. "I can do faces."

"Well, I've thought about it for much, much too long, and this is what I want," she said, smoothing the photos directly in front her, moving into one rich arc the birthday boys and the new mother and the groom feigning a getaway at the back door of the church. An usher and a priest were laughing as they pulled the guy inside by the sleeve of his rented suit.

"I want these people here, and I want them in a painting by you."

The words were said slowly, like she was using a language I was only beginning to study. "All of them, the people who have been the most important to me in my life."

She drew out from the pile a blurry shot of a woman standing next to a sign marking the Pink Shell Motel.

"I want them the way they are seen here," Mary said. "All in their prime—at whatever age that was for them. It's not always at age twenty-one, I'm sure you're aware. I want them depicted at whatever was the best point in their lives."

Here she stopped. The house gave one of those creaks that old places occasionally do. Outside, a single gust of wind brushed the trees at the edge of the back yard, like you might run your hand across the pipes of a wind chime. The icebox clicked on to defrost. Mary Ziemba kept going:

"I want to have them captured whenever things were the finest for them. Before life took from them what it was they truly needed, or gave them things they could have done without."

She straightened a stack, bringing together the edges, some with crisp white borders, others with images that ran right off the neatly scalloped cut of the paper. I noticed several held in fancy cardboard folders and a few that still bore the angled stuck-on black corners that once had secured them to album pages.

"Do you get what I mean?" she asked and leaned toward me, to make sure I was hearing her, even though it would have been impossible not to. "What I want is to put everybody together. I was hoping you could do that for me."

She looked straight at me, kind of like she was supposed to in the painting I'd already finished in my head—and that I now had to scrap. The breakfast table suddenly seemed too weak a piece of furniture for the great weight of so much memory. I am not exaggerating when I say that I could feel it all pushing against me and found I had to inch my chair back a bit to get myself some space.

I'd never assembled a collection of people in this way, but that didn't mean I couldn't. It probably wouldn't be any tougher than the few times over the years that Bobby Frydryk has called me down to his office at the police station to come up with a drawing of a suspect after being provided a scant few bits of information ("He wore black." "He had a mouth.") from a shaking crime victim. At least here I had these people's features—and I could have them there in front of me at my drawing board for as long as I needed them to stand or sit perfectly still.

I could feel Mary Ziemba staring at me. She wanted an answer.

So I gave it.

"I can make for you whatever you want. But I'll need you to separate them. I'll need a pile of pictures for each person you want included. I'll weed out what I need from there, but they have to be sorted in some way. Who's who. What's what. Since I don't know them myself."

She sat up straighter and said quickly, "I can do that. I'll start tonight. Whatever you need. Whatever will be helpful to you." She had on the same genuinely grateful expression worn by the man in the straw boater who stood under a misspelled banner reading "Your Our Hero."

"I want to thank you," Mary said, and she reached across the table and squeezed my right hand. Below our awkward grasp, a faded color shot of party guests attempting some form of a Greek dance snaked around a paneled basement. "You can't know what this will mean to me."

I couldn't. I'd just met her. And I'm not one to pry. If there was something I should know, she would eventually tell me. About these people, or whatever else was important. I've found that's the way it usually works. Spend enough time with somebody and they usually end up opening up to some degree. If they don't, well, maybe it wasn't your business in the first place. As much as I was there to make some art for Mary Ziemba, I was also there to do a job.

"Well, I'm glad then," I said. She could not know what this meant to me, so I let that go unsaid.

"I'll get to the pictures right away," she assured. "I'm around a lot. You know, the life of the retiree."

Another thing I didn't know. So I just said, "I do tend to work fast once I get everything I need. But if I've got a couple of months to work on this, then we have plenty of time."

"Well, time is certainly a nice thing to have," she replied, not so much to me as down to the table, where everyone she had ever cared about was looking up at her as they each enjoyed their own particular version of a bright, big, nice day.

3

Unc calls me at ten-forty-five every Sunday morning.

He tells me he would phone earlier, but believes the week-ends should allow for a little more sleep time for a young person like me and, of course, he wants to give me an opportunity to get to church at nine-thirty. He knows I've always preferred the English Mass at that hour, the one I can understand, to the Polish one at eight A.M. that he attends but that I can't translate. Thanks to the nuns who both taught me and employed me as chief bulletin-board decorator up through eighth grade, I know all the words to the prayers and the songs and can give them to you in an accent so perfect you'd think I worked at the U.N. But ask me to interpret what I'm saying and, unless it's the Our Father or the important basic of "I don't understand," I'm lost. Unc knows all the words from the childhood he and my mother shared, being spoken to all the time in Polish by their parents, who came to live here but actually were born over there, somewhere so close to the Russian border that over the ages, because of wars and other battles, our family was Russian, then Polish, then Russian, then back. Unc goes to the first Mass, where they speak Polish, which he says sounds and acts a lot like Russian even though it's in a totally different alphabet. And there he sits on the left, like all the single men used to do in the olden days, safely separated from all the single woman on the right-hand side by the neutral zone that is the center aisle.

On Sunday mornings, he figures that by ten-forty-five I should have had time to do all my worshipping, to also stop at the drugstore for my papers, to hit Pytka's bakery for a pair of powdered jelly donuts, to get back home, and to be ready to decide what I will be eating for supper.

"Okay, you can have your choice," is how he always starts it. "Not bad pickings today—what's your mood? Steak? Seafood? Chinese? Mexican? Eyetalian?"

I hear him expectantly shuffling, ready for me to ask what I always do, which is, "Well, what's the best deal?"

I know to ask that because I know that's what Unc is really looking for: A discount. A special. A bargain. A steal, even. He goes out to eat once a week, every Sunday evening, always to a local restaurant, and only to those that have printed in the Sunday newspaper circulars a coupon offering two meals for the price of one.

These places almost always are part of huge, national chains that have built one of their two billion identical locations within half an hour of Unc's side door. Their names are household, drilled into the brain through the incessant jingles he hears on his radio and sometimes, if the mood is right, sings en route to the week's destination:

"Bring your papa to Mama Mia's!"

"Follow the stampede to Steak&Stein!"

"Soupsamillion—Home of the Bottomless Bowl."

Their decorations are predictable. Brass railings and jewel-toned wall-to-wall guide you to squeaky vinyl banquettes bordered by fake ferns that climb toward the glow of plastic Tiffany lamps. The staffs are teenaged and inexperienced, and all too often bewildered if not just plain bored. If the servers do include some older workers, those are visibly annoyed by how they must fill in if the younger ones have forgotten to wipe down a table or distribute menus or refill water glasses or collect a check. Whatever the age, when they finally locate you in what usually is more than the "sec" the perky hostess promised, the waiter or waitress begins by offering you a variety of beverages served in oversized goblets or mugs or jelly jars, all bearing the restaurant's name and logo. And if you want to, for something like ninety-nine cents more, you even can take the container home. "Start your collection today!" urges the little plastic easel propped next to the rack of artificial sweeteners.

The menus are never simply two pages. Some are as thick as a telephone directory, with entire chapters of detailed choices highlighted by bold symbols earmarking those best for big appetites, dieters, vegetarians, coronary patients, diabetics, Jewish people, and children under the age of twelve. There's always a special of the day, and there's always some version of an all-you-can-eat deal from a soup-to-nuts plastic-shielded buffet that runs the length of the room.

Big families go to these places. Young people on dates. Businessmen on furlough from their damp rooms in the budget hotels nearby. And Unc and Phyllis and I go there. Though I don't know if there is a category we exactly fit into.

Unc is my uncle. My mother's little brother. Her only brother. And because he is that, when the wire mill closed the year I was born and made him unemployed for the rest of the years I've lived through since, what could my mother have done but what she did, which was to offer him a home under our roof? That home technically was in the cellar under our first floor, where Unc slept on a squeaking secondhand single bed near the water heater, came and went through his own private entrance up the cement steps of the bulkhead, and did his business in a special lavatory my father had ordered after seeing a little drawing of it in the back of *Yankee* magazine. "Toilet Flushes UP" was what the ad boasted, noting that the square little commode in the illustration was "Perfect for the basement!"

Everybody who knew Unc loved him, and as kids, Louise and Chuckie and I were pretty neck-and-neck with Phyllis at the front of that pack. He reminded me of a handsome pirate—as much as I knew of them from picture books. And that consisted of the fact that some pirates wore patches over their eyes, which was what Unc did over his right one since back when the wire mill was still open and a belt on a splicing machine one day snapped and, in a single, fiery instant, whipped across his face. Once while fishing off the foundation of the old power plant, my father confided to Chuckie, who passed it along to me, that there was an actual good and working eye behind the patch, but it was one that had been rendered so unsightly Unc felt it was better to hide it and sacrifice that half of his God-given sight than to disgust anybody who had cause to look at him.

He could have had sixteen gaping, oozing eye sockets and he wouldn't have lost us kids as admirers. We applauded that he did little else but garden and complete chores and make occasional small repairs for us and for people up and down the street, and didn't have to be anywhere special from nine to five most days. Having him around at home all the time was as wonderful as knowing there was a new half-gallon of ice cream in the freezer. Say something anywhere near the truth—nothing profound, maybe just something obvious and plain like, "It's Monday"—and Unc would say, "You know," and he'd pause before adding, "you're one hundred percent right." With him, if you were right, you were all that. One hundred percent.

As if you were perfectly correct and no one could argue otherwise. It was, for the one moment, like being the pope.

Like how everybody was one hundred percent right that Phyllis was Unc's girlfriend, yet we could never call her that in front of him or he would look so uncomfortable we would feel rotten even though we weren't sure just what we'd done wrong. Whatever Phyllis Dyl was to Unc, she'd been that since time began, showing up here and there in our family photo album as far back as when my parents were still shyly dating. In my favorite of those shots, Phyllis and Unc and my mother and father, all of them looking barely out of high school, sit laughing and even puffing on the cigarettes they threatened to kill us over if we were ever caught with. They tap their ashes onto the grass and weigh down the four corners of a checkered picnic blanket spread out at the foot of the hefty dam that keeps the huge Quabbin Reservoir in its appointed place and not roaring down the valley and drowning all of us in one unexpected and tragic instant.

I sometimes would ask my mother when were Unc and Phyllis finally going to get married. I just knew I'd be picked as a bridesmaid, and I wanted notice to plan my hairdo. That Lopata girl in Chuckie's class got to have French braids put in her hair for her brother's wedding—by a hairdresser who came to her house no less—and then she kept them in place and on display the entire following week. I'd long ago decided I would want French braids, only with real flowers entwined. My mother told me not to hold my breath. How she put that was:

"Phyllis has the great responsibility of her old parents to care for. Don't go expecting anything to change before God comes to take them. If then, even."

And you know what? She was one hundred percent right. It was back in Phyllis' youth that she was a young woman making great sacrifices for her parents over in the little brown cottage where she and Mr. and Mrs. Dyl all lived together at the end of Ruggles Street. And it is in that same home, still brown but now sided in wood-grain-imprinted vinyl, that Phyllis, her parents long gone on to their eternal reward, her youth just as dead, still resides.

I liked Phyllis from the start, and always thought it would have been fun to have her for an actual everyday aunt. Our only real one was my father's sister, known to us as Cioci Pups and inconveniently located way out in Michigan. It would have been wonderful to have called Phyllis "Cioci" rather than "Miss Dyl," as we always were supposed to and did, even when we became adults ourselves, all because she was pretty formal. And nervous. You could tell she was a little frightened whenever she first arrived at a place or event, but then she would settle down and could be entertaining if asked to recount a story or tell of her hobby, which was writing to the survivors of famous dead people.

This wasn't something that took up a whole lot of her time, as those you generally would consider notable didn't drop every day. She was lucky to even come up with a couple of them a month. But when she did, Phyllis would sit down at her typewriter and bang out the same six short lines:

Dear _____:
Please accept my sincerest condolences on the
passing of _____.
A bright light has gone out in the world.
Sincerely,
(space left here for Phyllis' actual handwritten
signature)
Phyllis Dyl

Phyllis just had to insert the name of the spouse or mother or child or brother or longtime love, then that of the person who'd been lost to them. She'd go on to sign her own name above the typed version of it, and she'd fold the paper carefully and slide it into the envelope addressed with as much detail as she could obtain or imagine (usually not much more than "Hollywood, U.S.A.," or "Washington, D.C., U.S.A.," or, many years later, in the case of Princess Diana, simply "England"). She'd then stamp it and send it off and sit back and await an acknowledgment.

People actually did write back, and Phyllis kept score of this in a notebook next to her typewriter. Over the years, the family of General of the Army Douglas MacArthur thanked her. As did that of Lyndon Baines Johnson, with the signatures of Lady Bird and of her two daughters using their new last names. The survivors of Louis Armstrong, Herbert Hoover, Gracie Allen, Jack Benny and Adlai Stevenson also had manners.

The family of Elvis Aron Presley returned a few inches of thanks. Mrs. Hubert H. Humphrey's message informed Phyllis that in his final days, the former vice president "was filled with joy, peace, and gratitude." Kathryn Crosby responded with a poem thought up by Bing himself, and—look—his autograph was right there beneath it, though, considering the circumstances, you know he couldn't have put it there himself. Ethel Kennedy mailed back some verses from the Beatitudes, along with a prayer card containing remarks her late husband had made on the death of Martin Luther King, two months and two days before somebody went and blasted Bobby away as well.

All these things Phyllis set into a binder, each card or letter glued to a piece of construction paper punched with three holes. If they had writing or printing on the back, she slid the responses into a glassine envelope that kept you from missing anything on the flipside. And all these she would show you if you ever had the interest and the time.

We three kids fought to be the first to read the newest note, or to receive whatever treat or surprise or attention Phyllis was lavishing. She never forgot us on birthdays, or even on smaller occasions like Valentine's Day and Halloween, a little basket or a wrapped toy or goody for each of us left in a twine-handled shopping bag hung on our side doorknob. She eagerly bought tickets for and dressed up to attend the events a child could only rightfully expect just a single one of its family members to be present at—weekday afternoon plays and science fairs, and lengthy concerts on warm spring afternoons when the weather is drawing you out-of-doors so strongly you nearly have to hold on to your chair to keep yourself in place. Phyllis, who other than grocery shopping for a shrinking list of her late mother's ancient friends, did not have a job and always stayed to the end. And at the end she always applauded quickly and softly through her white dress gloves with the teardrop-shaped pearl buttons at the cuffs.

She wore those same kind of gloves long after they went out of fashion. Including every Sunday, both to church and, later that day, to dinner with Unc and me. It was five months ago, the first Sunday after Jack took off, that Unc first called to invite me out with the two of them. The regular Sunday dinner at my parents' had been canceled that day, something that I took as one more little death. The meal never had been a fancy event—always a simple but juicy roast that we began eating at noon and finished by quarter after—but it was a nice and regular thing, and that particular weekend I was in need of routine. I understood, though. Like me, my parents were in shock from the news I'd hit them with the morning before. So they were headed down to Connecticut—the cure for everything from an idle afternoon to a roaring life crisis. It was my father's feeling that an afternoon at the slot machines would lift my mother's spirits.

"I'll be taking Ma down to see the Native American exhibit," he whispered in their code when he called early Sunday morning.

The two of them talked like that, never referred to the place by its proper name—Foxwoods Casino—because a word like "casino" would make it sound too much like gambling. And they didn't gamble, my parents liked to assure me whenever they called to tell me that's where they were headed, in case I found out their destination from somebody else and therefore got the impression they were trying to hide something from me.

And because I really and truly didn't gamble, I answered no when my father asked me to come along for the day, saying it might be good for me, but not venturing near the issue of why I might be in need of a treat.

"I'll be fine here," I said, because that's what I believed. "Win big."

Alice and Leo and Heather downstairs had gone off to a christening, reluctantly and only after I assured them I would be okay alone. I waved them bye out the window and went to pour myself a glass of water because I couldn't think of anything else to do. I sat down and flipped through an art supply catalog and bent the top page advertising the kind of computerized mat cutter you'd only find in the most professional and state-of-the-art frame shop. With the attachments, including the one that would allow you to create oval cuts, the price came to more than what my car had cost. But I marked the page anyway, like it was something I was considering. I put down the magazine and wandered back to the kitchen to dump out the water I'd decided I didn't want. I ran the tap to usher it down the drain, and watched as all of it circled away. I stared down the black hole and imagined somebody doing the same thing south of the equator, where I hear water swirls in the opposite direction, but where, I would imagine, people have to feel the same queasiness that people north of the equator do when the person they love ups and leaves. It had to happen everywhere. And the feeling had to be the same no matter if you were a deserted, heartbroken person in an igloo on a glacier, or a grass hut on some island, or a villa on a cliff, or a ratty bamboo shack dangling over a sewery river.

The next call came an hour later, from the same phone. But from Unc. Did I want to join him and Phyllis for supper?

"Sure," I answered so quickly and brightly that the energy in my voice surprised me. Guess I'd been more eager for a change than I'd let on to myself. In the past sixty minutes I'd gotten the creeping feeling that I really might not be fine at home, which was no longer so much my own place as it was becoming one of those cartoon puzzles that asks you to list what's missing from the picture. Everywhere I looked there was nothing where just days before there used to be a shirt hanging from the door, a book left on the couch, a husband slipping into bed in the middle of the night after three weeks on the road and saying my name softly like he was a breeze through the window I'd left open just for that.

"I'll come along," I told Unc. "But I'm not very hungry—you'll just be wasting your money."

"It's not wasting," Unc said, warming my heart. "I got coupons."

• • •

My parents went down to Foxwoods the Sunday after that. And the one after that, and the next one, and the next.

"It seems to help Ma," my father explained when they came by on their way home from the second trip and my mother was out of earshot, over at the icebox looking at the magneted snapshot of Little Ted and them only the summer before, eating their chicken dinners at the parish picnic, dark barbecue sauce smearing their faces. It had been 101 degrees that day, and while I put in extra time at the lemonade booth, and while Jack sat down in the pine grove taking requests during Lenny Gomulka's break, my parents showed off the boy they had never had any problem calling their grandson. Ten knives went through my heart seeing how sad my mother looked as she stood there in my kitchen, shaking her head almost imperceptibly, certainly remembering some part of all of the lovely images I'd just been calling up.

But my father was correct about their trips cheering her. She came back into the living room and launched into a story about how there was going to be a package deal offered for New Year's Eve and why didn't we all make plans now before it was sold out. Soon she started dropping Foxwoods information into every conversation. Telling me things like how much food you can get there for free, never seeming to realize, or acknowledge, the amount she was paying for it one way or another.

"They give complimentary breakfasts to the most frequent visitors and free lunches to anybody who arrives before eight A.M.—and, if you sign up at lunch, you can win a free dinner. So it really is like making money to leave after sunup on Sunday and spend the entire day." And this is the manner in which she told me that our Sunday dinners were on hold.

So I continued to take up Unc and Phyllis on the offer that

came over the phone line every Sunday morning. Those first two, and just about every one in the five months and four days up to this point, that's where I've been: sitting next to a car-toonish mural of meaty Italian women stomping grapes, or beneath a lobster buoy crawling with plastic starfish, or inside a booth constructed in the shape of a rickshaw, ducking piñatas, shouting above the strolling Oktoberfest band, sitting across from Unc and Phyllis. On the one day of the week that most people in the world land in some form of a family get-together, there we are, at Pasta Warehouse or Shishka Bob's, the three of us members of the local chapter of a national club of people who are all eating the same kinds of things off the same kinds of plates, using the same kinds of knives and forks and collector cups in the same kinds of seats and tables and dining rooms. Every single one of us getting our fill of the "Eat 'til the Cows Come Home" bar-b-q special at Lil' Joe's: T-bone steak, ranch-house baked potato, unlimited salad bar, corn-bread basket and nonalcoholic beverage, then, grand finale, the End o' the Trail Cow Pie with a plastic "LJ" branding iron spearing the decorative cherry. Price: $8.99 for one, $9.99 for two. Take as much as you want, until you feel like you've had enough.

Unc raves, rarely disappointed or the least bit underen-thused by presentation, taste, quantity, quality. Foodwise, he is as easy to please as somebody locked up on bread and water for ten years. He always makes a series of long *"hmmmmmm"* noises as he sets to work with his knife and fork, his napkin tucked into the holy chain he fishes out from beneath his undershirt.

Phyllis is quieter, but usually just as contented. Her meals end with a quick scavenging of the table—untouched rolls,

Wet-Naps, spare shellfish bibs, sugar packets printed with scenic New England destinations, unopened chopsticks that she will use to prop up the newest branches of her more vigorous houseplants—each find tucked into a Baggie hidden inside her purse.

The real leftovers are returned by our servers in sturdy foam garages, along with a check weighed down by a sprinkling of peppermint candies. It is then that Phyllis brings out a solar-powered calculator that she holds under the dim lamp of our booth. She enters the total, minus the half-off that the coupon granted, then adds my full fare and whatever tip she determined had been earned. The end result gets divided by three, which she says is only fair. Then she sets out the coupons and each of us counts out his and her third, to the cent.

"Let's hit the road," Unc then says.

So we do.

All the way home, there is still no need for the radio, as Phyllis or Unc fills in any silence by informing me of their connection to whatever we pass.

"Over there, Phyllis and I used to walk on a path along the river," he tells me. I find it hard to picture Phyllis dressed for the wild. I've never seen her in pants or shorts or anything with legs to it. But I did not know her back when, as Unc had the pleasure to. "There were no houses there at the time," he's telling me. "Just the railroad track. But we never once saw a train there. Only deer, if we went at the right evening hour. And one summer afternoon, we looked into the water and we saw a snapping turtle swimming to the opposite bank. Its shell was as big as the bulkhead."

"Yes, it was," Phyllis verifies, nodding.

Over there, Unc points out, just last Tuesday night, according to "On the Beat," his favorite part of the newspaper after the sports pages, two boys were taken into custody for trying to remove the sign for James Street. As James also was the first name of one of the boys, Unc figured it was a harmless prank, something to display in the bedroom.

"The point is," Unc says, "it makes me feel good to know that some people do crimes that are totally harmless. That don't really hurt a soul. Really don't."

"Unless you are looking for James Street," Phyllis corrects him, but as she says this she touches a hand to the crook of his driving elbow to show that she is not really being stern, only making a point that you couldn't really argue with.

About two miles before we get to her street, always at the point when we pass the icehouse pond where Phyllis says she once stood helpless, a shivering five-year-old on double runners watching an ice cutter disappear through a spot he thought was safely frozen over, she sticks her gloved hand into her neatly arranged bag and she brings out her key ring and holds the one for her side door. At the ready, like she is doing right now.

We pull into her driveway and she turns to the backseat.

"We'll see you next Sunday," is what she says without variation.

I tell her the same thing, using the same plural, even though there is only one of me.

Unc gets out and goes around the side to help her out of the car, despite Phyllis' not really needing such aid. I watch as he takes her arm even in dry conditions, to make sure she doesn't slip on the stairs to her porch. I watch as she unlocks the door and as he gently places into her hands the correct doggie bag. I turn and pretend to admire the neighbor's wrought-iron stair rail. With my eyes not on them, Unc and Phyllis will enjoy their one fast kiss for this particular day.

• • •

Claire O'Hare is why I am relating all that. She wants to know everything about me, including how I spend each day of the week. She even takes notes as I respond. But she assures me that's all part of her job.

She is the New Directions career counselor I nearly forgot I'd phoned the day before. The call from Mary Ziemba and the visit with her would have been enough to distract me from everything else, but at the suggestion of Alice, who, like me, rarely goes out on a weeknight, I followed the visit to Mary's with a late-night celebration at The Happy Tap. Right when I walked in, I bought a round for the house—a first for me. Okay, it was a Monday and there were only nine other people there, so it wasn't as big a deal as you might imagine. But it still was fun, and it was one of the parts I actually could pick from my memory the next morning. I wasn't in that great a shape just before ten, when I pulled my car next to the one already parked in front of Claire O'Hare's New Directions. My plan was to just stick my pounding head in the door and tell the person in there how I got some great news late yesterday, and I'm feeling a whole lot better about my career than I was when I called. So I won't be needing you after all. Something awkward like that. The way I was looking at it, this was true—Mary Ziemba was going to blast me out of my funk, I just knew it. Anyhow, the first session here with the counselor was supposed to be free, so it wasn't like either one of us was going to be losing any money by it never happening.

But Claire O'Hare had a big wipe-off board nailed to the far wall of her office, and on it she had written "TODAY IS THE FIRST DAY OF THE REST OF YOUR LIFE, LILY WILK!" The letters were all round and inflated, like the ones the cheerleaders poster-painted onto pep rally signs back in high school, "B-b-b-baby, You Ain't Seen Nothin' Yet" and other song lyrics of the day that really had nothing to do with the sport of football or our hopes for kicking the crap out of the hated Ware Indians. Claire had taken some effort to write her message for me, then had colored in each of the words with a different shade of marker. It looked great except for the yellow parts, which were so light you could barely make them out. All around the border she had drawn exploding fireworks. Rockets and sparklers and big happy blasts. The sign was kind of embarrassing, but it also was touching enough to make me feel guilty about breaking our appointment. Plus, the instant I pushed open the door, she rushed over to me out of nowhere with an enormous mug of coffee that took two hands to hold. So I stayed.

"The three Cs," Claire O'Hare, C.C.C., explained when she introduced herself complete with the string of them, "stand for Certified Career Counselor. I have studied long and hard, and this designation should make you feel more confident about having selected me to assist you with this most important process."

She talked like a brochure. That much about Claire O'Hare was sinking in so far. I took a sip and brought her into focus. She was around my age. Maybe a little younger. Tall, and what my mother politely would call big-boned. One of those on whom meat looks good. Her dress was a knit, straight and black and long enough to extend down and hit the ankles of some big-heeled boots. Her red hair reached her wide shoulders and bounced up into the kind of curls you can't pay for. The main feature of her face was man made, a pair of big black horn-rims that in our town made her look outdated, but in a big city quickly would crank her to the height of fashion.

Claire O'Hare invited me to inspect the C.C.C. certificate

framed and hung on the far wall, her name laser-printed onto it in Old English typeface, along with the fact, in smaller and easier-to-read type, that for a series of Saturdays in January of 1986, this woman had sat through sixteen hours of career seminars at the Holyoke Holiday Inn. On either side of the certificate were laminated road maps that looked to be clipped right out of a gas station atlas. They were part of the find-your-road-less-traveled–we're-all-on-the-same-journey theme I saw continued on the lamp table, where several small compasses were displayed, and on the door, where somebody had done a rather lousy job of painting a big black one, and around the turtleneck of Claire's dress, where a tiny gold one pointed north/northwest while she asked me to sit down next to her computer so she could fire at me the first of her million questions.

I answered yes, that I was the Lily Wilk who had called to make the appointment. That I was thirty-nine. That I lived at the corner of Springfield and Anderson, one floor above my best friend, Alice Baldyga, and her husband, Leo, and their Rocky's Fish Market, which, despite its name, has no owner or employee named Rocky and actually sells just fish-and-chips dinners and only is open Thursdays to Saturdays, so there is nothing near the daily commotion you might imagine such a place generating.

She wanted to know my schooling, so I told her of my four years at Westfield State, where I studied what I considered to be the drawing and painting and history of just regular art, but after four years of this was awarded a diploma reading "Bachelor of Fine Arts." She asked my marital status, and I answered I was single. Even though I had my own set of certificates to prove I was, I didn't add that I was divorced. I'd yet to pronounce the word. Say it, I imagined, and you'd have who knows how many people asking you details—for how long, and maybe even why. "Single" normally won't get you much interrogation, unless the inquisitive people are related to you.

"Now comes my favorite question," Claire announced. She put her hand to her chest like she had to calm herself from the excitement of it all. "What is your current occupation?"

"Artist," I answered.

"Ar-tist," she repeated.

As with every other fact I had told her, Claire typed this word into her computer. Slowly, using a hunt and peck that grated on me. I wanted to shove her hands aside and do the typing myself, even though I probably wouldn't be much better at it. I left her alone, and she continued on, repeating then entering syllable after syllable, echoing my answer as she hit the keys. Then she dropped her hands into her lap and swiveled the chair until we were nearly knee to knee.

"That must be so interesting," she said, and the way she strung out the "so" sounded genuine enough to convince me she meant it. I got the impression this was not the same remark she made to the laid-off security guard or to the disgraced former bank vice president or to the twenty-five-year-old living off parents tired of his expensive search to locate the meaning of life on their credit cards.

"Yes, it can be interesting."

Claire made a face like somebody had just slipped her a glass of milk gone bad. "*Hmmm* . . . These words . . .'can be.' Not a good sign [here she waved a finger at nobody in particular]. Listen to what you're saying. Listen . . ."

I cocked my head, thinking back to my answer. My mind was fuzzy. I tried to hear something, but it was only the soft hum of the electric wall clock that, instead of numbers to designate the hours, had only the first letters of the words "north," "south," "east" and "west."

"You said 'It *can* be,'" Claire reminded me, and I was grateful. But I still didn't get her point. She must have caught that because she went on to give it to me: "Your answer wasn't that it *is* interesting, but that it *can* be—which means it sometimes is, but it isn't always."

Well, of course it wasn't always interesting. If my work was consistently so fascinating, I never would have made this appointment. But I didn't put it like that. I just said, "You're right."

"And that's why you're here."

"Right."

I watched a smile stretch across Claire's face, and then she slowly swiveled in her chair to point at the wipe-off board. Beneath the big message to me there were small yellow letters I hadn't noticed before. They spelled out the words she read to me right then:

"So start living."

It was a perfect place to end this. My coffee was nearly gone, and the inch left was cold. Surely the next client soon was going to come through that door, seeking a portion of Claire O'Hare's guidance. It was the right time to stand up and extend a hand and say nothing more than that I'd think about what she'd said, which I would, knowing all the while I had no need to return.

But I didn't move.

The compass clock ticked, its pointy red second hand haltingly progressing east, then south, then west, then, finally, north. Then heading back around the world again.

It was the moment in the hairdresser's chair when the trim is done and you're all set to take off the plastic cape and then the stylist comments how "It looks very nice, but, you know, if

it was my hair, I'd do something totally different." And you figure, well, I don't have to be anywhere for another hour, and
what's the big deal? It's only hair. It'll grow back. So you say to
her "Well, tell me what you'd do." So she tells you. And then
maybe you let her do it.

There in the chair at New Directions, though all ready to
leave and never come back, I continued to sit. It wasn't even
lunchtime. Mary Ziemba had asked me to return to her house
at three that afternoon. What did I have to lose by asking one
question?

So I said to Claire O'Hare, "Tell me what you'd do if this
was your life."

4

I live above the Bicentennial Queen.

It has been a long time since the Bicentennial, so unless you have been around town for quite a while or ever had a reason to go flipping through the crackly plastic photo albums stored down at the historical society's headquarters, you might not realize that the woman behind the counter at Rocky's handing you your little red plastic basket of deep-fried scrod and crinkle-cut crispy fries every Thursday through Saturday night is former royalty. Someone who, in front of as much of the town as could jam itself into the high school auditorium one Friday night twenty-three years ago, dressed as the Liberty Bell for her swaying, clanging interpretive dance set to a short cassette of patriotic tunes. Someone who really is no better looking than anyone else I know but who easily whupped nine other contestants including the favored and beautiful Sally DiNucci and her babushka and her bare feet and the fake baby at the breast during her multiple-accented recitation of a monologue titled "I Am Every Immigrant." It was Alice who by the end of the night was wearing the red-white-and-blue sequined crown and holding the matching scepter and carrying off the envelope containing the one-hundred-dollar United States savings bond. It was Alice who one week later was enthusiastically waving from a folding chair bolted to the top of a giant Declaration of Independence hauled down Route 20 by Snarkie Cambo's Chevy pickup during the big parade.

She might look to you like nothing more than Alice Baldyga, wife of Leo Baldyga, daughter of Edziu and Genevieve Szczpiorski, best friend of me, Lily Wilk. She might never, ever mention the title, because it never really gave her the big head her mother warned her it would. But if you go into Rocky's, you can see her crown and scepter on display inside a long shatter-proof plastic case Leo had made up just for that purpose. You have to really go looking for it, kept safe high up on its own wooden shelf, on the left-hand wall, next to the speaker through which is announced the number of the dinner that's now ready. If you dragged over a bench and stood up on it, you could read the red plastic plaque that Leo got engraved at a stand in the mall. I will save you the trouble:

> Beautiful and ornate crown and scepter
> presented to Alice Szczpiorski
> —NOW ALICE BALDYGA—
> Town Bicentennial Queen, 1976.
> (Jewels not real.)

"Leo is very proud of me, but he also doesn't want us to get robbed." Alice leaned over and whispered this to me after she and he yanked on the rope that pulled off the beach towel that unveiled the case during a private ceremony held at the end of the same week the two of them repainted the interior of the fish market, a couple of months after the Szczpiorskis came to the conclusion that running the business was a young person's job, and that they were not young anymore. In this way, their only child, then halfway through an undeclared major at UMass and nowhere near old, was handed her life's work: owning and operating Rocky's.

Alice and Leo and I all attended the parish school together, and the town high school as well, but Alice and I really clicked when we turned fifteen-and-a-half and our shared birthday month landed us in the same drivers' education class.

Back at that time, she was best known for nothing more than having five whole consonants in a row at the beginning of her last name. "SZCZPIO" was all that could fit on the plastic punched-out label stuck to the rusting black mailbox next to the doorbell I rang every Tuesday night for the six months I walked with her to Walulak's corner. There, a driving school car would pick up a group of us kids and bring us all to the school's tiny classroom next to a Portuguese bakery in Ludlow that had in its window huge models of wedding cakes so grand that they grew not up in size but across, two tall layers connected to the two next to them by a plastic bridge on which a tiny bride and groom stood contemplating what they had just gotten themselves into.

Alice was never ready when I arrived at her house, even though she knew I was coming, and I'd have to sit in the living room and watch her mother tat embroidery floss around hanky edges and listen to her tell me how all the things being described to us by Harry Reasoner on TV, no matter how terrible or horrific, were nothing compared to what she had known back as a young girl in a death camp.

"You see that bird?" Here she'd point to Alice's parakeet, a jerky pickle-colored thing they sometimes allowed to fly around the room at will. "It would have fed six of us in camp."

If I picked a thread off my clothes in front of Mrs. Szczpiorski, she would lean over and grab it from me, then push it into her sewing basket. "You kids don't realize," she'd say. "Enough bits of thread, you can make yourself an entire shawl."

Mrs. Szczpiorski scared me. I knew of a couple other people in town who once had been held in the same kind of a place she had, but they seemed to have found the ability to talk about at least a couple of other subjects. Weather, sports, neighbors, the new family that's been showing up in the front row of church wearing hats like it's 1960 all over. Some of them, you'd never have known they were in the camps if your parents didn't whisper to you to shut up in front of them about how much you like to watch *Hogan's Heroes*. Or unless these people were handing you something in the warm weather, when their cuffs were loose or rolled up, and on their forearms or wrists you saw the blocky blue-purple numbers that would remain there for the rest of their lives. But Mrs. Szczpiorski wasn't the silent type. She threw out her stories nonstop from the moment she let me inside. I'd eventually tune her out, checking my watch against the time shown on the big clock hanging high above the radiator.

The Szczpiorskis once told me it might be the only such work of art in existence, and that would be easy to believe. The face of the clock was fitted into the table part of a metal sculpture of the Last Supper. It was a tag-sale find bought from the family that year-round sells reconditioned vacuum cleaners on the front lawn next to their mobile home out near the old drive-in. On the hour, a different one of the apostle figures would pop up stiffly for however long it took the chime to sound out the proper number of rings. I should say everybody but Judas got to do this. For good reason, he did not get any special attention. Instead, he, along with Jesus, would stand up with the rest of the apostles at both midnight and noon. Alice always came downstairs about ten minutes after six o'clock, when Saint

Thomas was already settled comfortably back in his seat, probably doubting something.

"Is it six already?" she'd always ask me, like she couldn't believe it, and her mother told her that it was, and that it actually was about ten minutes past, if she wanted to know the truth, and the girl, which is what she called me even though she'd known my name since when I was in first grade, the girl has been sitting here patiently waiting for you for fifteen minutes already.

"But I had to do my haa-ir," Alice would whine, like that was something else she hadn't expected.

"I don't know why you want to drive a car anyway," her mother would shout as we rushed out, still pulling on our jackets. "You'll only end up killing yourself."

Then she'd yell after we'd shut the door, but I could still hear it: "And the girl too."

It was my idea that we—me and Alice and Leo—all move into the empty apartments in back of and on top of the market once it became Alice's. I was still at home, and for the two months since they got married, Alice and Leo had been living for free, Unc-style, in the Szczpiorski's cellar.

Mrs. Szczpiorski sat on the stairs and wept the morning that Leo drained the water bed into the utility sink Alice previously had covered with a board to use as a nightstand.

"You don't realize how good you have it here," she told him. "This place is a palace compared to how I had it in the camp. It's the girl's fault. [Here she pointed at me.] She put this crazy idea in your head."

Pulling the tape from the two Bruce Springsteen posters she'd decorated the oil tank with, Alice wanted to know "What's crazy about making use of a perfectly good, vacant apartment?"

"*Aaaahhhh,*" is all Mrs. Szczpiorski moaned in reply, and she waved us away, crossed herself, and stomped back upstairs.

The first thing I told Alice she needed was a new sign to finally replace the old flounder-shaped piece of wood that once had hung proudly over the door. The original had cracked long ago and had been taken down and leaned against the back of the building, where over the years it became the victim of weather and dry rot and bugs. People who were going to go there knew where Rocky's was anyhow—they didn't really need a sign. But why not make the place look nice? What I had in mind was the new sign, murals, and a big, illustrated menu for the wall behind the counter. Plus a sidewalk one to announce the specials and snag the people who were driving past not even realizing how hungry they were until they saw the words "FRIED FISH."

The more I did for them, the more Alice and Leo knocked on my door. They needed a sign for the new promotions, like Alice's idea to give you a free order of fries for every ten you purchased, even if that took you a year or more to do. And they wanted some seasonal decorations painted on their front windows—elaborate scenes of fish raking leaves or fish making snowmen or fish lying on the beach tanning their scales. They liked my idea of sinking old tires into the small front garden and painting them yellow to look like the onion rings that were new to the menu. They couldn't wait for me to letter "Buoys/Gulls" on the door of the bathroom required by law. They thought it was great how I put out big quahog shells for ashtrays, replacing the ancient, chipped glass ones that had come with the place. They liked most anything I came up with because the customers commented on all the imaginative decor and were happy. And when customers were happy, they spent money.

How Alice and Leo paid me for all this work and genius

was with the rent on my very own place. It was a box, really, nothing fancy, a basic living space slapped onto the roof of the market by the guy named Rocky when he was first getting his business off the ground and needed the extra income of a tenant. Whoever rented it got one huge living room, one bedroom good in size if you had nothing larger than a double bed, one thin kitchen appointed with toy-sized fridge and stove, and a half bath, plus, out the kitchen door, a front porch for relaxing on. The back stairs led to an assigned parking spot on the driveway, and I don't know whether Rocky offered this to his renters, but I was told by Alice and Leo to feel free to do anything I liked to the yard, along the lines of plantings or purchasing outdoor furniture or whatever. If you did not require that much space or luxuries in order to be happy, and if you did not mind the greasy-smelling exhaust and noise from the Frialator three days and nights a week, it all could be paradise.

"Consider this place your home," Leo had said on our first night there. And Alice added, "For as long as you want it."

Alice was there when Jack resurfaced in my life that steamy Sunday afternoon at the Yarmouth Clam Festival. It was the summer of my short-lived painted T-shirt period, which Alice actually had inspired the year before, when she returned from a Fourth of July weekend at Horseneck Beach wearing the ugliest painted shirt, a twenty-five-dollar price tag dangling from its sleeve.

"Whaddaya think?" This is what she'd asked me when she barged in my back door and spun so I could admire the blots of color somebody had slapped onto both the front and back, and the left shoulder.

What I thought was: There was a fortune to be made in this, from suckers like her.

So I bought a ton of shirts, on my Visa, through the mail, from a wholesaler on Orchard Street in New York City who used curses in regular business conversation. My porch would be jammed with the big cardboard boxes the UPS man so kindly would lug up the back stairs for me, and I'd empty them as fast as I could. Depending on the season I was thinking of, I dipped into my big new plastic jars of fabric paint and adorned cuffs, necklines, backs and fronts with fall foliage, Christmas trees, hearts, pilgrims, schoolbooks, Old Glory, pumpkins, sailboats, suns, moons, and any other corny thing that might sell to tourists, because it is true that people on vacation have money to burn and they'll buy anything you can come up with. Then I'd send out deposits to rent tables at craft shows, and I'd go set up my wares and I'd listen to people sneer how they could make the same thing only they didn't have the time, but they should try because, hey, look how much she's asking for this and maybe they could get rich.

They'd take the shirts off the hangers and press them against their fronts, and they'd look just about ready to get out the wallet when their kid in the stroller would spill his bottle of something on another shirt and they'd pretend they didn't see the stain and would leave quickly. Will the paint come off in the washing machine, people would ask, like I would make and sell something that could only be worn once before disappearing. What's so special about these, they wanted to know, and I didn't know what to say. Then I, and Alice, who I made come with me once I realized what a bore I was in for, would cheerfully chant, "They're all hand-painted!"

The whole experience was pretty awful, and I can't even add that somebody would buy something sooner or later, because that is not the truth. Some days nobody would buy anything. Some days it would rain and the event would be canceled and we would learn that only after driving two and a half hours. Or threatening weather would move the festival from the highly visible town common to the smelly high school gymnasium nearby, where nobody but the janitor knew it was taking place. Never would the day be a flop simply because we didn't bring enough merchandise—selling out was never a problem.

Time crawled at most of these things, and I painted to keep awake. That day at the clam festival, I was hunched under the table getting a tube of purple when I spotted a pair of feet wearing big red slipper-type shoes that ended in curled toes from which bells dangled. Alice and I had been yelled at by the organizers because our tablecloth did not reach the ground and did not hide all the boxes of stuff we'd stored beneath, so from under the table I pulled the cloth down until the feet disappeared. And when I crawled out from underneath, I saw Jack Murphy for the first time in my adult life.

He was wearing a xylophone on his head. This is the image that, until the one afternoon last April, took up more space than anything else I carried around in my heart. You know, when you think of a loved one and they are fixed in the eye of your soul and heart, maybe sleeping peacefully or looking at you in the firelight with one of those perfume-commercial gazes that coming from anybody else would look dumb? Well, when I called up thoughts of Jack, I could see him only with a xylophone rattling on his head, a pearly white accordion strapped to his front, a trumpet attached to the top of that, a flute clamped to his left wrist, a circle of bells on his right one, a tambourine dangling from his belt, a cymbal strapped to the inside of each knee, and a wide drum on his rear that he beat by kicking himself.

"Any requests?"

He asked this, and I asked for silence. I didn't yet recognize him, and I generally can't tolerate strolling entertainers—mimes, jugglers, musicians who want to show off their balance and illusions and ultimately pull some kind of farm animal from inside your blouse. I seem to be a magnet for them, usually the one in the crowd they pick to focus on while they do their tricks and acts and numbers. I usually turn away, or walk away if there is a clear path out. But there was something about this one that not only made me pay attention but ask for some Creedence, if he knew any, which he did, and soon the crowd all joined in the chorus about our being stuck in Lodi again. People gathered near, but it was not to look at our table. They were enthralled by the entertainer in the red-plaid trousers and the thick, blue, long-tailed coat buttoned despite the July sun, the guy playing, blowing, shaking and kicking his way through the song, all while focused on me.

The people clapped. Alice clapped. Even I did. I couldn't help it.

In response, he bowed, walked up to me, and said two words: "Lily Wilk."

I got a start, hearing my name coming out of a total stranger. Then he made it clear he wasn't that.

"Lily," he said, smiling. "It's Jack."

Jack Murphy. With that thing rattling on his head, a pearly white accordion strapped to his front, a trumpet attached to the top of that, a flute clamped to his left wrist, a circle of bells on his right, a tambourine dangling from his belt, a cymbal strapped to the inside of each knee, a wide drum on his rear that he beat by kicking himself, and a wedding ring on the fourth finger of his left hand.

I looked from that finger to his face, which was Jack's all

right, only with the touches of getting older that we all had by then, even a wave of gray in the black hair at the one temple I could see. But on him, age was like the wine in the corny commercial—it didn't make him simply older looking, only better. And he'd been pretty good to begin with. Louise always had been after me to go out with him. To her, he'd always been what she called a "drive." As in somebody who would drive her up the wall from being so fantastic looking and all.

"Oh, my God, he's such a driiive I don't see why don't you just grab him." She would whine like this while I'd be getting ready for one of the thousand outings I made with Jack after we got our licenses and began to visit every area gallery and museum we could find. Together, that had been our interest: What were real live artists making? What had real dead artists accomplished in their allotted time? How did they all do it? What was their inspiration? What materials did they favor? How did they not give up despite being poor or depressed or shunned or criticized, all those great experiences that stunk while they were happening but that ultimately built their heart and character? The many possible answers to all these we would debate afterwards, in a nearby ice cream shop, or in the closest parking lot, nibbling the smoked cheese cubes and carrot sticks we'd lifted from the modest buffets at the show openings. We each were dating other people off and on in those years, but they never appreciated the things Jack and I did, and always ended up breaking it off because they couldn't understand or believe how the focus of a relationship between a girl and a boy could be simply a deep, intense yearning to learn, to wonder, to admire, to stand in front of a work of art and simply breathe it in. Sometimes with eyes closed, even. Often with one person's hand finding one of the other person's and holding on as both represented the receiving end of the message or statement or emotion that some printmaker back in the sixteenth century was sending out still.

"Jack and me, it's a whole other thing than wanting him as a boyfriend—you couldn't begin to understand." I'd say that, or something equally haughty, as my answer to Louise, who would walk out of our room shaking her head.

I was thinking that day at the clam festival how Louise would be collapsing if she could only see Jack Murphy now. He was like the Easter dress Phyllis once bought for me—a flowy floral print that was nice but that needed something. And the something, I finally figured out, was to have all its petals and leaves and stems outlined by me in thin black laundry marker. Only after I did that could anybody else understand how yes, nice, but yes, sort of ordinary the dress had looked to begin with. Now it was truly something to behold, the contrasts, the colors stronger for being separated by the lines I'd made, by the shapes that were created by my work and time.

Well, Jack now was like somebody who'd been edged with a marker, or with something like that, further heightening his appeal, emphasizing even more the plusses that had been there to begin with—the definite oval of his face, the gentle swell of his lips, the little happy dents pushing in on either side of them, the fringy black hair still flying around on it own course, the wire-rimmed glasses that circled the mysterious dark caves into which were set faded blue eyes the shade of the stonewashed denim clothing that in the years since I'd last seen any part of Jack Murphy had swooped in and out of fashion. They were the same eyes that had taken in God only knows what scenes of life since the last time he used them to look at me, which was a late August afternoon just before he left for art school and for what turned out to be for good.

I finally had taken Louise's advice that day, on the burning hot vinyl of a flowered chaise lounge on the sunny deck cantilevering off a locked-up A-frame on Brown's Pond that Jack told me belonged to some relation who liked him and invited him to use the place yet wouldn't trust him with a key. Even years after we lost touch, I'd drive out there every once in a while and I'd park at the side of the road and I'd admire the wide water and the sweeping hills and the big oaks and the jagged geological formations jutting up into the shoreline, all the things that had been invisible to me that first visit, when the only thing I'd cared about was Jack Murphy and our first true kiss, which melted into the slow whisper that told me he'd wanted that from the first time he saw me.

"Jack Murphy—you look fantastic!"

Alice was nearly screaming the words. Jack looked down at his trumpet, appearing embarrassed or something close to it.

"Thanks," he said quickly. "Alice, right?"

"Alice Baldyga now."

"Shoulda known," Jack said. "Leo was always one nice guy. Tell him I said hello—if he remembers me."

Alice said that she would, and added that Leo of course would remember Jack. It was he, after all, who in our junior year, as a surprise meant for Alice, had paid Jack to delicately paint her name in a heart on the hubcap of the spare tire bolted to the back door of Leo's dark blue Ford Econoline.

"We still have it—the hubcap you painted." Alice sighed, and I knew she was telling the truth—I'd seen it on the wall of the basement, the blue paint and its silvery white accents still looking electric despite the rust and pits on the metal.

"Oh, yeah," Jack said, whether or not he recalled the job, or cared. I remember that Leo had paid him five dollars, which went for gasoline the next Saturday, when Jack and I drove all the way up to the Sterling and Francine Clark Art Institute in Williamstown to overdose on its Impressionists. Now, years and years later, Jack was facing me and staring intently, in much the same way he had when I sat that day on the museum's barber-clipped lawn and weighed the virtues of natural light against the kind that can be created in the studio. "So how about you, Lily?" he was saying to me now.

"Me?"

"You're still painting, I see."

He motioned to the T-shirt in front of him, the one with the Easter rabbits hopping all along the bottom edge. The week before, I had given in to Alice's nagging that I could sell a million if I'd only add "Some Bunny Loves You" in bubbly script. I was so embarrassed right then I wanted to crawl back under the table. Jack was standing there with an entire orchestra hanging off him, and I was the one turning some obvious and sweaty shade of red.

"My first summer at this—don't think I'll do it again. I'm painting on my own; this is just something for a little extra money—you know." That was what I rattled off to him, hoping to recover some dignity in his eyes.

I do real work, was what I honestly wanted to say. You should see it. You should come by and see it. You know I can do things much, much better than this.

"Lily has paintings hanging in the post office," Alice bragged, singsong, like we were on a playground. She looped her arm through the one of mine that hung helpless as Jack stared right into my brain and looked around inside it the way he once had the great skill to do. "She sells them sometimes, even. People come in and buy them."

"That's great," Jack said. He was holding the edge of the bunny shirt now, and was running his fingers slowly over the preshrunk fifty percent cotton/fifty percent polyester. "That's just great."

He said this again, and by that time I couldn't remember what he was referring to. I felt like I hadn't had any sleep at all, even though the night before I'd gone to bed at ten, then slept the whole way up here, three hours out cold in the backseat while Alice drove, happily, because Leo always hogged their wheel. Then I was hearing Jack say, "So, is Alice filling in for your husband today?"

The question, even though I got asked some version of it regularly, caught me off guard. It was weird coming from somebody my age. Usually the people who noted that I wasn't "taken" were my parents' friends, the people who didn't so much want to see me married off as wanted to be invited to both a Jack and Jill shower and a two-day wedding, complete with an open bar and prime rib dinner. Jack was fishing here, and it flattered me.

"I'm not married," I said. And Jack went, "Oh." That was when he smiled for real.

Turned out that he was almost in the same boat as me. Or at least close enough to the same vessel that he could jump from the dock and swim to it without exhausting himself. That's what he told me in the refreshment tent, where we foolishly ordered the festival special—steaming cups of clam chowder sipped at a picnic table near a big fan that blasted air not much cooler than the one that wasn't moving at all, and that was freezing compared to the temperature slowly crawling its way up in the space between the two of us.

"I'm having a tough time taking off the ring," Jack said quietly and down to the fresh green paint on the picnic table. I didn't know that feeling, but I nodded like interviewers do on

TV to show they're listening. Because I was, to every syllable of his circling, lengthy summing up of what had been his life with Sylvia.

She was Sylvia Nelson when they met, Sylvia Nelson-Murphy after they married, just as, in some kind of headache-inducing attempt at making all things equal, the ceremony had transformed Jack into Jack Murphy-Nelson. They'd met down at the Rhode Island School of Design, which is supposed to be such a great place but which really can't be because it didn't accept me when I applied. Jack it snapped up in an instant, wagging in front of him the incredible offer of two full years of tuition and the promise of equal help with the final two if he agreed to a work-study program selling sketch pads and such in the school store. We wrote each other for a time, but until that day at the clam festival, I never saw Jack once we began college. He spent his school-year breaks in Providence, waiting tables, and his summers somewhere down near the shore, doing yard work and some loose form of baby-sitting at a rich family's vacation place in exchange for a garage apartment where he could paint things to sell to tourists because it is true that people on vacation have money to burn and they'll buy anything you can come up with.

Sylvia was studying fashion design at RISD, and she and Jack got together a couple months into their first year there, right around the time he stopped writing to me and didn't so much as acknowledge the small India ink self-portrait I'd sent with New Year's wishes after matting and framing and wrapping it to present to him during the first Christmas break he never returned home for. Right around that time Sylvia came looking for him to ask him to paint up some fabric that she'd later cut up and sew into the one-of-a-kind clothing she just knew was going to make her famous. The project interested him, and Sylvia interested him, and before you know it, they were spending all their free time going around to craft shows, peddling the simple boxy dresses she'd sewn up out of the ninety-nine-cents-a-yard muslin that Jack had decorated with all sorts of wild shapes and scenes and even some blotches not unlike the ones on Alice's shirt from Horseneck.

Three summers before the day we remet, at one of those same kind of events—a Fourth of July celebration at a small but tourist-ridden town over in Vermont—Jack came to own all the instruments he had carefully and skillfully removed most pieces of just before we ordered our lunch. A musician had been performing right next to Jack and Sylvia's booth and collapsed halfway through his version of "My Way." Jack helped the emergency personnel unstrap the instruments that wheezed and clanged and jingled through the unsuccessful CPR attempts, and when they carted the man off in the screaming ambulance, Jack was left there, upset, shaking, sitting in the dust, Sylvia trying to comfort him, the two of them surrounded by the cast-aside elements of what had made that one man a band.

"Take it . . . I don't want to see any of it again," the man's widow choked over the phone line when Jack finally tracked her down a couple days later, offering to return everything once the hubbub of the funeral had subsided. "It would be like . . . like looking at the pistol that killed him. Can you understand this?"

Jack answered that he guessed that he could, so he kept the instruments as his own. Once in a while he'd take them out and fool around with them. And after he got the hang of playing one, he would strap on another and add to the sound. But other than at his own parties, and only after several drinks, he never played the whole band at one time and in public—until he had no choice. Which was what happened after Sylvia's business took off and she got her clothing displayed in real stores and had to rent a studio and hire two helpers full-time and it all made her so busy that she and Jack had a hard time getting along. He no longer was asked to paint the fabric, and they separated and began divorce proceedings. Jack was forced to make a living on his own, which he was one year into that day in Yarmouth, the latest stop on a tour of the same summer festivals at which he and Sylvia once had hawked shirts like the one he was wearing that day. Plain, unbleached cotton with a repetition of fluttering olive and copper leaves. The physical design of it was nothing to note. The paint and the shapes Jack had made were what grabbed your eye.

I pointed. "Nice."

"Old," he said. "Got a million of them. Shirts, drawstring pants, shorts, tanks, jackets, scarves, hats—and dresses, jumpers, and wraparound skirts, if I'm in the mood. Never had to go shopping for clothes. That was one good thing about us."

I decided to change the subject. The way the "us" word had grated on me was unsettling. "So what are you doing with your own art?"

Jack motioned to the instruments carefully stacked next to him and said, "With this here, I don't really have the time. There's a lot of driving, and now no one to share it. Like I'm heading for Nova Scotia when this thing ends at five. The ferry's too expensive from Portland, so I'm driving all the way up to Bar Harbor to catch the one there."

Suddenly I was at the wheel of Jack's car, on the road to a place I'd never been. In the backseat, he stretched out in a sleep that had to be his first sound one in the long months since he and Sylvia had split. He would wake hours later, already some-where in a foreign country, and he would lean into the front and whisper close how he hadn't felt this good in ages. And it was all because of me, he would add. And I would say it would always be this way—once I had the chance to drive over to Orange and tell Art, my boyfriend at the time, that I'd decided we weren't right for each other after all. I would have to finally admit that I was hanging around with him only because I thought it would be cool to say how I once had a guy with his name, who lived in a town that was a color.

But now, in real life, Jack was walking around to my side of the table. The hard edges of his knee cymbals pressed into me as we hugged fast but nice like long-ago friends might in such a situation, without an onlooker having any reason to think there might be anything more going on. Now, in real life, he was digging through a zippered blue-and-brown cloth wallet that had to be part of some failed accessory line. He picked out a white card on which raised lettering read "JACK MURPHY, ONE MAN BAND" above his address and phone number. Now, in real life, he was saying that if I gave him my own address and phone number, he would send me a postcard from up north.

Even though I knew you don't need a phone number to write somebody, I gave it to him anyway. The card arrived a week later. A photo of a beach with a high bluff, a lighthouse in the distance. "Greetings" was the word in white printing that floated in the perfect blue sky. I flipped it and saw the familiar handwriting, and message: "You are still a treasure."

Alice and Leo weren't home either when Jack left me. He knew their schedules and plans and habits almost as well as our own, and he'd selected the day that the two of them were going off to buy all the remaining napkins, paper plates, take-out containers, plastic cutlery, and tiny packets of salt and pepper from a friend's foundering grinder hut out near Framingham that had a Burger King spring up next to it nearly overnight. Between the consoling and the packing of the truck, they weren't supposed to be home until Heather's school bus arrived in midafternoon. That gave Jack four hours from the time they left to the time any of us was supposed to return. A little less than one hour for every year of the stuff he and Little Ted had accumulated at my place. Taffy Mendrek, who lives across the street from us and is on some kind of mysterious disability and does nothing all day but watch what everybody else is up to, later on told me she'd seen two strange guys helping Jack carry a series of boxes out of the apartment throughout the midday. Since Jack was present, she knew it was not a robbery, something she would have loved just to have a reason to try out the town's new 911 system. She said the three of them fed into one station wagon the cartons and the computer and the stack of shirts on hangers, the few stray books, a couple framed things, the industrial-size box of the favorite Cheerios that I'd recently bought Jack at the price club. Next time Taffy Mendrek looked out, all of them were gone. Including Jack.

That's when my life came to the point in the TV miniseries where Victoria Principal, or Melissa Gilbert, or Valerie Bertinelli— or Lindsay Wagner if you've tuned in to a true classic—throws herself into her work, both because she needs the money and because, finding herself deserted by her man, she has nothing else that she really loves. Or maybe the career was her first love in the first place. You usually don't have to stick around to the end of the series to find out if that is so—these programs are not too dramatic, not very cryptic, usually spelling the plot out for you in giant capital letters by the third commercial. You can bet on that just as you can bet on a happy ending. In real life, though, it's not something even my parents would put money on.

• • •

"No, come in here," Mary Ziemba says when she lets me into the kitchen and I start to head for the breakfast table.

She pushes a swinging door to the right of the one I'd entered through, and she waves me past. My heart beats even faster than it had on my way over, when I couldn't believe I'd ended up spending four and a half hours at what was supposed to be a fast visit to Claire O'Hare's. I'd left myself only about ten minutes to get to Mary Ziemba's. Now I am here, and I'm hoping it's her gallery that she's guiding me to.

I've pictured them in my mind for ages, the wonders she owns. Even though I know only the barest-boned descriptions, I can see them: Cassatt's sundappled children, the calm golden sea of Homer, the rounded lines in the pencil sketch of the big man's head by the elder Wyeth, the exact brushstrokes in the barn roof by his son. The rain that further darkened the black-and-white city street Stieglitz stood on for that sixtieth of a second, and the staggering wealth of colors O'Keeffe managed to find in the tiny overlapping of one pinkish white petal shading another.

I prepare myself to stand in their glory.

"Everything's on the table," Mary says, killing my hopes. "More space for us to work in here."

It's only a dining room that she leads me into. A very nice one, though. But still only a dining room. Long and historical-looking, like a famous dignitary maybe once had a meal or a drink here, something from a tour on the Home and Garden channel, fashionably beat-up flooring and paneling, and a stone fireplace so tall you could almost walk inside it. Suspended from somewhere inside its chimney are all the iron arms and hooks and pots that would help you to cook a meal there, if you wanted to go to all that trouble in this modern day and age. A big, busy wreath of highly flammable dried flowers hangs above the mantel, a sure sign to me that nobody ever lights a roaring fire just feet below. The only furniture interrupting the wide floorboards is the dining room set, of old knocked-around wood as well, one long and simple and shiny table ringed with ten high-backed wicker-seated chairs. It is on two of them that we settle.

In the center of the table are the five piles of photographs I quickly counted the minute Mary flipped on the electrified pewter candles that hung over the table. The box of pictures she'd shown me the night before had been full, and I was relieved that Mary had edited the contents down so well.

"There are five people," Mary confirms. She holds up that many fingers to make the number clearer. "Five that I really want in the painting. Plus me, so six. Six in all, but me you can see here before you. For the other ones, it took me most of the night to go through the pictures and pick out the best from those I already liked. Would you believe I didn't get to bed until after three? That's three in the morning, I should say. I'm beat."

She didn't look it. Her appearance was the same as the day before: eyes no smaller, or puffier, or darker, her face no more lined. I saw nothing to give a clue she'd been up much of the night. But then, I thought, how did I know how fatigue appeared on this woman? I'd only really been face-to-face with her just twice; I had no frame of reference. So I said nothing— I'd been up much too late myself and wasn't looking that great at this point in the day, fresh from giving the story of my life to a complete stranger. I thanked Mary Ziemba for her hard work in selecting the best photographs, and I asked if we could get going and see who she had here.

She smiled and pushed the first stack toward me.

"My sister." Then she added one word, which she gilded with pride and pronounced like she was slowly pulling open a curtain to reveal something so fragile it can only be displayed and exposed to light for thirty seconds of any hour:

"Flossie."

In the first three photos—the black-and-white and the fashions and the general look of which smacked of the terrible war years that had to be so awful but that, more than fifty years later, my parents have yet to stop rhapsodizing about—Flossie was captured in some version of the same pose: seated, her right leg over her left knee, fingers interlaced, and the two hands stationed on the left hip. There she was, in a yard or a field, in sweater and pants and boots, on a camp chair set in front of a fire. Then at the edge of a low brick wishing well, in a dotted cap-sleeved spring dress. A locket on a chain. Hosiery. High heels. Then indoors, at the far end of a bar, a skirted suit, simple flat hat, clutch purse, half a glass of something dark in front of her, a striped tapestry on the wall behind.

In each, Flossie smiled from a face that was much more interesting than her sister's. Where Mary's looked to be the product of trip under a rolling pin, Flossie's consisted of dramatic angles and planes, like she had been formed from clay with six or seven quick and artful strokes. Dark hair with a fine wave held its place despite being brushed up and off her face. Full brows shaded intense eyes. Her upper lip had subtle versions of cartoon peaks, as it had once been the fashion to paint on. But you could tell she came by them naturally.

Flossie had to be in her early twenties in these shots and around that, more or less, in the others that Mary had selected.

In the formal portrait branded in the corner by a golden stamp reading "Four Corners Studio, Three Rivers," she looked up and to the right, glowing from within like one of the chiaroscuro paintings I had to name and date in the mind-

Lily of the Valley

numbing series of slides that were my college art history exams. Under the studio lights, Flossie's hair was the ribbon candy my mother would buy for the table every Christmas—rippled, exotic, translucent lengths of sugar finished with a burnished glow you want to stroke.

"She's something," I said. And Mary laughed a little, like this was no news to her. She placed in front of me a snapshot, Flossie at a kitchen stove. You could guess it was not her normal place, and perhaps that alone was the reason for her being photographed at that instant. A lace-edged pinafore protected a fancy dress decorated with bold flowers. She stood on heels that would kill you if you spent all day on them. She laughed into the camera lens as she stirred something in a huge black pot, her hand holding an oversized wooden spoon, delicately, probably so she would not damage a nail.

Beneath a sign that read "ALL TRAINS THIS WAY" and a long arrow that directed passengers to tracks down the hall, young ladies Flossie and Mary wore tailored winter coats, a corsage pinned to the lapel of each. They smiled sweetly and held hands. It was my first look at Mary as someone other than the person seated across from me. She had much the same features as she did in the present, only with the layers of years removed. Her hair was blond and ended in a flip back then, and with the same bangs she had now she resembled Rosemary Clooney from the videotape of *White Christmas* that Alice likes to run nonstop during her holiday parties. People had to have mentioned this likeness to Mary Ziemba at some point in her life, and I wondered if she felt flattered. She struck me as the kind who wanted to be known for being herself, and not first off as an imitation of another. Maybe I was only supposing that. Still, it would have been a compliment.

"You were going somewhere far away?"

86

"Flossie was."

"But you both have corsages."

"That shows you something about Flossie," Mary said, pointing at me. "I got her one because she was leaving. And she got me one because I couldn't go."

I looked closer at the picture. There was a touch of sadness that I hadn't detected before in the faces, or maybe Mary had just put that into my head. Whatever, I now could see this wasn't a trip for two. And that it might have been the beginning of a lot more than just a simple week away.

Mary slid over to me another picture. Flossie, in a dark skirted swimsuit, probably navy, embroidered with a big white anchor that held down her chest. She was seated high up on a lifeguard's chair, smiling broadly and pointing her hand at the words "SANTA MONICA" stenciled onto the life preserver hanging from the side.

"That's the day she arrived out there," Mary said.

I asked, "Vacation?"

"No. She went there for work."

I didn't need to ask what kind. In the eight-by-ten of a stage holding about a hundred chorus girls in abbreviated white tuxedoes and sequined Uncle Sam top hats, one teeny figure three rows from the back and seven from the left was circled with black ink.

"Me!" was printed next to the circle, in case there was any question.

Same circle, same announcement, on the five-by-seven of only a dozen dancers, all dressed for safari—khaki jackets and shorts, tooled riding boots with metal plates at the toe that must have transformed them into tap shoes. Flossie was in the front row here, third from the left, joining the others in pointing a hunting rifle high over her pith helmet.

Then, a small snap of a mermaid. A suit of shimmery scales. Long fake hair that fell past a fish waist, a huge tail that curled gracefully where feet should have been showing. A necklace of shells, a trident, a crown of starfish. "My 'Princess of the Sea' Audition" was written on the back, in Flossie's hand.

"She got that audition" Mary told me, pointing to the picture and nodding.

Flossie had been the glamour girl of the family. It was easy to guess that. No afternoons on hands and knees in the garden, no mornings pulling the vegetable cart up hills or over rough pavement, wheels sticking in trolley tracks, bad kids swiping things if she didn't keep watch. Flossie probably had nothing at all to do with the kind of life that had turned out to be what had made her sister so well known. But that seemed to make no difference; their connection was clear.

"We liked the same things," her sister said, and she went on to say her sister was the kind of person mad for egg noodles.

For tea.

For complimentary shades of red.

For the kind of snow that is like little crystals when you push your mitten through a drift of it.

For bingo with real money as the prize, if any place was so generous as to be offering it.

For the idea of the Caribbean.

For even something as simple as the rich creak that wicker makes when you settle onto it.

For synthetics that need no ironing.

For children under the age of four.

For films starring beautiful women who get rescued by men who are almost better looking.

For mystery novels with plots not too taxing.

For quality hand cream applied just after nighttime prayers.

For fancy stationery.

And for her sister.

Who told me, "Flossie was the first person ever to really know me. I'd like you to start with her." Mary pointed again, as I was beginning to catch on was a habit of hers. "Put her somewhere up front in your painting. She'd like that. Up front. That's the place she belongs."

5

I once made a picture of my own sister. A long time ago. When I first came to realize that not everybody's was like the one I had.

It was a watercolor of Louise at age nine, walking toward me from the mailbox, wearing the tattered orchid gown one of the Pilch girls sewed for herself when a military boy asked her to a formal dance ages ago. The hem has lost all its stitches and is now held up with a line of old diaper pins that have faded yellow plastic duck heads for the part that shields the needle's point. A red patent-leather belt that is way too big, and that my father had to make extra holes in with an awl, pulls the dress around her waist. She has plain white flip-flops on—no borrowed heels because my mother always warned us that wearing shoes that are not your size can be dangerous. Louise has made these plain things ornate with some of the gift bows she collected whenever anybody in our house got a present. On her left foot she has taped a big, full, satiny yellow one that looks like a chrysanthemum. On her right one there is a red bow decorated with flocked poinsettia shapes. Neither one of us girls at this point in either of our lives is allowed to paint any of our nails. So on her toes, Louise has pressed a thin layer of red crayon as a poor substitute.

Since she first learned her days of the week, Thursdays always have been dress-up days for Louise. And this was a Thursday afternoon in late August. I first noticed her in this particular outfit while I was sitting on the front stairs sorting through a pan of raspberries Unc had picked hastily because the rain was coming fast. Bruised clouds swelled from behind the woods across the street. The light was getting greenish as Louise approached me slowly and, with both white-gloved hands, held out a big gray envelope.

"Look," she breathed. "It's from him."

Nobody ever heard of such a thing in those days, but Louise that summer had added to her two ambitions the desire to become a girl astronaut. My parents shook their heads and actually did ask her, "Whoever heard of such a thing?" But the dream really was their fault to begin with. They were the ones who, one month before, had woken us and made us slouch into the living room in the middle of the night to watch the fuzzy image of Neil Armstrong bounce down the ladder to the surface of the moon. My mother excitedly snapped photos of the TV set with her Instamatic, and my father shoved a slippered foot into any of us who were starting to doze.

"Wake up," he'd shout. "It's for your own good. This is something you'll tell your kids about someday—that you saw this with your own eyes, something people said could never be. A man on the moon. Just think of it. This, here, this is why you should go to school and become as smart as you can."

"If they're so smart," Chuckie asked, "why couldn't they land there during the day, when everybody would be awake?"

I thought that was a good question, but my father just gave him a kick.

Down on the floor, I lay with my toes hooked into the

dangly drawer knobs of my mother's hope chest, on top of which our RCA sat beaming what the little white capital letters on the bottom of the screen assured us were "FIRST LIVE PICTURES FROM MOON." Unc leaned forward from the edge of the hassock, his elbows poking into his knees. In front of him, Louise sat up straight and still, arms hugging herself, eyes big like somebody was telling her a ghost story. She had far from what could be described as a scientific mind, but she was suddenly and totally taken by the space mission. The next day, she wrote a letter asking Neil Armstrong for his autograph. She didn't make the letter out to him, as she knew he was busy up there in space. She wrote it to Walter Cronkite, who every night appeared on the same channel where each morning you could find Captain Kangaroo, and who always seemed to know where to locate the astronauts any minute of the day, on several occasions prior to their missions even sitting right next to them in person and asking all kinds of questions. Louise figured it made perfect sense that Walter Cronkite would be the one who could do her this favor. And the day that I painted her picture coming up the walk was the same day she went down that walk to get the mail and came back to show me the big dark-gray envelope addressed to Miss Louise Wilk, with a return address of CBS News in New York City.

All of us who were there that afternoon—Chuckie and Unc and me—gathered around and watched her slowly pull up the metal tab that held the envelope closed. She reached a trembling hand inside and slowly slid out into our view an eight-by-ten black-and-white glossy.

Of Walter Cronkite.

With a big felt-tip autograph on the corner:

"Walter Cronkite."

Chuckie licked his finger and tried to rub off some of the ink that made up the signature. Nothing happened.

"It's printed right on there—it's fake! Ha!" He pushed it back at us and walked away.

Louise blubbered into my tank top, and when she finally got it together enough to speak, she choked out the words, "I didn't want his picture . . . I didn't want his name . . ."

"If he was going to do the signing, you'd think he could have at least written it himself." This was Unc speaking, somebody who was trying to help, but who only upset Louise more.

"Maybe now you'll give up this stupid astronaut stuff," Chuckie yelled as he rode his banana bike across the lawn, popping a wheelie as the back tire crossed the walk. Blowing her nose into Unc's hanky, Louise nodded and said, reverting to a baby voice, that she would forget about it. And she added the word "forever."

But by the next Thursday, she apparently had some second thoughts. She woke early and quietly, and I never heard any of her rummagings as she went looking for everything she needed: her good, white cotton pajama pants from the dressy set Phyllis had bought for Louise to spend the mumps in, the old white-gray dress shirt that Chuckie had worn each and every day of third grade, my white vinyl snow boots with the fake fur around the top and silver snowflakes for zipper pulls, and a pair of grayed once-white garden gloves. She put all this on and slipped over her head the enormous goldfish bowl Chuckie kept turtles in when he found them, and then she used half a roll of my father's widest masking tape to seal the mouth of the bowl to the neck of her shirt. It was her Neil Armstrong outfit, to be worn on the four-foot stepladder already set up on the driveway, to climb, then to ceremoniously descend, and set foot on the moon.

But Louise had done such a good job of binding her shirt to her helmet that the glass soon began to fog and she couldn't see. She began spinning around the backyard shrieking for help, only nobody in the house could hear her, we being inside, behind all those walls and windows, and Louise's head being outside, under all that thick glass.

My mother later asked us to all thank God for Hope Kapinos, who, also early that morning, was outside, next door, under her clothesline, hanging her and her sisters' freshly washed unmentionables. It was she who spotted Louise—or at least something that looked like Louise—swirling and flapping and making muffled noises while headed right for a collision with our flagpole. Hope claims that she ran—and we all would have liked to have seen that because she then had to be a million years old at the very least—across the garden, and she grabbed Louise right before the fishbowl smashed into the pipe.

It was one of those many times my parents yelled that somebody could have put an eye out, but there was no way in the world you could argue that they were exaggerating. One collision and I didn't want to think about how awful it could have been, all that tragedy taking place while I was still safe in bed and stretching, listening to my joints pop and making loud yawns just to irk Chuckie, who I know hated that and who I knew could hear me through our thin shared wall. I went back upstairs and hid in our room as, down in the kitchen, my parents yelled, "What do you want to do, kill yourself?" and otherwise blasted Louise for playing so foolishly, and with glass yet.

People ask me what it was like to grow up with Louise, and I answer, "Never a dull moment." Because it truly never was.

"I bet," these people say back to me. "I never knew anyone so creative. That must be where you get it."

They say this even though Louise is one year younger than I am, and therefore could not be anyone I inherited anything from. And any artistic skills she might have, I would point out, didn't really surface until she was thirty-one, the year she was facing eviction for nonpayment of rent on her place out in Watertown, already having tried and failed at being a personal shopper, and a time-share hostess, and a cable-television-billing-center office manager, and a home-party Crystalware pitchwoman, and a wife, and a wife one other time. There was no big golden future on her horizon the morning she was out power-walking and got bit by a misleadingly docile terrier mix that turned out to be owned by a theater guy who asked what else he could do other than speed her over to the emergency room and pay for the nine stitches on the outside of her calf. And Louise answered how she didn't need anything else but a new job—even though it is hard to imagine thinking of such a thing when you are in terrible pain and a piece of you is hanging off and needs to be sewn back on. But that's what she thought of and said. And now, seven years later, because of what she said, she is chief costumer for the Boston Theater Company. And now I am often referred to as the sister of Lu Wi.

It's Lu now. Not Louise. Wi. Not Wilk anymore. When she entered work in the world of drama, Louise thought such a change would fit her new life. "Everyone around me seemed so exotic—and I was, well, blah." This is how she explained it when she came home and told us that she had become Lu Wi—legally, with the seal-affixed court papers and everything. My mother didn't much care about this decision—at least she never said she did—but my father was very disturbed by it. He normally got upset even when somebody with a Polish name pronounced it the American way. Like Freddie Byc out by Junction Variety, who'll give his name to you and then will add brightly, "Just like the pen!" when, correctly, it sounds identical to the word that I on occasion have called Jack's ex-wife, the *y* rightfully being pronounced like a soft *i*, and the *c* accented to make the sound "tch."

"It's only for my image in the working world," Louise kept telling my father. This was seven years ago. I know that because Louise came home with this news the same weekend I finally broke it off with Art. I was moping, and secretly happy that Louise was using one of her rare visits to make a scene and stop everybody in the family from looking at me and asking me what had been my problem with the boy—that at least he was employed, and there are worse things a guy could do than assemble .45s down at Smith & Wesson, something I did not believe true.

"You're ashamed of your heritage," was all my father would say back to Louise when she gave another piece of her defense. Louise said that she was not, but it's clear she just loves it when she arrives somewhere and people say to her that from her name they were expecting someone Chinese or Japanese or the like. And Lu Wi waves them away and says, "Oh, everybody thinks that."

Why shouldn't they before they meet her? The name has done more than make obsolete the navy blue crewneck my parents ordered stitched with "Louise" during the preppie craze. It has set the image for an entire life. Lu Wi's message machine asks you to wait for the sound of the gong. Her see-through rice paper business card bears a series of Chinese characters that translate to something about finding who we truly are, rather than living by what we have been labeled. The apartment she shares with the mysterious husband she married in some kind of Far East ceremony to which none of us got invited is a back-drop from the *Shogun* miniseries, or a pricier version of The Golden Bowl, where Unc and Phyllis and I always ask for sec-onds of those little fried noodles they put out on the table to dip into duck sauce even before they give you a menu or water. Lu Wi's home has screens for room dividers, straw mats for rugs, pillows for chairs, tables with abbreviated legs, handleless cups for tea—don't even ask for coffee because one bean of it has never made it through the door at which you have to remove your shoes before passing through, and she even pro-vides a variety of different-sized canvas slippers to put on once you're inside.

Lu Wi grew her hair long just so she could keep it up with chopsticks, and she dyes it from our family's brown to a shiny black. There is nothing she can do about her facial features, which zoom her right back to her still-warm Eastern European roots. Yet she tries, spending a lot of money on cosmetics made out of rice powder. She drives a Honda and didn't much like it when I informed her how I'd read that nowadays they make them in New Jersey. When she is out in the world, her clothes are of simple lines and silk. At home, she wears a kimono and walks around slowly and delicately like Unc did after he had a plantar's wart removed. She speaks of peace and serenity, and of how Westerners—by that she means anybody but her—would do well to follow the Eastern paths to enlightenment. It goes without saying that she no longer attends real church.

Over in Watertown, the prospect of being damned to hell does not crowd my sister's mind. Over in Watertown, her stereo plays music that is little string plinkings with no particular melody the uninitiated can cling to. Over in Watertown, the music sounds like how she once was, back when she mattered to me: directionless.

But now Louise has a path. A purpose. A life. A big-deal career. And she never, ever comes back home.

Or even has the time to receive visitors. Or to return messages left after the gong.

"It's a fast-paced life you would never understand," she said the time a couple years back that Alice and I chaperoned Heather's Girl Scout troop to Louise's company's production of *Cinderella*. It was a matinee and we got someone to bring us backstage and locate my sister as she came out of the rest room behind the big pumpkin coach. She looked embarrassed and hugged me halfheartedly with only one arm like the other was broken or something. She'd plucked her eyebrows nearly to extinction, and I was fixed on them as I listened to her recent schedule of show deadlines, fabric-buying trips, woes about living in a co-op, search to find a suitable acupressurist now that her regular one has moved. It was Louise, Louise, Louise, with not a single question to or comment about me except that she didn't want to take up our time—she was sure we had to be leaving soon. Right?

It would have been nice to have a sister's shoulder to cry on when Jack took off. I called her at the time, not knowing what I was going to say, but once she surprised me by actually answering the phone, I blurted out a whole lot more details than I should have to somebody who didn't care.

"Another will come along and it'll be fine again. I gotta go." This is what she said to me. Like I was going to have to live in some kind of limbo, as if in order to truly breathe I had to be hooked through plastic tubing to someone else I considered family. I wondered all the rest of that night if that was the kind of person I'd turned out to be. And I came up with the thought that maybe she had something there. You couldn't see them, and they're nothing that you'd actually trip over, but pieces of me indeed fell off when I read the note from Jack, and when I realized how that also meant good-bye to Little Ted, and when I came to the conclusion that the Louise Wilk I knew no longer existed. And I certainly did feel kicked in both lungs when my mother and my father upped and moved to Florida.

That happened because they hit it big at Foxwoods. At a slot machine in the no-smoking hall, exactly seven weeks after their first therapeutic visit.

They won on a Sunday morning, of course, just after they made their dent in the breakfast buffet. It was on my mother's fifth quarter of the morning. The first had resulted in some-thing like two peaches and a pear and a seven and a cherry, though I'm not certain of the actual fruits involved. The second had been some similar salad. Same with the third and fourth. But the fifth: seven, seven, seven, seven, seven.

Ding-ding-ding went the machine. My mother's was mak-ing this noise, but she didn't realize it. To see who'd won, she glanced at her neighboring players, to the left, at the old legless *babci* drawn up in the wheelchair, to the right, at the young woman breaking the rules by bringing in the baby that now was shrieking from all the noise. Ding-ding-ding. Lights flashed on a pole that extended from my mother's slot machine and rose slowly up to the ceiling to announce that a winner had been crowned, right here. Then the coins began to fall. And they fell and they fell and they fell.

People gathered. Some of them could be heard swearing, how just minutes ago they'd tried that very same machine, or at least one very near to it, and nothing like that had hap-pened to them. Some of the people who came to see what was going on handed my mother their big plastic change cups for her to collect in. One man rushed to help her scoop and kept assuring her, "You can trust me, lady, I'm an honest guy. You can trust me."

"But it was more than some small change that you wouldn't mind a stranger helping you with. It was a lot of money." That's what my father said when they told us the story that night, after they called me over to the house saying, "Come quick, but don't worry, nobody is sick or anything like that." When I arrived out of breath and terrified even though I'd been told I wasn't supposed to be, my father said, "What I was thinking when I noticed the commotion was, 'Whoever that is, they're getting a lot of money.' You could hear it falling from across the room, as noisy as that place is to begin with. It was steady. Like a waterfall. Money just pouring down. And the money—turned out it was your mother's!"

We all ate at Dominick's the following morning—my parents and Unc and Phyllis and me and Alice. Our first time ever in the round aqua corner booth where Father Krotki sits each Wednesday at lunch to enjoy a medium-rare moonburger, a selection touted on the menu as being "Outta this world." The rest of the time the table and seat is marked with a typed-out placard reading "Reserved For Celebrity Guests." In the fading color enlargement that hangs over the space, Ted and Joan Kennedy share a plate of *golombki* during a campaign stop. Dominick and Julia themselves stand posed to the left, ready to offer a plate of the *pierogi* they pinched the night before, once they learned from their state representative friend that the famous couple would be passing through town and would most likely be hungry by then.

There, on the same vinyl that Ted and Joan once warmed, we celebrated. When not being interrupted, that is. Even though the win had taken place in another state, by early next morning word already had snaked through the town: Nobody had an idea of the exact figure, but they did say in low voices, did you know that, suddenly and wonderfully, Casimir and Dorothy *bogaty?*

They're rich.

"Rich enough to buy a Rolls-Royce," Joey Fijal called over from the counter.

"Rich enough to get a vacation place on the Cape," Mr. Mleko yelled from the coatrack.

"Rich enough to eat lobster there every day," Lori Kozniewski said as she put down another pot of coffee.

"Certainly rich enough to fund the rest of the drive for the new chapel out at the cemetery." Eva Plattner threw this at us as she and her husband passed. Nobody said anything back to her.

"Well, certainly rich enough to retire in Florida," Dominick himself said brightly.

And my parents, both at the same time, replied, "You're a mind reader!"

That was the first I heard of it. Sitting there poking at the still-fluid yolk in the egg I'd ordered over hard. Everybody said I should get more to eat than that, but I never have been much of a breakfast person.

"Who cares if you aren't going to eat it?" they asked. "Get whatever you can think of, because it's all going to be free of charge."

"Yeah, I know," I said. I'd been there when Dominick rushed over and shook my father's hand and kissed my mother on the left cheek and then announced that all our breakfasts would be on the house. All because my parents had won a lot of money. They now could afford to treat the entire restaurant, but they were going to get food for nothing.

"Florida?" I pronounced it like I'd never heard of the place. Of course I knew what it was, and I had even visited there. On my honeymoon, one full week in Walt Disney World that Jack had the good fortune to win in a fund-raising raffle at a school fair he'd worked the fall before our wedding. He'd tried to finagle a cash equivalent of the trip, which would have been nice but wasn't possible. So when we made our wedding plans, we decided to use it, the seven free nights in a ground-floor room in the budget-wing section of the Contemporary Hotel, where we could board the monorail right in the lobby to go use our all-day passes to Tomorrowland. On the carousel, as I was riding one romping stallion in front of the one Jack sat on, the clean-cut attendant in lederhosen first made sure I was holding on tight and then told me I looked great that afternoon and then asked me if I would be interested in a real ride after he got off work.

"Yes, Florida," my mother was saying, and she was beaming a great big smile.

"For good?"

"Well, it's not really somewhere you go just for weekends," Dominick stuck in, like he had any right to still be standing there, let alone to be part of the conversation.

"Unless you're a Kennedy," said Lori Kozniewski. Everybody but me laughed at her comment. And they laughed again when she added, "Or a Wilk!"

None of it was funny to me. I know—I was nearly forty. An adult by anybody's definition. But at this point, I didn't want two more pieces of my family to vanish from my life. It was as simple as that, even if some might find it hard to understand. Another bump to the card table on which I, over the years, had been assembling the pieces of my life. Another smack and there they go, shooting off into the air, and even after you find most of them and put them back into place, there are some you suspect are still under the couch or may have been carried off by the dog to be eaten or chewed beyond recognition or repair. I bet you can be eighty-nine years old and still feel that way, that you want around you the people you are used to having around you. The people who know you best. And when one or two or three of them up and leave for whatever reason, even at eighty-nine, or in my case, thirty-nine, even if you don't make one outer sound, inside you still turn into a kid who's whimpering, Don't leave me—stay, stay, please stay.

"You'll have your own room, whatever kind of house we end up in," my mother said, and she put her right hand on mine as I still held my fork even though I didn't want any more to eat. As was her custom for special occasions, my mother was wearing the gold band with the small, square, pale-green stone, the ring that she had found at Hampton Beach back when I was in second grade and she caught her left baby toe on it when we were dragging all our stuff back to the car after one long hot day out near the state park jetty. Of course we brought the ring over to the white-brick lifeguard station in back of the band shell, and a big tan guy who told us he was in charge of the place even though he had no shirt on instructed my mother to leave her name with him in case nobody claimed her find. On a pad he found near his telephone, she printed out the information in her usual all capitals, even though she asked, "Who wouldn't come looking for such a beautiful piece of jewelry?" The answer was nobody, because nobody ever did. And at the end of the summer, my mother received a postcard to come and pick up the green ring if she wanted it, as the lifeguard station had no more cause to hold it and really no place to store such a valuable when they closed up the station for the winter months.

• • •

"Come with us." Years later, in the celebrity booth, my mother was begging me in this way. Her green ring sparkled and looked as it always had—like it simply was made for her. I guess sometimes things you stumble across end up being just that.

"Florida is far away," she told me. "A new place—new things to paint. Think of all the flowers there! The boats. The sunsets. You could sell your paintings to tourists. People on vacation have money to burn and they'll buy anything you could come up with. This may be just what you need."

Exactly what I needed was a mystery to me. But when I inserted the word Florida into the blank, that didn't seem to be the answer. No lights, no horns, not the faintest ding-ding-ding.

"Please think about it," my mother asked when I didn't reply, and I nodded that I would, even though I didn't need to. I didn't know too much at that point, but even as more of them were being scattered around me, I was becoming aware I had pieces to pick up here before I ever could think of picking up and going anywhere else.

6

It was Chuckie who first said I should give drawing lessons. But it was not out of any confidence that I had knowledge and skill and genius to share.

"Nobody's going to want to buy any of your old drawings," was what he told me soon after my abilities were revealed. "They want to be able to make one themselves. If you want to get some money out of this, that's the only way it's going to happen. You have to teach."

With Chuckie, that's what everything came down to. He loved money—saving it more than spending it. Even way back, as a kid. Acquiring it and plinking it into an empty Clorox bottle and once in a while pouring it all out onto his bed and spreading it around with his hands to make one big sea of change and crumpled bills. Then he'd call, "Wanna see something?" to anybody who might pass his door, and he'd show them just how very rich he was.

I have to say he was a hardworking kid, and he came by most of the coins respectably, much of it from his cut of the sales at the summertime table of garden flowers we were paid to mind on the front yard, stocked neatly every day with whatever Unc picked from the garden just after the sun came up. Bunches and arrangements were five or ten cents, or a quarter for the grandest ones. We would collect payments in the drawer of a red toy cash register after handing over the flowers displayed in cleaned-out food jars that people were not beholden to return to us.

Chuckie also profited from the evening and Sunday-morning paper routes he had on three streets other than ours, and he did regular work for some neighbors who preferred that he, not they, rake their leaves and cut their lawns and clear their snow and weed their flower beds and once a spring pick up all the fallen branches and bits of sticks the winter had thrown onto their properties. Occasionally, when he got one of his big ideas, Chuckie did something sneaky to get even richer, like when he was in the fifth grade and Catholic Charities time rolled around and he put on his school uniform one Saturday and took a Maxwell House coffee can door to door on the other side of town. Or the Halloween he left his pillowcase home and carried around only a small cardboard box on which he'd not too neatly written "UNICEF." My parents never found out, and neither the diocese, nor the U.N., nor a single poor person ever saw a penny of the impressive amount of coins he collected these ways and saved for his own rare and personal use.

He was not all stingy, though, as was demonstrated secretly when I was nine and my parents signed Louise and me up for the polonaise lessons being offered by the Polish Women's Alliance every second Tuesday night of the month. Louise and I were members of the club's girls' organization, which had something to do with insurance policies and never held meetings that we knew about, except at Christmas, when the ladies threw us a nice party on a Saturday afternoon and we could select whatever fancy box we wanted from the pile of them heaped beneath the silver-fringed Christmas tree that changed color continuously thanks to a red, green, and gold plastic disc rotating in front of a nearby spotlight.

It was at the previous year's party that the ladies got the idea we all needed dance lessons. And they were probably right. But it was Mrs. Slowik's idea that we learn the polonaise, and that she would be the one who would teach us. She wasn't a dance pro, just somebody who had learned the steps during her one and only trip to Poland, made the year before, when she got word that her great aunt had died and that there was a chance some amount of acreage would be up for grabs.

Mrs. Slowik took her position seriously. She came to the lessons dressed in a traditional costume she'd brought back from her visit. Her squarish torso was laced into a black-velvet vest ornate with the kind of embroidery you normally only see on priest vestments. Her flowered skirt stopped below her knees and showed you how her thick calves were jammed into patent leather boots lashed up with thick ribbons. She'd turn on a record of the polonaise and stand on a wooden case from Cascella's Soda and she'd wave a yardstick to the beat, yelling, "ONE two three, ONE two three, ONE two three," as we all made our way around the room repeating the lunging steps.

Louise was my partner. Since the lessons were held on Thursdays, Louise's dress-up day, she came to the classes looking like a tiny version of Mrs. Slowik. Hers wasn't another of the outfits pulled together from stuff around the house. It was an actual costume that Sister Consolata's sister—a sister sister rather than a nun sister—had brought back from her own visit to Poland a couple years before.

It had been first prize in a church raffle the previous October. Wojcik's even donated one of its children's mannequins, and it was dressed up in Sister's donation and placed in the church vestibule, between the holy water font and the

old wooden table that always held a collection of things wor-
shippers had left behind: the unmatched mittens or gloves, the
key rings, mantillas in their little plastic envelopes, rosaries and
umbrellas of various colors, small toys and pacifiers. From the
time that costume went on display, the late end of July, to the
festival in the middle of October, Louise went to church every
chance she got. We had perpetual adoration, which means the
Blessed Sacrament was displayed nonstop and the church was
open twenty-four hours for anyone who might feel the need to
come on in and pray even at three in the morning if they
wished, so Louise visited constantly. She rode her bike down
there once, sometimes twice, a day, bringing along a nickel to
light a candle and beg God to allow her to win the prize,
promising Him she'd never, ever again in her whole entire life
ask him for anything else, including that she be let into heaven.

This part of her visit got expensive, and Louise soon was
knocking on Chuckie's door for financial aid. She needed
money for lighting a votive a day, plus several times a week she
would buy herself a fifty-cent raffle ticket from the pad of them
on the lost-and-found table. Chuckie gave her whatever money
she needed, at a rate of six cents back for every five he gave out.
He made her sign a paper that said she agreed to pay in this
manner and that if she failed to reimburse him in a timely fashion, his household chores would be hers for an entire year. He
made it look official, typing it out, and peeling a fancy glittery
seal off the cap of one of my father's liquor bottles to glue to the
agreement. He called me into his room to witness as Louise
printed her name on the correct line, and I had to sign on
another one that I had seen Louise willingly enter into this,
though it all quickly had become another thing for her to
quiver her lip over. But Louise wanted the outfit, and, guess
what—hers was the name Sister Superior drew from the pickle

barrel full of tickets rolled onto the stage at the end of festival. It was not her handwriting, but who cared—it was her name.

I found out years later from my mother, who had found out years before from Father Krotki, that Chuckie one day that October had walked to the rectory to meet with him personally to ask what he could do to assure that Louise would win the dress. Some cash donation was arrived at—I never found out how much—and a couple weeks later a couple of men were carrying the mannequin into the ladies' room so Louise could try on her prize. She reappeared to great applause and many flashbulb pops. Next, she marched next door to church and said a private prayer of thanks, tearfully admitting to God then, as she did to me about a week later, that she never had thought she was a good enough girl to get exactly what she prayed for, as this was the first time in her life it had worked. After all that, she got in our car and went home and wore the thing to bed.

By the time I found out Chuckie's part in this, I had no way to tell him how great I thought all that was. He was off working. Chuckle's childhood love of money grew into a calling that none of us could really understand but that the stories in the investment magazines he'd once in a while clip and send home would tell us was something important along the lines of "pouring firm financial foundations for the shakiest of the emerging nations." That's where Chuckie went off to live. In emerging nations. Places you never heard of, even if you, like we, studied the globe with great regularity.

When I was in the third grade, my father narrowly beat brainy Ethel Heneghan from the street next to the French school in coming closest to guessing the number of jellybeans that filled a new plastic gasoline can displayed in the window of Belanger's Hardware. He won the can, the beans, and a previous year's model of a World Nation Series globe.

The can he put in the garage, because it's always wise to have spare fuel for use in the snowblower and lawn mower and to wash your hardworking hands with if nothing else will clean them. The beans he hid in the pantry, up on a high shelf, to be touched only by my mother, who rationed them out to us four per day wrapped in a small leaf of tinfoil and tossed into our schoolbags until the supply ran out in a month. The globe he got the bright idea to set up in the bathroom, in the vacant space right beneath the toilet paper roll.

Chuckie, Louise, me, we all got A's in geography the rest of our years in school. We could in a second find for you all your major and minor countries, bodies of water, land formations, and currents, along with being able to spin the thing and put our finger on the exact location of the Yellow Sea or the Bodele Depression or the Ross Ice Shelf or Franz Josef Land, or a whole bunch of other places I'd never heard of until they were revolving there next to me. Some bad flu seasons we'd all agree to study a particular area—say the South Pacific or everything above the 60th parallel. No other kids we knew held in their heads the wide range of fascinating geographical facts that we did. And those who asked us why bother with all that, well, years later, we could point far away, to Chuckie over on the other side of the world, and we could say to them that was why.

The globe was the reason Chuckie went off to do what he did for a living, and why he lived where he did in order to do that. When he graduated from UMass, he had no plans except to travel off to some of those places he'd previously seen only in our bathroom. They were, of course, so much more fascinating in real life, once their individual peoples and languages and architectures and landscapes and foods and music and wildlife were right there in front of him. He returned home to get a master's degree in business, but then moved on, to a long series of faraway places that had in common the fact that their names were unpronounceable. And that they needed a lot of help. Chuckie was there to give the kind he knew best: help with money. How to get it. What to do with it when it arrives. How to save and spend and make more, with an eye to what you want in the future. One picture we have is of Chuckie in front of a farming co-op he helped found, hoe in his hand, the arms of shoeless smiling men flung around his shoulders. Good works like that were what he spent his grown-up life doing. This was why we never could see him. Rarely heard from him, and often couldn't contact him if we wanted to. But somebody on a staticky phone line was able to reach us right after we'd had our fifteen-minute meal one Sunday afternoon the May before Jack took off, to ask was this the family of Mr. Charles Wilk? I thought about the name that we never used for my brother and answered yes, it was, and they asked me to sit down. There was no chair near the phone, so I went to the table, and my mother told me to please get out of her way as she carried the big platter empty of meat past me just as whoever it was on the other end of the line said they didn't know how to tell me this but Mr. Charles Wilk's train had derailed and was incinerated somewhere south of the Gulf of Ob and Mr. Charles Wilk was not found to be among the survivors.

This is why, when I want to see my brother, I think back to when we all were alive and living under the same black-shingled roof, Chuckie passing by in the hall on the way back from brushing his teeth before bed, stopping to stick his head in my and Louise's doorway, reminding me for the dozenth time that "If I could get away with it, I'd teach people how to do art. What could be easier than standing around pointing and telling somebody what to do?"

I didn't agree with him then, but a couple years later there I was, standing around pointing and telling Pammy Franklin just those very things.

"She just draws and draws and draws. It's all she cares about."

Pammy Franklin's mother tells me this as she pours me a cup of coffee even though I have asked her not to go to the trouble because I don't drink coffee. I am twelve at the time. Nobody drinks coffee at age twelve, unless they live in some foreign country.

"Really, I tell you," Mrs. Franklin says as she offers me the cream and sugar. "She just draws and draws."

She gives me all this while beaming at the one and only daughter who landed in her nursery after a drought of four boys, the girl seated next to me at the kitchen table that first night I went over there, a character out of one of my old picture books: long white-blonde hair, a red-and-white checkered dress, her Mary Janes and lace-trimmed knee socks crossed at the ankles, all of her propped up on a chair made higher by volumes E, F, and G of a children's encyclopedia on top of which she perched to indeed draw and draw.

One piece of paper, one triangle cat face drawn on it, then pushed aside. The next, a ray-spiked sun, shoved over. A sailboat, a vase of flowers, a clock reading noon or midnight. All rejected. Next, a long car, then a thin tree, both of those slid over to the pile of completed ones. She was showing off, anybody could see. Working her pencil but sneaking a peek at me out of the corner of her eye to make sure she was the center of attention. When I caught her looking, she grabbed angrily for a clean sheet. She was a little brat, I could tell. I wanted nothing to do with her. But what I wanted didn't matter this time. Pammy Franklin's father was some rich guy who owned an athletic

footwear factory in the old Ware mills and who'd recently made
it known that he had his heart set on acquiring the bowling
lanes down the street—even though Mr. Rolla hadn't once
expressed a wish to sell the place. Mr. Franklin was visiting
there one of the slow afternoons I was busy painting all those
multicolored candlepins flying across the high cement-block
wall to the right of lane eight, and he came over to compliment
me and to ask me what would I think about giving art lessons
to another talented young girl?

My very first thought was, if this girl was so talented, what
did she need lessons for? Really, what it came down to was that
I just didn't like Mr. Franklin, as I just didn't care for the few
people I knew who appeared to have any good amount of
money. Even early on, that was a problem for me, much the
same way poor people are a sticking point for many of those
who are better off. I just couldn't abide the ones I knew to be
wealthy, though they weren't many. So when he asked me to
help his daughter, I answered Mr. Franklin only that I always
had to ask my parents before I did anything. Because I did have
to. And my father, when I told him what Mr. Franklin had
wanted, said of course I had to do whatever the man asked—
that Franklin soon could be his boss and nobody would be able
to protest if he fired everybody and hired all his brothers and
sisters and kids in their places. Then my father would be out of
a job and where would we all be? In the poorhouse, that's
where.

So in the interest of saving my father, there I was, sitting in
what Mrs. Franklin called their breakfast nook, way past sup-
pertime, assessing a possible pupil—and her mother, just
because I couldn't help it. On the day I met her, Mrs. Franklin
wore a black, flowy bell-bottom pantsuit, all fitted to her skinny
Jack Lalanne frame. Her curly hair—fake blonde—was frizzed

into a thick Afro. A flat circle of hammered silver nearly choked her toothpick neck, another one curled around her wrist. Smaller versions had been shoved through stretched-out holes in her earlobes. Her nails were long and colored in a grayish silver paint that sparkled beneath the cantaloupe-sized lightbulb of the kitchen lamp suspended from a chain. It wasn't the season for them, but she wore high-heeled sandals, and the color that coated her toenails matched that on her fingertips. She smelled of spice and of something good on fire. Nobody I knew had a mother like this, especially not on a Wednesday afternoon that was described to me as being perfect for our meeting because she wasn't going anywhere or doing anything—anything but watching Pammy, that is, of course, you know.

We both watched now as the girl switched from sketching to scribbling, covering one piece of perfectly good paper and the one after that with fast tornadoes of gray lead.

"So, Pammy, do you like to draw?" I asked her in the compelling tone I often had heard used by Miss Penny on TV when some less-than-cooperative kids landed in her *Romper Room*.

For an answer, Pammy shrugged. I took that as an easy out. I said, "I don't think she's interested, Mrs. Franklin. . . ."

"Oh, yes, she just doesn't like to use her words. Only to draw. She's a visual person, you know. She'd draw all day, if you let her. But, actually, we only want you to teach her for three or four hours at a time."

I point to Pammy Franklin when people ask me why I don't teach. In all, I was sentenced to her for two entire years of Wednesday nights, allowed to quit only because Mr. Franklin one day changed his mind about the bowling alley and instead brought his considerable investment capital and power to hire and fire over to a squash club on the road to Stafford Springs.

Claire O'Hare clucks and shakes her head. She touches me on the shoulder of my painting smock and tells me, "Now I understand fully."

I am glad because I know I went on and on when she asked me the question. I tend to ramble like that when I'm nervous, or when the topic strikes a particular kind of nerve in me. Like this one apparently did.

"Chuckie was right—I probably could have made an okay living teaching. But I wouldn't have enjoyed much of it. I just like the doing. Not the talking about doing. Or the showing. I don't have the patience. I'm watching the person I'm supposed to be instructing and usually I just want to take the paper and pencil and do it myself."

"Those are good observations," Claire tells me. "It illustrates you know yourself well. Also, that's why I all the more appreciate your doing this."

The "this" was giving lessons to Claire O'Hare.

It was her idea, brought up on our one and only other visit, the week before, when we talked for so long that I had to up and leave in an instant to go and see the photos Mary Ziemba had selected.

Claire O'Hare is very interested in how it had gone at Mary's. She sees this commission as a turning point, an opportunity that will pay off in ways I can't yet imagine or understand. That is what she told me at the end of that one and only session, when I had the time to listen, and she had the advice to give as to what she would do if she were me. In answering, Claire first had squinted her eyes for a while, like she was a psychic tuning into the message being tossed out by some passing spirit. Then she relaxed her face and said, "You know what? This certainly doesn't help my business, but I'd say you really don't need me."

I thought that was pretty good—kicking out a client who, when I looked around the vacant waiting room, obviously wasn't just one more chore added to her overloaded plate.

"Not that I couldn't help," she punched in, "but maybe this isn't the time. Wait until this new job is over with. Things could be changing all along the way."

"I've had enough change," is what I told her.

"Wait, you'll see," is what she said back.

This was her job, to be encouraging. So I just took it for that. Even if, with me, it was obvious she wasn't fishing for a new client.

What I did for people—what I usually did for people, that is—was to make for them whatever they wanted. And Claire wanted the chance to sleep in a swamp.

She'd seen a bedroom like this on a new television commercial for some kind of sleeping pill and couldn't get the image out of her head. Then she met me, the person who could help her make this possible. "Your telephoning me—it was just meant to be," she kept saying, and I nodded my head even though I wasn't sure if I agreed.

"The woman in the ad takes one or two of the pills and—bingo—her bedroom turns into this. Have you ever been to Louisiana? I haven't—South Carolina is the farthest south I've gone, and it's kind of like that, but Louisiana—tropical, bushy—is more that way, I guess. Anyhow, in pictures there are these swamps, which have to be muddy and dirty and buggy and full of things like alligators or crocodiles. Well, take out the bad things and what you have left is this beautiful water and dreamy trees surrounding you, and a big giant moon. That's what the woman's bedroom turns into when she takes this pill."

Claire O'Hare went on to tell me how she wanted her drab

old room to be transformed like the one in the commercial, where the ceiling fixture fades into a veil of cirrus, and waterlilies bloom in the corner where a pile of laundry once was heaped. The carpet is flooded with warm blue water across which a peaceful swan cruises. The bed, cradling its now-blissful sleeper, floats in this paradise.

"Too much of a project for a beginner, right?"

She was right, and I told her so. I also told her not to expect it to be finished overnight. How that was only the way it happened on TV.

"You're the expert," she said, and I appreciated her acknowledging that.

I made her my Friday morning. It was the best day of the week for both of us. Mondays and Tuesdays were pretty busy for Claire. Haggard people who were coming off a weekend of obsessing to themselves or fighting with their spouses or lovers or whoever about how much they hated their lives all wanted to plunge right into making some changes. And they demanded their appointments ASAP—Monday would be best, but if not Monday then how about something early on Tuesday? If not early Tuesday, then how about later in the day? Not Wednesday, though. It would be penance for them to wait that long to begin the search for their new direction. As for me, I didn't really like to deal with many people until halfway through the week. So Fridays were perfect. At least they were until Mary Ziemba called and gave me this big piece of work, filling my head full of people who bumped against one another, crowding around to tell me about themselves. With her help.

The second person she introduces is shown in a wedding party. Mary must point him out to me from the ten people—

girl, boy, girl, boy—lined up in front of the photographer's ornate backdrop of painted columns and vines and stained glass.

"Here," she says. "Did you ever see anyone so dashing?"

He is in the second couple from the left, the one standing just behind the bride and groom, so I am assuming he is the best man and that the maid of honor is the girl whose wrist he supports gently. If I am correct, then they are the "honor couple," a term I never heard before I was half of one when Alice and Leo got married. They teamed me up with the exchange student from Italy that Leo's family ordered the summer we were to be high school juniors, not really out of any great interest in people from another land, but so that Leo could get a similar trip, in the reverse direction, the following June.

"It's no surprise he was chosen as best man," Mary Ziemba was saying, meaning the guy in the photo. "I am not going overboard when I say there is no term more fitting."

She was pointing again, to the peaceful-looking well-postured man in the military uniform. The photo was black and white, but you could tell the outfit was something like Flossie's safari-scene khaki fabric made into creased trousers, shirt and tie, with a short line of bar pins above the left pocket and some kind of circular patch on his left shoulder depicting a star taking flight by means of a pair of wings.

"Best man," Mary Ziemba said. And she tapped a pencil eraser on his hair.

I searched the faces of the women. I saw no Mary, no Flossie. I looked at the man's face. Angular, but not sharp. Small eyes under long and thin eyebrows that ran the same length as the wide mouth farther down on his face. His nose was nothing to make note of, same with his ears. Whatever features he had were overshadowed by his carriage. Standing straight as they must have forced him to in the service, eyes front, and chin proudly up, making the other four grandly tuxedoed men in the group—including the proud groom— look like nothing but slouches.

I gave this opinion to Mary Ziemba. That whoever this was, he really stood out. She smiled, relieved, like I had just figured out something she'd been trying to tell me at the top of her lungs.

"Now you see," she said quietly. "Simply from a photograph, you can tell a little something about a good brother."

Davy was twenty here, and an Air Force gunner for two years already, most of that time flying countless missions over Germany. The one and only time he was shot down, his parachute landed him in France. In a rye field belonging to a farmer named Zabawa. Davy was known for his detailed, lengthy, eloquent letters, and he wrote of this day on a page that arrived with some of the words covered up in black by military officials who feared he might be leaking important information.

"Think of it," Davy's neat architecty printing asked his family. "A Polish kid from the middle of nowhere lands in the field of a Polish man in the middle of a war."

The family thought of it, Mary Ziemba said. And it made them laugh before they all started crying nearly at the same moment.

"I never saw Pa weep before that day," Mary told me. "Not even when Davy left and all you could think of was this might be the last time we ever can have our hands and eyes on him."

Davy had built the cart Mary rolled through town. "That was the kind of talent he had," she said. "He made furniture, but much of his work was fixing, repairing the pieces people already owned because who in those times could afford new? He worked with mostly secondhand wood, and that's what he made the cart from. Tony next door was knocking down an old well house. Davy ran over and took what boards the termites hadn't yet gotten to. The wheels he put on the cart were solid rubber, and new. Don't ask me where he got them, because he never told me—though here I am not hinting that he stole them or anything of that nature, because I like to think he wouldn't. Somehow, though, he got them for me. You can have everything else second hand, but start with new wheels, that's what Davy said to me. He said they would get worn down soon enough, if I was going to be any kind of a saleswoman. He wanted me to roll them down to nothing in the first season. He wanted me to really make a success of it. He and Flossie were always interested at the end of the day: How many streets today? What did you run out of first? I have some time to help you—what can I do? The first night, I came home with nothing left except for a couple of cucumbers I hadn't realized were soft. Davy loaded me and Flossie in the cart and ran us around the yard, hollering and whistling. He pushed us out to Main Street, past the open door of Saint Stan's bar. Men in there called out how they'd take one of us, or what was the price for two? We were screaming at Davy to get us away from there, but he was laughing and he took his time wheeling us past."

Mary Ziemba said that Davy liked to dress in the few good pieces he bought when he began getting paychecks from his extra jobs at the drugstore and over at the Springfield Armory. The good student wanted to go to college once the war was over, later writing his dreams of this in the letters he regularly airmailed back to his favorite high school English teacher, who was among those who saw him off when he left for overseas two weeks after graduation.

And who saw him return a year and a half later, for a long-awaited but too-short leave.

"Everybody in the world was getting married in those days," Mary told me. "You didn't know what would happen next. In your life or in the world. I am not exaggerating when I say that. You really didn't. Things were crazy. So people rushed with their plans if they already had them, or they made some plans quickly if they didn't have any at all. So many people knew Davy was coming home, and that he'd only be home for a matter of days. So they held their weddings then."

That explained the photos stacked before me, each protected by a different type of folder that opened to turn into an easel you could stand and display. In these cases, they showed off group portraits that contained Davy. Or couples he was half of.

He took his place in precise rows, or in carefully posed groupings, behind the in-laws seated in carved chairs flanking the bride and groom. After a few photos, I began to get good at instantly picking him out, his face beaming from a back row, one time earning a place of honor next to a bride, his right hand propped on the arm of his chair, his left on his knee, holding a long and unlit cigar. In one lineup, he was not the only military man. The groom himself wore a plain uniform with no jacket, a "2" on his shoulder, the top half of the number dark, the bottom light, and I wondered the reason for the difference. In the couple behind Davy and his date, a short man had on a sailor uniform, a letter *C* and an eagle on his sleeve. Only one usher in this group was in a tuxedo, and he looked barely fourteen and definitely nervous and out of place with all these daring men who, obviously and to unknown degrees, had traveled from here to witness a place most certainly so different from this small town that it might as well have been located on a whole other planet.

I spotted Mary in one group posing on a front porch. There was more of a mush of people than exact rows of them, but up by the left pillar, there stood Davy, his hands on the shoulders of Mary, who sat in a chair in the lower row, wearing a shiny ruffled dress that almost reached the ground. Her hair was curled for the occasion, and she tilted her head to make contact with her brother's wrist.

In another photograph, it was just Davy and a bridesmaid. She was much taller and had two fat, braided buns of hair growing from either side of her head. She was out of focus even though it appeared the two of them were standing side by side. Perhaps she had moved—she looked uncomfortable, her bouquet cumbersome, many ribbons tied with ferns hanging from it and nearly reaching the floor. All around the feet of the girl and Davy lay soft, fresh, new petals.

In all, there were six group portraits shown to me by Mary. Another four with Davy as part of a couple.

"It was the best few days," Mary Ziemba said. "Parties nonstop. Either a kind of a quick meal, or the actual reception with music. One wedding just blended into the next one. We made the most of the time, I tell you we did."

I knew the next part: "And then the men went away."

Mary Ziemba nodded.

I went through the photos again. There certainly were enough of Davy for me to do my job. In each he had the same stance. Consistently happy and young. The short line of bar pins above the left patch pocket on each of the shirts he wore. The wings on his shoulder poised to take flight to an unknown future.

7

One Sunday long ago, just after we'd all eaten and cleaned up everything from our big and fast meal, a long, dark blue car with license plates from The Garden State pulled up in front of the vacant lot that edged the left side of our house.

"Thank God for the lot," my mother would instruct us often. And we would. It blessed us with privacy. How wonderful to look out at the unbroken green expanse, certainly, but if it wasn't there, we would have the crazy Mlekos right on top of us, and then we would have to listen to their fights on Friday and Saturday nights at a much, much louder volume that we already had to from far away, where they sounded like nothing more than a TV drama turned way down. That alone was worth an extra Hail Mary at bedtime—or another hour of outside work. My father or Unc or Chuckie, whoever was doing our yard at the time, mowed the lot to keep it neat and tidy even though we did not own it. The lot had been there untouched when my parents bought the house, and nobody had ever come by to tend it in the years since. So, in that way, it became ours. According to my parents, and the history book the church put out once, it was in our blood to care for it. People who came from our old country were famous for revering land. It was all they had over there, and when they came over here, they were able to afford only the crummiest pieces. The rocki-est, the most uneven, and the least desired. Yankees laughed as they sold acres to the Poles and made what they thought was money for nothing. But entire families pitched in—children, certainly, and even the women, something unheard of at the time—and the richest farmland around was created in this way. A lot of it is still in use, and that's where my parents used to head on weekends when we were in need of cabbage and pota-toes and apples and onions.

We did not farm the piece that was next to our house. We simply admired it and took solace from it. As for the work it entailed, there were the tips of seven big stones jutting from it, and the hardest thing about caring for the lot was that the mower was forced to make a weaving pattern to avoid them. We used those rocks as freedom spaces for tag, as misplaced bases for ball games. I dreamed of keeping a pony on the lot, and in my mind's eye I had planned out the location of the split rail fence and the small barn near the edge of the woods. I knew the patterns I would ride over the grass, using the seven stones for my landmarks. I could do a figure eight easily, and then worked out a version of a cloverleaf. Soon the ground would be etched with the paths the pony and I would make. I could look down from my room and see them there already. And then the big car pulled up one summer Sunday when I was eleven.

I saw my father go out to it, to meet the two men who stupidly threw their cigarette butts into the dry grass the sec-ond they stepped out. They were dressed in good suits, one blue, the other tan, and they stretched their arms widely and shook out their legs like they had been seated for many hours.

By the time the rest of our family had made its way out there, the men had pulled a big white sign from their trunk.

"LAND FOR SALE" and a long phone number was printed on it in shiny black paint, uneven but good and big enough to get the point across.

"The lot was their uncle's, long, long ago," my father explained to my mother when we got out there to join him. "He's dead. Now it's theirs. And they don't want it."

"We've been meaning to get up here for a year," the taller man said to us, reaching into his breast pocket for a pack of Lucky Strikes. I thought how in my dresser I kept a pack of candy cigarettes in a similar box. The tips were pink in a fake flame, my favorite part. "It's just that this is a long trip."

"We'll put the sign up," the other man informed us, "but we'd appreciate if you'd keep your eyes and ears open for buyers. Feel free to tell everybody that we'd like to sell this. Maybe you'll get a neighbor for yourself finally."

He said this like it was some kind of a good thing, and then he winked at us kids.

"Maybe," he added to my father in a lower voice like he was giving out a secret, "there'll be a cut in it for you if you find us somebody to take it off our hands."

In response, my father nodded once.

"How much are you asking?"

The man in the blue suit said the figure: $7,000. The heads of my parents and Unc jerked back like a yellow jacket was flying fast in front of them.

"It's none of my business," my father said, "but I should let you know that nobody around here pays anywhere near that for a lot this size."

The men looked at one another and smiled. It was clear they thought they knew much better. You almost could see the word "yokel" forming over their heads, inside one of those balloons with which cartoon characters do their thinking.

"We'll take our chances," is what the man in the tan outfit told him. Then nobody said anything, and then Debbie Dymek's family's car passed and honked at us all, at our entire family plus some other people standing out there on the edge of the road. I waved, then put my hand down fast. This didn't seem like a time to be doing anything happy looking. I was noticing that my parents weren't asking the men in, or even did they want a drink of something in the heat. Neither were they saying anything like "Good luck" when our meeting apparently was over.

"Good-bye" is all my father said, and he led us back to the house, all of us leaving the two people there lighting up new cigarettes and looking uncomfortable far from their kind of home.

That night, I slept in small portions, worrying how one day soon I would look out my window straight into somebody else's. I wondered if this was how a city started. I was awake again when my clock said one-thirty and I went to kneel at the window. There was half a moon lighting the world, and it helped me to see that, as of that moment, nobody had even made one action toward putting a house there. I leaned my chin on the windowsill and watched how the details came to life as my eyes adjusted. The brightness of the birch bark. The gray of the sidewalk. The seven stones sticking up like iceberg tips. The white of my father's sleeveless T-shirt as he crossed the lot, quickly, swinging his arms like he had been instructed to march. Where could he be going, and at this hour? Then I realized his destination: the sign, also white in the night. And I saw all the words and the numbers yanked from the ground in one swift movement, then flipped over my father's shoulder and carried back to the woods, where I heard some sharp chopping noises, then silence. Then slow footsteps up the stairs. And the soft click of my parents' bedroom door closing to the scary and uncontrollable world outside.

Something in that memory is the closest to my main image of my own father, of him being a frontier type, a Daniel Boone out there on our own personal prairie, always vigilant, worthy of his own picture-book series and television show, protecting our land, and us all. But the people I tell this to don't always go on from there to ask me more about him. They suddenly only want to know about the lot. Did the men ever come back? If they did, did they ask about the sign and where it had gone off to? Did they paint and erect a new one? Did anyone ever respond to it? If so, who was the buyer? Were we happy with them as neighbors? And just what does the lot look like now?

I tell them nothing ever happened. No men, no sign, no sale, no construction. Unc now mows the lot, picks up the odd bit of litter that blows in from the road, and gives a good raking at the beginning of the spring and as many times as is needed throughout the fall. I have no reason not to believe that the men from New Jersey still own it. But they never showed their faces again as far as any of us know.

Mary Ziemba, who of course is well-schooled in business things, says they probably just never paid taxes on it and that the town must have then taken over ownership.

She tells me, "You should go down to the Town Hall and ask about it—you probably could get it for cheap."

I tell her I'll mention that to Unc at dinner on Sunday. With my parents gone off to Ocala, the house is now his. They had wanted me to take ownership of it, me being their child and the one still in town and, though they did not point this out, the one who was in a situation where she could use such a nice bit of news as she was being handed a home for free. They wanted to put the place in my name legally, but, of course, to stress that it would be Unc's home for as long as he wanted. I said no. I had moved on long before, and as much as it would have been comforting to have been back in my old room, sitting in the middle of the night with my chin on the sill, nose to the screen, it made no sense to me to go in reverse. So because the house is Unc's, any decisions about the lot would have to be his. I live far down the street, and when I moved into my apartment, there already was a tall white house right next to me, so close to mine that on summer nights with my windows open I can hear the snorings and tossings of either Mr. or Mrs. Pugh, whichever of them is causing the noise. It's one thing to have a house right next to you from the start. That's a fact and you know nothing else. It's another to for all your days have known the pure stretch of grass, and the rocks, and the twilight deer, and the dreams you set in that space, and suddenly there is an instant ranch house with half the grayed white siding never applied, and an old car up on blocks, and trash including potentially explosive aerosol cans being burned illegally in the backyard, and suspicious neighbors who shun your well-meaning offers of free and quick-spreading perennials to at least give some color to that dirt front yard.

Mary Ziemba gives me a name for all this.

"Change. That's what it is," she says. "Nobody wants it."

I don't respond. My head is still back up there in the window of my old room. Louise stirs and opens the right eye that isn't hidden by her pillow, and she whispers my name like it's a secret. Then she drifts back to the coveted peace of not being aware that a single bad thing ever existed.

That was the same serene look on the face of the third person Mary Ziemba pushed in front of me.

He looked like Babe Ruth did—if Babe Ruth had been an old man who I'd say was at least eighty, and who had to learn to cope with a left leg that bowed out considerably, and who was forced to support himself on the left side by one of those metal crutches that grabs the upper part of your arm. His head was round and meaty like that of the Babe Ruth I've seen in pictures, and this man had his hair greased and combed back in a pretty much identical manner. He was dressed in a suit that was tight-fitting and short in the legs and arms, but he was one of those who illustrate well how clothes do not make the man. As he stood on the stern of a ship or boat, it was apparent he was simply very pleased to be where and who he was.

"He built boats for a hobby," Mary Ziemba told me. "Small ones." And to clarify further, she pulled out a hazy snapshot of the same man at a messy worktable, the sturdy hull of a model ocean liner growing under his massive hands. There was a window behind him, so he was mostly in silhouette, though the backlit effect probably was because of a simple camera and not any intentional artsy effort. I still could make out the upturned nose, the big round head, and the pointed right ear.

"All his life he made those boats," Mary said. "From scratch. No kits—no directions or books. Just by figuring. He had that kind of a brain. Now, these days, with the way they regard the handicapped, he could have been anything he wanted in life. Or at least his way in the world would have been assisted to some degree. But he was born at another time, with a bad leg, so he was restricted, held back. It's as simple as that. If he had been encouraged to, say, go to school, I just know he would have invented something to save lives or make some kind of noticeable difference, or somehow else change the world. But the way I see it, he ended up doing that in the corner of it that was his home."

His name was Aleksander. Mary Ziemba called him Pa, the man who owned a big yellow boardinghouse down near the river and worked all day without the help of any Ma. It was the family's first home in this country, and Mary and Flossie shared one of its seven bedrooms with a long string of newly arrived mill girls who just needed a place to stay until they got their bearings. Whatever they could afford to pay was all Pa asked of these hundreds of girls to whom, in the days prior to occupancy limits or fire regulations, he gave blankets and a space to sleep on the window seat of Mary and Flossie's room, or on the floor of the second pantry there never had been use for, or the dead end of the upstairs hall, or in the empty and otherwise wasted bed of a boarder out of town for a wedding. The Christmas story of there being no room at the inn never sat right with Pa. "What does a sleeping person take up but a couple of square feet, and who am I to turn anyone away?"

"Half a year we had a family of five in the attic," Mary said. "Five people in a space where you really couldn't even stand up straight except for the middle part by the chimney. And then not even totally, if you were tall. The family came to us at the end of the summer, and it was the only space Pa could offer. I don't know how they stood the heat. But they were so grateful and even came back a few years later to visit. There were six of them that day. The newest one, a little boy with one tooth, whom they introduced to us as Al."

When she had the time in those days, and when nobody was curled up there in her way, Mary Ziemba said she liked to rest for a moment on that window seat and enjoy the view of the big furrowed field that fanned out toward the river. She told me how Pa tended a small triangular patch of soil in the nearest corner of it. And it didn't take much time for me to guess that this was what eventually became Mary's garden, the first sprout of what would become the Grand Z.

"I cleaned houses when I first arrived—some mill owners' places, and the houses of the foremen and the others who were paid the best." As Mary told me this, she ran her finger over the shiny finish of the table. There was no dust to be seen.

"I'd come home from all that work and feel like I couldn't even lift a fork to my mouth. Then I'd spot Pa out in the garden and I'd get a whole new piece of energy. I don't know if it reminded me of home or what—to tell you the truth, back there I always tried to get around having to go into the barn, away from doing the farmwork, which is why I knew best how to clean. I kept myself busy and indispensable inside the house, where there were no animals. I am not fond of animals, which is why I pulled my own cart—not that I would have had any money to buy a mule or ox. I am fine with just myself and the land—once I gave it a try, thanks to Pa. It always has been like rocket fuel to me, even back before there were rockets. It was something that powered me like nothing else. I'd be out there in that field with him for so long that somebody would have to come out and drag us inside for our meal before somebody else made our food their own. The garden he started I enlarged, bigger and bigger, rows so neat in the pointed area of the field that the farmer who owned it said he didn't care if we used because it was hard for him to get his tractor successfully into that portion, it being shaped like the tip of an iron. We took care of it ourselves, and soon we were growing more food than the house could use. Pa waved a big radish at me one day and said, 'There's money to be had here.' That's when I started bringing it around to the houses, nearby at first. I know he really would have liked to do that himself, but I was the one who had the blessing of two good legs. Davy built me the cart, and off I went."

She reached over and held up the picture I'd been looking at. Pa on the deck of the boat, looking content as anybody ever could hope to be.

"See?" she asked me. "This was the first time he took a ride on the water since the day he arrived here. There were lots of years in between, and the second trip was a much more comfortable one than the first, as you can imagine."

In case I couldn't, because it's pretty easy to guess I've been right here in America from the first day of my life, Mary Ziemba filled me in on the man's big trip. Nine queasy days in a canvas hammock wildly swinging over two other hammocks in a skinny little hallway between the constant din of the engine room and the busy galley meant just for the crew. This was the kind of makeshift passage you ended up with if you were either the last person to get a ticket, or if you were on time but you had very little money, or if you had enough money but also had to foot the bill for the rest of your family. Pa didn't see daylight for the entire trip, being so sick. In one of the bits of time that he did feel better, he actually stood up, and he peeked around to the galley and got his first look at a person eating spaghetti. It looked to him like a pile of worms. And for the rest of his life, no matter what kind of sauce or other disguise somebody put on it, he was not interested in pasta of any shape or form.

The second ride was a two-hour steamboat pleasure cruise out of East Haddam. A Father's Day gift in 1964. Mary, by then having more than enough money to afford such a treat, rented the entire upper deck for a cruise down the Connecticut River.

"It was the least I could do for him," she said. "We tried to make it a surprise. We told him we were going to a farm. He loved looking at horses, so he was raring to go. Every pasture we came upon he'd ask, 'Is this it? Is this the one?' Nobody would answer, and when we'd pass the gate, he'd say to himself, but loudly, 'Guess not.' I think he was getting a little annoyed in the end. Finally we got to the dock and all we heard was, 'I'm not going on no boat.' It took us nearly an hour to get him out of the car. Then we had to ask the captain if he would be so kind as to come out to the parking lot and assure Pa that he'd be going nowhere other than the upper deck. No enclosure. Full sunlight. Not a wave in sight."

"It's really the finest conditions," the captain told him. He had on the uniform and the cap and everything, was looking as official and professional as you'd want somebody to. The captain told Pa, "It's the best day you could have."

Mary picks through the stack and pulls out proof that Pa eventually boarded. A shot in the wheelhouse, with the captain. Pa smoking at a railing, taking in the wide, treelined river. Another one, same day, a group shot of twenty or so people, and I recognize Pa out in front, Mary on his left. Then she shows me the one I'd seen first. Pa on the deck. No enclosure. No boundaries. Full sunlight. Not a wave or any other disturbance in sight, on the water or in life.

Mary still held the moment exactly:

"What he said to me was, 'I want to tell you that I am simply glad to be here.' That was when I stepped back to the proper distance and snapped the shutter."

8

Ten years after we both learned to drive, not that that had anything to do with it, Alice had a baby.

And one day, not right after she had the girl they named Heather, but about half a year later, she and the baby and I were all sitting in the backyard one breezy afternoon and Alice sees that a couple of the white fish-market aprons have blown off the line, so she goes to run and pin them back up.

"Watch the baby," she orders me as she heads off.

So I do. I am sitting next to its little cloth, the one on which the baby is lying on its back, strong and kicking and punching something invisible that I can't see but that she stares at with such intensity I believe it's there. I watch her do that, like I'm supposed to.

She takes a good right-hook shot at the wheel of the stroller that is on the other side of the towel. The wheel is a filthy thing to be playing with, so I offer a toy instead. A ring of pastel plastic keys that I imagine must fit the pastel plastic locks of a pastel plastic house somewhere in a pastel plastic town. I dangle them over her face and she makes a noise like *"eeeooo."* Then with the strength of a couple of grown men she yanks them out of my hand and shoves into her wet little mouth however many keys can fit.

Alice is back by now. I tell her, "Wow, she likes to grab things."

"Yeah," Alice answers. "It's so fantastic. You give her something and she holds on to it. That's totally new for her. She'll take whatever you hand her and she'll hold on to it and entertain herself. All by herself. It's just wonderful."

"Oh, I bet," I say. "Then you can go off into the kitchen and get something done, or maybe sit down and take a rest."

Alice gives me a look like I just taught the baby the F word.

"What I meant was," she tells me slowly, "it's wonderful to watch her do this. To just watch her—that's the thing." She stops here and looks at me to see if any of this is sinking in. "To see each new step in her life. It's, it's indescribable. Leo and I can just sit and look at her for hours. All these discoveries. That's what I meant."

"Okay," I say, still trying to understand the fascination. "I'm doing whites tomorrow. I'll take any aprons that got dirty."

Alice doesn't hear me. She is looking at the baby, who is looking back at her. She's just transfixed, and asking me, "Isn't this wonderful?"

I say, "Uh-huh," just to be polite. The way I see it, it's like how there are dog people and cat people. There are kid people too. And I never was one of them.

And then I met Little Ted.

Little Ted. Who was truly and really little the first time I saw him, coming out of Jack's wallet. So young that his age was still measured in months.

"Eleven months," is what Jack had said, all smiling after he brought out the squarish picture. He offered it to me, so I took it in my hands and looked from the pudgy little awestruck face up to the bigger and leaner and proud one across from me. It was another of those moments, when I was hit by the fact that somebody who I considered just another one of us kids now was somebody's father. It happens often enough—more often as time goes by. They pop up everywhere. On the street, at the Grand Z, in church just last Saturday afternoon during the sign of peace. I turned to shake the hand of the young woman next to me, then reached around her to acknowledge the man holding their baby. And who was it but a big, tall grown-up version of Georgie Papuga, up to then frozen in my mind as the kid who once found 17 rolls of quarters under his parents' bed and put them in a wagon and took all us kids downstreet to buy kites and Creamsicles and wax lips.

Suddenly, though in reality decades later, Georgie Papuga was a father.

Well, now Jack Murphy was one too. Something I learned roughly one year after the clam festival, at our first in-person meeting since that day. In between, there had been a postcard a month from the many places he and his instruments had traveled—states in the Northeast during the summer, ones in the Southeast in the winter—picturesque shots of shoreline and woods and municipal buildings that flipped over to tell me funny things about the requests he'd gotten or reviews of the interesting kinds of food you can find in parts of the country that are not your own. He left out the biggest news from the past twelve months, which he told me on our second face-to-face meeting, that August day in the middle window booth during the lunchtime-specials period at The Golden Bowl: a reconciliation attempt with Sylvia two winters ago had been a flop in every way except in resulting in the breathtaking surprise of the petite and ruddy infant somebody had photographed next to a bag of Domino sugar just to give you a better idea of his unusually small size at the time.

"He was born early, actually about a week after I saw you," Jack was telling me. "On my way down from Nova Scotia, I had to get to a music workshop on the Connecticut shore. I stopped by my place for clean clothes; there was a phone message. That the baby was here—two months early."

He handed me another shot. The same infant, only bigger. Dressed in a roomy, soft-looking, one-piece sleeping outfit of the kind I've always thought they should sell for adults to wear all day, making them so comfortable that they most certainly would find themselves happier just from that. The piece of clothing the baby wore was decorated with small footprints, various shades of blue on a background of organicky-looking ecru-ish fabric.

Thoughts tripped over themselves as they charged through my head: Jack = father. When we remet, he knew about the baby coming. He didn't say anything. But why should he have? It wasn't my business. Even though, now that I knew it, it sure felt like it was.

I was thinking all that, but what I was saying was "nice outfit." And Jack was telling me that it was Sylvia's new line, baby clothes stamped with the footprints and handprints of this same baby. Not by his actual hands and feet, because that would be cruel and messy, but with a rubber stamp made from his actual prints. And as he grew, she planned to stamp larger and larger clothing—toddler, preschooler, grade schooler, on up, until, Jack guessed, the baby would no longer be a baby and no longer would be interested in participating in such a project.

He kept calling it "the baby," so I asked the inevitable and Jack answered: "Little Ted."

And I looked at him like most people must look at him when he says this and Jack assured me, "No, not Little Jack, Little Ted. The name is really Ted, after Sylvia's father. Sylvia stuck on the 'Little,' to make more of a difference. His grandfather is big, and he's little—not that they're in the same room that often that somebody might confuse them. Just to make it clear. You know."

"Okay," I said. This was a lot to process. I'd spent two whole separate days shopping for the right thing to wear to the lunch we'd planned when Jack wrote on a postcard of Colonial Williamsburg that he'd be performing at the Kielbasa Festival in Chicopee and visiting some relatives and would I have time to meet when he was up here? Now I was sitting across from him in a fortune for me—a rayon tank that cost me sixty-five dollars, flax pants that weren't much less expensive, and sandals that were seventy dollars at half price. I was concentrating on not dropping any of my Tofu with Three Different Mushrooms while digesting the fact that, even though he was free and clear of Sylvia legally, in Little Ted the two of them forever would have a living, breathing link stamping on their lives his footprints and handprints and whatever other parts of himself that he felt like.

That day Jack wore old denim cutoffs and a peach T-shirt that was a souvenir from the New Orleans Jazz Festival two years before. Ask me any other thing, any other bit of detail, and I can tell you the correct answer because I recorded each in a photo I took with my eyes because I didn't have my camera with me, and even if I had, I don't know that I would have had the nerve to use it so I later could examine the black plastic windup watch worn on his right wrist in the manner of some people who, like Jack, are left-handed, and that of some other people who just want to make themselves look different; the plain brown belt made of braided rope and buckled with something that looked like a small seat-belt catch; the old shorts that were frayed and had a sprinkling of tiny battery acid holes across the right pocket area and onto the fly; how his legs were surprisingly tanned for a guy who walked around in long, funny pants for a living; how they ended in enormous feet cradled in properly sized tan suede Birkenstocks you just knew he wore year-round despite the weather.

How he knew his way around a plate, neatly chopsticking his Mushu Chicken into one of the little pancakes it had come with, rolling it all up and dipping it in the small white dish of chocolately-looking sauce and biting off a big hunk of the whole deal without losing one piece of it. How he liked his Coke with no ice and one lime because ice diluted the taste and the lime made it even sweeter without adding any more sugar. How he encouraged me to have a dessert and even though I didn't have any room left and I said yes but only if you'll split it with me and I asked for the coconut cake, strayed my fork onto his side of the plate, and tasted one of the crumbs that were his; how when we were finished he took three or four separate balls of crushed-up paper money out of his pocket and began unfolding them to find out what they were so he could pay for his share of the check. How he said no no no no but eventually let me place my Visa card onto the skinny black tray that held the bill holding more facts: that our server had been Mike B, our location had been 3, the time had been 1:14 P.M., the date had been 8-13, the check had amounted to $21.61, and my tip had been a generous $5 because of my good mood. I took the yellow copy home to keep in my prayer book so each night I could add to the stack of my wishes that whoever or whatever else he had in his life right then and there, Jack Murphy soon would be adding me to the mix.

People say I am a great stepmother. I say thanks, but that I didn't start out that way, that I never thought I could be captured by a child, but that everybody has to have at least one exception to their rule. And Little Ted was mine.

I was Alice transfixed by Heather all over again, and on that first day I met Little Ted it suddenly was as clear as anything to me how you could stare at a child for endless hours and gain the world from it. Over the years of watching him print the first letter of my name, spear the peas out of his mixed vegetables, curl his hand around the side of his neck while he slept, widen his gray eyes when I pushed my thumb back to touch my forearm like I can do, and then beg me to do it again, the warmth created in me came from out of nowhere. To think back how, fearful of running out of things to occupy his interest, I'd hardly slept the night before his first visit. I was thirty-four and I was going to marry his father and there I was, petrified of a five-year-old. Like all worry, when you get right down to it, this was wasted. Little Ted was the kind of a kid who could inspire a population explosion. And, lucky me, I could go around telling people that the small, perfect boy they found themselves staring at in wonder was mine. He even for a couple of months performed the miracle of getting me to wish for a kid of my own.

"But we have Little Ted," Jack would say.

"No we don't."

Legally, Little Ted was the son of Jack, and of Sylvia. Don't ask me how that happened—by this I mean how such a gem could have come from those two. But somehow they had created a boy who silently would walk over and softly take your hand and slowly lead you to the paper cup of dirt on the windowsill where the seed he'd hidden in there only two weeks back had turned into a strong, bright green stem and a sturdy pair of darker leaves, then another, unfolding for a determined rise toward the sky. And this boy would look at it, and then at your face, to make sure that this was hitting you as it rightfully should be. If he brought over somebody who just didn't get it—somebody who was seeing only the cup and the seedling and the wet soil—Little Ted knew it.

"Look," he'd say. "Look, don't you see?" And he'd stand there and wait until the person did.

Jack had legal custody of Little Ted one weekend out of every month. For me, those were the days in our marriage that were outlined in sharp black marker. I always felt we were more a couple when there were three of us. The other days and weekends were nice enough, but busy. I would do my work at home and in town, and Jack would give music lessons, spend time at the computer or on the phone promoting himself, prepare to leave for a weekend trip, or decompress from having another one over with. I'd accompany him when my schedule allowed, living and breathing the daydream I'd had at the clam festival, Jack stretched out in the back seat, me driving somewhere I've never been, and when the car stopped finally, he would lean into the front and whisper close something sweet. And I would say it would always be this way.

He was a good husband. This is something he plainly told me was his aim because he regretted not being that for Sylvia, whom he softly referred to by her old nickname of "V" when he brought up the subject, which he did often enough to long make me suspect in the dark and chilly corners of my mind that maybe there was an unfinished something between them. But I never asked, of course. Asking would have brought it up, opened it, made it real, maybe gotten him mad. And I didn't want Jack mad. I wanted him happy, as you'd want anybody you loved to be. And he was, and we were, especially for that one weekend every month that Jack made sure he was around and that Little Ted was with us, and we lived like how I think many normal people do. We went to the mall, to the video store, to the lake, to the snow hill, to the outdoor Mass at the shrine to Saint Anne where afterward, to get the disturbing part out of the way first, we'd walk in reverse the path lined with the stations of the cross. We cooked our own big meal on Sundays. Or we took out fast food. Always, we made things. I bought an old lidded box from the junkman down at the train station and painted the name "Little Ted" in large gold letters onto the red that I'd covered the rest of it in. I added fake gems onto the ends of each letter, like it was some treasure chest. To me, this boy was as much a wonder. My heart would fly straight through the ceiling when he'd arrive, and he'd tear over to the corner of the living room where I kept the box. Each month we'd add something new from our safari to the drugstore, where we'd stand in the same spot I occupied when I was a kid admiring all the supplies there in front of me, on the shelf below the Ace bandages, the support hose, and the various paddings for the ugly things that tend to grow on your feet once you get old.

There it all was, right in front of us: Pads of white paper in sizes from pocket to sheets you would need a small table to hold. Fat, banded rainbows of construction paper. Dozens of already-sharpened colored pencils. Jars of thick and vibrant tempera paint. Fancy plastic cases of watercolors dried into oval jewels. Shrink-wrapped ribs of modeling clay. Long vinyl envelopes that closed with a pearly snap and held every shade of Magic Marker you would ever need, or would ever be able to think up.

With Little Ted at my side it was easy to recall imagining the thrill of running a pencil along the cardboard stencils of the entire alphabet sold in sets that included punctuation marks and numerals zero to nine. Cutting the letters out with one of the shining silver scissors offered with both rounded and pointed ends. Taking a wide brush from the cellophane packs holding trios of them and dipping it into either the white Elmer's or the amber mucilage—maybe even into the dangerous rubber cement that wore on its label a skull and crossbones. Selecting the first of the sixty-four new Crayolas. Painting and gluing and cutting and coloring, and then going to the end of the aisle, to the four stacks of four different sizes of gold-rimmed picture frames that just waited for the day when you finally came up with something you decided was good enough to put on display.

I'd get him his choice, and we'd return home to create things until way past his bedtime. Crowns, buildings, villages, planets, bugs, spaceships. Jack would join us, and soon we'd all be there clipping and pasting and painting and stringing together our own particular versions of lines and circles and squares to make the world as no one before had ever viewed it.

We took him to some of the places we'd traveled to back in high school. At the big museum in Springfield, we walked past paintings of stern elderly men in dark suits, agonized saints being put through all forms of bloody torture, women lounging on picnic cloths spread beneath the falling blossoms of flower-laden trees, ships at sea with all sails unfurled and the gigantic tail of a whale right in their paths, and massive battle scenes where the soldiers' mounts displayed so much fright in their bulging eyes that I advised Little Ted to look away.

Out at the one in Boston there was a room of nothing but cases of gold jewelry that had been dug out of ancient graves, and it was stressed that no machines had been used in the making of their links and parts so small and intricate that you would need to have the hands the size of an ant's to put them together. A long hall after that was lined with cases of palest green pottery all the way from the Orient. Plates, bowls, tea sets, vases, each of them perfect, unbroken and not even with a nick or smallest crack, even though they were something like five times older than our country and had to be mailed here for this exhibit.

In the Berkshires, at the dead sculptor's home, we took in the sight of life-sized naked people frozen in the whitest stone, their mouths calling out words we couldn't hear, their arms tireless after centuries of reaching out into space, their hair still holding a good curl, their most private parts shielded by hefty pillars or distracted cherubs or conveniently crawling vines.

We went all over, or we went nowhere but home, the streets around it, the winding path down to the river. One of us on either side of Little Ted, holding his hand for as long as we could get away with it, until he finally broke free to charge ahead and chase a cottontail in the grass or a duck sunning on the shore. I don't know much about science, but I imagine there has to be some kind of element or chemical or gizmo that you can put between two substances to better connect them, to refine how they are joined, to bind them even better than if they are just pushed up against one another. If there is such a thing, Little Ted was that for us. The object in the middle of Jack and me that made the two of us a better one.

"Lily," Little Ted said on only the fourth weekend he came to stay, "you're a flower people don't often see."

The following week I repeated this to about a million people. When I told them, in between the first word and the rest of the sentence, I made the same thoughtful expression Little Ted had worn on his face at the time. Like he was awaiting transmission of the rest of his thought. I'm sure I was making people sick—I'd been on the receiving end of enough of these kinds of tales to know how they can leave you if you really don't give a care. But didn't my listeners know that Little Ted was no ordinary kid? He wasn't, or I wouldn't have been bothering them with any of this.

"Does he like the Red Sox? The Boston Red Sox?" Mary Ziemba was asking this.

I knew where the Red Sox lived, thank you. "Yes," I answered. "He likes the Red Sox." I always thought I would take Little Ted to Boston for a game. Now I can't take him anywhere. I don't even know where he is.

"Then maybe he would like my Tim." Mary Ziemba is handing me a photo of a short teenager in a Dutch-boy haircut and a baseball uniform. "They'd have that much in common to start off."

My eyes are fuzzy. I wipe at them. Into focus comes the photo being shown to me—that of the guy who's number six on the Boston Red Sox.

His uniform is a fake. Even I, who don't know much about the sport, see enough of those guys on TV to know that it's not a real team member we're looking at. And considering the young age of the person wearing it, this had to be someone new to a college team, or maybe only on the high school varsity.

"It was taken on the day they gave out the uniforms down at the high school," Mary Ziemba says. "He had to come to work right after that, and he ran up to my office to show me. Varsity! He stood there, breathing fast from the run up all those stairs, so pleased."

She was fanning out a stack like a hand of cards, and she located a photograph of the boy swinging a bat, left-handedly.

"Here," she said. "Look at how thrilled he was. That he got a new uniform. That he got the number he wanted."

Mary Ziemba told me that six once had been worn by a guy named Roy White, an unsung left fielder for the New York

Yankees in the sixties and seventies. Even though Tim was going to be on a team named after the Red Sox, he wanted this guy's number.

"I remember him saying how this Roy White was a little guy," Mary Ziemba said. "Tim was a little guy then too, and I think that was a lot of the appeal. Like how he also admired Bobby Kennedy, who always looked so small when he was standing there with his brothers. He—Roy—was a switch-hitter. A Catholic. And black, in contrast to his name. Tim told me all that when he showed me this jersey. I don't think I could come up with any other statistics about any other player or sport. But these ones I know. Because they meant so much to him, and that's what he said to me that one afternoon."

Mary even knew Roy White's batting stance, and she stood up to demonstrate.

"A little knock-kneed," she said, and she posed in that fashion. "He'd hold the bat almost on his hip." She did the same with a bat I couldn't see. "Then he'd go whoosh!"

Tim looked to be about as old as me. In my mind, I swooped through the Grand Z aisles of my teenhood, checking out the faces of the stock boys who managed to stand out for me even years later. There was the tall, curly-haired one who kind of looked like a cuter, younger Tony Orlando and who of course was always busy pricing stuff in paper goods whenever my mother would send me in for an emergency four-pack of toilet paper. Of course I had to get the kind she had a coupon for, and of course that was the brand he was replenishing at the time, and I had to wait for him to move so I could reach over, and he would turn around at some point and apologize for being in the way and would ask if there was something he could get me. That guy I remembered. And Leo, of course. He worked there for the three weeks in high school that he and Alice did not date due to some big fight that today neither of them can put their finger on the cause of. For that period, he quit Rocky's—it would be too difficult to be around even Mr. and Mrs. Szczpiorski—and in an instant he could be found bagging groceries at the end of the second express checkout. Every other day, Alice chokingly begged me go into the Grand Z and buy twelve items or less just so I could have the chance to ask Leo if he was okay and, more importantly, was he seeing anybody yet? It killed me to ask that last question because, even just from spotting me with my couple cans of Beefaroni or jar of Tang, and knowing fully why I was there, Leo had to run to the maintenance cabinet and mop at his eyes with a Handi Wipe. Other than the Tony Orlando guy and Leo, there was Amy Dale's older brother, Dale Dale, if you can believe two parents would do that to one defenseless little baby. And there was the nice retarded man with the one ear higher than the other, hired by Grand Z decades before it made good publicity to have a mentally and physically diverse staff. He's still at the store some days, handing out flyers and wishing you a most pleasant morning or afternoon, depending on the time of day. Those were the sum and total of the stock boys I remembered from that era.

"My son worked mostly at night," Mary Ziemba said. She often called him that when she spoke of him. "Son," not Tim. Just son. You could tell she enjoyed using the word.

"'Son,' I'd say," is how she'd start off another story, or explain the significance of another picture. Like the one showing him and another boy stacking neat pyramids of huge navel oranges, a shot taken one night just before each boy claimed an end of an aisle and practiced fielding.

"'Son,' I'd say, 'Son, if I catch you throwing fruit again,

you're out of a job, and I mean that.' He'd answer something like 'Then I won't let you catch me.' And he'd wink. I'd have to give him an evil eye, but I really didn't mean it. They horsed around only after the store was closed, so no shoppers ever knew how their purchases once might have been mishandled. The boys liked to play football with loaves of rye bread. Hockey with ant cups and tuna cans. Badminton was Jiffy Pop pans and a bulb of garlic. They bowled with frozen capons—the tenpins were cans of Ajax and Bon Ami. I'd sit up in the office and look down on all the mayhem, and I have to admit, I let it go on for a little longer than maybe I should have before I got on the loudspeaker. But you could say they were being boys, kids, teenagers, whatever. And that was enough to buy them a few more minutes from me."

Tim went to the junior prom with a girl who looked to me like one of the flat-faced Topolskis from down by the egg-box factory. They were not to be confused with the regular-looking Topolskis from out on the road to Red Bridge. The two families were not related, even though they shared the same name. The ones closer to our house had heads shaped like most everybody else's, and the kids in that family hated when they were asked if they were cousins to the other Topolskis, who weren't odd when viewed straight on, but in profile resembled a melon sliced in half, with Mr. Potato-ish facial features stuck onto a sheer vertical wall.

"That's a Topolski girl," Mary Ziemba told me, tapping her finger several times on the ruffly dress colored in a lilac that matched the bow tie around Tim's neck, the thread accenting the big ruffle down the front of his shirt, and the hanky artfully pleated and tucked into the breast pocket of his white tuxedo.

"She was one of the ones from out by the egg-box factory," Mary Ziemba added, like that was necessary.

In the five-by-seven, Tim and the girl were turned toward each other on the sloping yard in front of Mary's house, holding hands and looking extremely lovesick. In a smaller print, Mary was at his left side as he posed in a graduation gown, his tilting mortarboard hung with the golden tassel that in my day told you he was a student above the average.

His mother began to point that out, how smart her son was, and she recited a list of awards and scholarships he had collected. I didn't catch it all. I was too busy doing math, which I am not that great at even when I have full concentration, never mind when somebody is telling me a whole story out loud and right next to me. I learned from the banners hung in the background, and from the little golden number attached to Tim's tassel, that the year of his high school graduation was 1980, the same year I'd finished up at Westfield. I counted eighteen years back from his graduation, and placed Mary in her forties when she had Tim. Ahead of her time once again. Like the more-publicized older movie stars giving birth today, Mary Ziemba was starting a family just when many people her age were becoming grandparents.

"And he was the first boy to win the Betty Crocker Award," Tim's mother was saying. "For fine achievement in the area of home economics. He was handy in the kitchen all right, but I think, more than that, it was all that time spent in the grocery store. Not right next to me, but in the same building, under the same big roof, working with me in that way. Those were the nicest times, when I could just look down and see him there."

She arranged Tim into one neat pile and looked at me. "I think that must be like how God has it—not to sound as if I think I'm anything like God, mind you. But the whole idea— sitting up there behind glass you can't be seen through. The person down below looks up and it's just a reflection of themselves, a mirror is what they see. But behind the glass, some-body who loves you more than anything is watching, and is hoping the best for you, and cheering you on, and loving you even when you are doing something you shouldn't be."

How many things must Mary Ziemba have seen from that sneaky vantage point? People browsing, comparing, counting the money in their wallets, worrying that what they'd collected in their carts wouldn't be enough for the week, flipping through painstakingly alphabetized coupon files, clicking prices into those little red plastic counters that every savvy shopper carried before calculators came around. People show-ing off a find, directing a stranger to a cheaper but just-as-good-tasting brand, alerting a stock boy to a spill or broken jar that could be hazardous, offering a fast recipe that doesn't need to be written down—all that's needed is one or two of these cans here, a box of rotini, some butter, nothing could be easier. People smacking their kids for being unruly, peeling a low price off one item to stick over a higher one, opening jars to sniff con-tents or maybe even dip a finger in and try, stuffing into their coat pockets loose candy bars and small cans of creamed corn and single packets of hamburger. Grocery versions of all the worrying and exploding and good and bad that we're all doing every day. Most of the time—if you ever knew it in the first place—forgetting there's somebody up there watching from the other side of that decorative glass.

Even when the somebody is your own mother.

9

I didn't exactly leap at the offer when Wally Wazocha asked me to paint a mural in the second of the two viewing parlors down at his funeral home.

I had the same thoughts that surely most people would at first—that it would be a lonely job, and that it would be creepy. As a kid, I'd hear my parents say they were going off to a wake, and I'd think it meant the dead person was going to be somehow awakened for those couple of hours, allowed to say their final good-byes and settle their affairs before going to sleep for good. When I was twelve and attended my first—Joanne Mleko's *babci,* so ancient that she always talked about old-country dragons and knights like she'd known them personally—I was greatly disappointed. The talk was all one-sided, with no answers to the questions of "Why did you leave me?" "What am I to do now?" and "How will I ever go on?" that Dziadziu Mleko and Joanne's mother and even Joanne herself were pitching at her overly made-up face. Babci Mleko just lay there clutching her rosary, pursing her candy-pink lips, still and lifeless, like a big doll with the batteries removed. Every dead person I've knelt in front of since Babci Mleko has struck me in that way.

The thing that swayed me was Wally saying I didn't have to work when the place was closed, which shows you how professional he is, that he is more than well aware not everyone in the world is as comfortable as he about hanging around a funeral home. The painting he wanted would be on the wall in the lesser-used of his two rooms, the one closed off from the other by a sliding canvas screen. Eventually, if he liked how this one came out, he might want me to do a mural in the main room. But for now, I was to try my hand, as he put it, like this was some hobby I was just starting, in Parlor II. Unless there happened to be two wakes at the same time, or if a particularly enormous crowd was expected, that room would remain closed off by the thin sliding partition. As long as I used paints that wouldn't smell like paint, and as long as I made no noise, which of course I wouldn't dream of, there would be no chance of me disturbing anything going on in the main parlor.

"Check the obits," Wally said. "If a wake's on, just come over. Use the flower entrance."

So that's what I did. I could put in a good four hours a day, working from two to four and seven to nine whenever Wally had somebody on display. Even though I couldn't see them, I had a constant stream of living and breathing company right on the other side of the screen. To be sure, many of them were upset. But many others—especially those who camped out as far away as possible from the casket and the action at the front of the room—weren't that broken up, usually attending only for the sake of appearance, and their running commentary was as good as having a radio playing while I made progress on "The Eternal Serenity."

That's what Wally called the painting the very first time we talked about it, the night last May when I frantically phoned

him after coming home to hear his message. The only words
that had registered were these:

"I'm calling from Wazocha's Funeral Home."

The dead faces of every still-living person I really or even
mildly cared about blew past me. Roulette at Foxwoods. I actually shook as I waited to learn where the little red ball that is
God's hand had landed after its skips and bounces and nerve-
wracking final hops. But all I heard was this:

"I want you to make me a mural."

"It's going to be called 'The Eternal Serenity,'" Wally said
when I arrived at his house to hear more details. "I hope you
don't mind that I've already come up with a title for it, before
you even started painting it. But this is something I've had on
my mind since I took over the place from my uncle last year. I
just know how I want it to look. I tell you, if I had different
kinds of talents, I would have painted it myself long ago. "

Wally had told me I should come by his place in late afternoon, which I had, just as the first of the final rays of the day
were starting to disappear behind the tall white pines at the edge
of his property. We'd had rain that day. The wet air filled the
light with a haze you could almost reach out and pull your fingers through, and all around us the drenched leaves dripped
happily. Unlike a lot of funeral people in our area, Wally didn't
live right above his place of work. Instead, his place was a regular kind of home, high up on Baptist Hill, far up at the top of one
of those driveways that is so steep that three or four oil cans full
of sand are stationed at intervals along the incline so he can get
himself back up to the house on icy nights, and so he can get
himself back down the driveway without becoming one of his
own customers. At his home way up there, Wally told me that
he wanted the mural to be of his backyard. Only showing God,

instead of Wazocha's founder, his old Uncle Wojciech, there that evening, sitting for dryness' sake on a beach towel placed on the fancy wrought-iron chair next to a huge and burbling water fountain of the kind normally only seen in the center of a town.

"This is where I want people to think their loved ones have gone on to," Wally said to me. "Nobody knows for certain what heaven looks like. Everybody has their opinions. I'm taking the liberty here of giving one vision of it. Mine."

"I can think of worse places to end up." I said that because even people who had a tough time with the idea of an afterlife would be tempted to dream of landing here forever. Especially at that time of the day and year, with the light the shades of a peach skin and the scattered trees tripping over themselves with blossoms, the great lawn as green as it was ever going to be, the arbors live and almost moving with new growth, the terraced perennial gardens shooting up bulbs straight out of a flower catalog, all of it being admired by us, two people still living on earth and standing there on what Wally called a palazzo but what you or I would refer to as a deck.

I looked at Wally Wazocha right then, and the thought came to me that I never really had seen him in natural light. Maybe he was thinking the same thing of me because I was startled to find he was looking back into my eyes when I went to check the color of his—brown with little spokes of gold on the left one—and I quickly moved my gaze down his long nose to the wide and thin lips that right then opened to form the word that was the question, "Champagne?'"

It would be easy to slide into some kind of love with Wally Wazocha, slowly and quietly, by the light of the dim, recessed pink-hued bulbs, amid the carnation-scented air, to the strains of the unobtrusive organ dirges played by a fancy stereo system housed back in the office. From behind the screen, I listened to his understanding tones as he dealt with the bereaved, how he sounded like he truly knew how it felt to experience a death, even though he has confided with a knock on wood that he has yet to lose a single person even remotely close to him. He still could be so convincing as he said, "Yes, yes, oh, I'm sure, yes, I know," when he had never been anywhere near the receiving end of a life-altering three A.M. phone call from the police or the hospital or the sister-in-law. Just as he said, "Yes, I know how you feel," when I told him how in one way or another I lost not only my brother, but my parents and my sister and my husband and my boy.

"I know, I know," he said, despite that he didn't, and that he knew I knew he didn't.

That didn't matter. It just felt good to be comforted, even if it was by somebody who'd once taken actual college courses in that. You'd have to have something wrong with yourself to turn away Wally Wazocha, dressed most days in the tailored suits that, as long as they were solid black and were not worn for recreational purposes, could be declared tax deductible.

But Wally was busy all the time. Since people die all the time, his was not the kind of business for which he could buy one of those orange-and-black CLOSED signs to hang from the stained-glass window of the heavy front door while he went off on a lark. He worked a lot. As I did too, making slow progress on "The Eternal Serenity" while going through much of my own personal disruption. I couldn't see myself in a funeral home forever, but it was nice to live in another kind of world for a while, surroundings quiet and clean, everyone using low tones except for the occasional wailer, the sound of the passing traffic muffled by the thick white-brick-faced walls. And there I was behind my screen, painting an image of peace for those who were in desperate need of the tiniest slice. On my own side of the parlor I'd take my break and sip from my thermos of tea and sit back in one of the thronelike chairs reserved for next of kin, and I'd look at the border of peonies and the doves splashing in the water and the setting sun that was leaving with the cross-my-heart promise of popping back up tomorrow morning, and I'd try to reach for a piece of it for myself.

"That's good, that's good," Claire O'Hare told me. "You need that. Everybody needs that."

"You missed a spot," is what I answered.

I'd been telling her the story of my Wally commission while we were adding the big dark trees all around the walls of her bedroom. She was adding them, I should say—I'd outlined them earlier, now she was filling them in with a blue so dark it was almost black. I lay on the plastic that protected her bed from any paint drops, and I ate peach yogurt from a small container while I watched her work and reminded her to slow down when she got to a tricky part, like the gnarled branches from which she later would attempt hanging a delicate silhouette of Spanish moss. I was doing next to nothing, and I was getting paid for it. Chuckie would have approved.

Claire liked to dress the part of an artist. For our classes, as she called them, she'd come to the door in this pair of big white coveralls, matching painter's cap, white high-top sneakers she'd bought special just so she could get them dirty with various splotches of color. She'd knot some kind of little scarf around her neck, and maybe add a cheap pin she'd bought just for this, a golden paintbrush or a silver palette with colored rhinestones representing blobs of paint squeezed out along the edges. I was the only one who came by during our hour together, so at first it was kind of sad to me that she would go to all that fuss. But then again I felt a little envious that she would do all that costuming just for the enjoyment of it. Not because some great crowds were going to be looking at her. All that, just to please herself. It was a quality I'd like more of, but didn't feel I right then had the strength to go searching for.

"How's that?"

Claire asked me this after filling in a part she'd missed, a curvy branch that was important to the scene because it was meant to bring your eye up to the big full moon glowing above it.

"Great," I said. It would have been better if I, instead of her, were doing it, but her efforts weren't that bad, made with a steady hand that did not really stray from where it was supposed to go. You could not ask for much more than that.

Claire started in on the next trunk to the right, brushing more of the paint over the rich midnight blue we'd rolled on all the walls and the ceiling as well. We'd accomplished a lot in the month since we'd hauled everything but the bed out of the room and sentenced Claire to sleeping on the living room futon for the duration of the project. She said she didn't mind. That it was a thrill for her to wake up and creep over to the door of the bedroom and open it to get another look at how things were changing in there. "I know nothing would have happened overnight," she assured me when I gave her what I guess was an odd look, "but I just love the idea that I'm soon going to be resting in someplace different. All because of the work I did myself."

"And the few things that I did—don't forget that." I said this as I stood up and took the brush from her. I ran it down the opposite side of the trunk in two long lines, leaving a lighter thread in the middle that gave the effect I shot for: Suddenly, moonlight was reflecting off the bark.

"You're good," Claire O'Hare told me.

"I know," I said, because it was true. Actually, the day after I finished painting a fake doorway in an upstairs hall at a fancy home in Monson a couple months ago, an overnight visitor walked right into it and knocked her head so hard she had to go to the emergency room for three stitches. That's too bad and all, when you consider the pain and trouble involved. But when you think more about it, it's really a compliment. That people could look at something I made up out of nothing and think it was so real that they could walk right through it and into whatever they thought was on the other side.

"It's all the practice you've had," Claire said. She was talking slowly because I guess in her brain she could not make words and move her hand to paint at the same time, something that was second nature to me. She was concentrating down at the root area now, painting in the base of the trunk as it sloped and disappeared into the floor. "Wish I had those years of experience in my own work."

Claire only had the dozen years behind her because it wasn't until 1985 that she came across the newspaper advertisement that made her who she became. I didn't find this out during my one and only session, because it is not the kind of thing that a professional probably wants her customers to know right off the bat—that she was once as lost and as wandering as the people who now are coming through her door. But I guess that really is good, because she can honestly know what it's like. Not just imagine or have studied case histories of it. But to actually have lived for a time in that low point, which was where Claire's ego was existing at the time she was selling tickets down at the cinemas and working another part-time job picking people out of the phone book to call and ask if they were interested in a special on vinyl replacement windows. Then she spotted the ad that asked her if she was interested in changing her life and the lives of others. She thought about it and answered that, you know, once the question was posed to her, she thought she really would. So she read down to the part where she was asked to send twenty-five dollars for the booklet of instructions on how to go about doing this. Her boyfriend warned her that it was a scam, that the booklet would probably just tell her how to place ads in her own paper asking people to send their twenty-five dollars to her. "You're always thinking the worst," is what Claire told him, and she wrote out the check.

"And when the booklet arrived, you know what?" Claire placed her brush on the tray and turned around fully, so I knew it was important.

"What?"

"He'd been right. The advertisement was nothing but a way to take advantage of people. Just a little folder that gave you examples of different ways to word the same ad that I'd seen and responded to. Different lead-ins: 'Are you sick and tired of your work?' 'Bored with nine to five?' 'In need of a new career?' 'Hate your boss?' You could take your pick if you wanted to run one every week or month."

"Did your boyfriend tell you he told you so? That he was right?"

"He wasn't that type," Claire said. "But I didn't give him the chance, anyway. I was so embarrassed that I never showed it to him. I just ripped it up and threw it in the fire. I can't say that right there was the moment, but it was shortly after that, thinking about how easily I mailed out twenty-five dollars on the off chance that I could get some good advice. That told me how much in the mud I was. And I decided it was time that I start acting my age, not the size of my shoe. To do something with myself. To help other people who were as stuck as I was. As directionless. That's where I got the name New Directions, you know."

So she went to the library. Looked up some reputable career counseling companies. Wrote and found out how she could learn from them. Took the courses when they came to the area and set up camp for a weekend in the Holiday Inn. Got the C.C.C. certificate now framed and hung on the far wall of her office. Took out the ad telling people like me that people like her were out there, ready and willing to help—a beacon, a road map, a needle on a compass, knowing the way, and being so kind as to share the route. For twenty-five dollars a session. A real deal, considering how, with Claire, you were actually getting something for your money.

"So," she was asking now, "you think you could go for him?"

"Who?"

"This Wally."

I gave a laugh. "He's nice and all, I don't know. We had a pizza once. In his office. He played the Electric Light Orchestra. It was pleasant. Then the phone rang. Some lady who wanted to know how to have her sister shipped out here from Denver. For burial, you know, not vacation. Then the phone again. Dead guy at the hospital. Wally had to run off and fetch him. That's what it's like, I guess. You never know from one minute to the next what your day is going to be like."

"Who does?" Claire asked. "Is this straight?"

"Nothing in nature is straight."

This was a fact I'd read in an art book Unc had bought me for the first birthday after my abilities were revealed. I'm not at all sure if it's true, but my quick and assured delivery of the fact had to make me sound like I knew what I was saying: The appealing and calming idea that nothing in this world, even if it was made by God himself, truly is perfect. So there was no need to kill yourself trying to be.

10

For my First Communion present, there was nothing I wanted
more than a television set.

Not just any set, but the tiny ice-cube-shaped one with the
orange-red casing and the beige frame squaring the olive
screen, the Motorola that in the spring of 1966 sat flatly silent
on the kitchen table in the window of Topor Furniture, a cardboard sign—PERFECT FOR YOUR GRADUATE!—poked through by
silver antennae.

Like a space-age centerpiece it rested in the center of an
avocado runner that split in half the dazzling white Formica
surface and matched the color of the bumpy place mats and the
scratchy-looking napkins and the Naugahyde swivel chairs. A
plastic tree with thick, shovel-shaped leaves grew from a white
ceramic urn to the left of the table. In the painting that hung on
the textured plaster wall behind all of this, a big-headed, big-
eyed boy slumped at a street corner, his small hand sadly
strumming a tiny mandolin.

Nobody ever turned it on, but I often stood in front of the
window, staring, fixated simply by the burning lure the set held
for me. I dreamed of reaching through the glass and pulling the
on-off button and twirling the UHF and VHF to the channels
that held my most favorite shows. I wanted it like I had wanted

nothing before—far more than I secretly yearned for Sandra Chudy's palomino, or for Beverly Martowski's inborn gift, even back in first grade, to sing as fine as anybody you could hear on a store-bought recording. Irene Yocz, who was the richest girl in my third-grade class and probably in my whole town, had her very own television in the professionally decorated bedroom that she was not required to share with even a single one of her four siblings. Not only was the set all hers, but it was a color model and was able to capture all kinds of reception, wired as it was through a tiny hole in her glitter-painted ceiling, up to her father's monster of a roof aerial, a threatening web of shiny chrome assembled into the general shape of a huge arrow and aimed in the direction of faraway Boston, which was where, Irene said her mother said, the nearest people of any true intelligence made their home.

The TV is the first thing I remember aching for. And mourning over. Because I never got it. On the afternoon of my First Communion Sunday, my parents presented me a twenty-five-dollar savings bond and a plastic picture of Jesus, his Sacred Heart appearing to burn with actual moving flames if you cranked a dial on the side.

When my mother excitedly chirped, "And here's what you've been waiting for," I already had my eye on the nearest electrical outlet. That's when they placed into my hands the picture of the big-headed, big-eyed, boy slumped at a street corner, his small hand sadly strumming a tiny mandolin.

Mary Ziemba likes the story, I can tell.

She asked me the question, and now she in turn gives me her own reply.

"Well, what I first wanted," she tells me after clearing her throat, "wanted more than anything, was a chocolate heart."

Back when Mary Ziemba first got here, there was a confectioner on the first floor of the house that now is right after the driveway to the AMVETS, the little blue Cape where the guy sells flats of impatiens off his porch and smokes through his throat.

"It was a small, family business—just their front room, really," Mary says. "The Pulas—do you know them? They made candy in their kitchen and put it out on trays in their front window. Just after lunch they'd move them back, out of the light of the sun. But if you came by before that, you could go up on their porch and look through the glass and admire what they were offering that morning. If you had the money, you could go inside and get what you wanted."

Mary Ziemba never had the money. Not for something like candy, which truly wasn't essential for living even though some days I and probably a lot of others might argue otherwise. But she did glance over at the window every time she was pulling her cart up that portion of Main Street, and once in a while she'd give herself the treat of going up on the porch and taking a good long look.

"Every time I did, there it was. The other things changed each time—the rows of caramels or butterscotch drops, peppermint sticks, licorice. But in the center of the big tray there was always a chocolate heart. Just about as big as your palm. Not flat, but fat and rounded, so that it would be the same shape on whatever side you turned it to. And polished—I don't know how they do this—to look like fine wood. Or marble, if you've ever seen the brown shade of it in a church or museum. I loved how they always set it on a shining red pillow, to point out how much more precious it was."

The Pulas wanted an even dollar for the heart. An impossibility for a poor girl. But that didn't stop Mary from her regular looking at it, and admiring and dreaming.

"What I didn't know was that while I was outside looking in, somebody on the inside was looking out," said Mary.

This is how I got to meet Michal.

The photo she showed me was very old—gray and yellow, rather than the black and white it once had to have been. There was only the one picture, and she didn't let me really hold it. She had no problem with me placing close to my eyes the huge dancing-girls group that contained the pinhead-sized Flossie. Or shuffling through Davy and sorting through the Aleksanders or staring at the Tims and trying to remember his face in real life. But with Michal, there was a difference. She'd sealed him up in Ziploc, and even that she handed to me at the farthest edge, like touching the wrapping would somehow bring him harm. I wanted to pull open the bag, to get my best look at the man. To figure out if I'd need to use something like a magnifying class to truly portray him. But I got a definite feeling from Mary, who was looking both sad and ready to pounce at me, that I shouldn't even move. So all I did was look through the freezer-safe plastic, under the little white box where you can print the name of the food you're storing and the date you filled the bag.

Michal was alone on a long and straight dirt road. Standing in the direct center of it. Trees on each side, after a curb of tall grass. He was far enough away that it was a challenge to make out his facial features, which amounted to small, hooded eyes and a flat bit of a nose that ended at a handlebar mustache. Suspenders held up his trousers, which were high-waters that broke at laced-up boots. His shirt was white and had no collar. The cuffs were rolled up once, and his hands hung at his sides. There was a lumpy bag leaning against his right leg. The shadow of it, and of him, fell in a pointy shape to the left, just

SUZANNE STREMPEK SHEA

touching the edge of the road. It struck me here that people in the olden times either liked greatly dramatized poses or, as was the case with this guy, they didn't make an effort at all.

I looked at Mary Ziemba.

"This is all you have?"

"This is all I have left of my husband."

And then there was a big space that I didn't interrupt because I could tell plain as day I shouldn't. I let her go on when she was good and ready and done with her own staring, which wasn't an hour later, just seemed like it.

"I know it's not much help, but this will have to do," she said.

"I'll copy it," I told her. "I'll have it enlarged; that'll help me somewhat."

When I said this, Mary winced. "I really don't want the picture leaving the house."

I thought for a minute. "But I'd like to take at least a copy home with me. I've got everything underway there."

One month after Mary Ziemba's first call, preliminary sketches of Flossie, Davy, Aleksander and Tim were finished to my liking, all very nice if I did say so myself. I'd wanted to wait and get a look at all the subjects before deciding where I might place them for good, to see where they might fit the best in the grouping I was creating. With Michal, the set was complete, and my real work would begin, that first pencil mark of many to be covered by translucent layers of color that one day soon people everywhere would stand in line for hours just to look at and study and be struck by. Then they would travel all the way home in stunned silence, reflecting how they had been changed in some vital way by the sight of a thing made by my own right hand.

I liked imagining that. A lot.

• • •

With the other people Mary had introduced to me, I could see some reason why it had been a fantastic day or time for them. With Michal, the occasion or reason for Mary's choice wasn't so obvious. I was guessing the road he stood on was leading somewhere—how could it not?—but the question was, was the guy coming or going?

I didn't ask. I don't like to pry, even if it's killing me to know. I busied myself by closing my pen and flipping the cover on the little notebook I'd been bringing to Mary's in case there was something important I should take down. I'd yet to write anything that I'd honestly consult later, but I figured having the pad with me made me look that much more of a professional.

"Will you copy it and get it right back to me?"

Her nervousness wasn't lessening. So I said, "You can come along, if you want. They have a fantastic copier down at Roberts; it's as good as taking a photograph of something."

And that's how Mary Ziemba ended up in my Toyota, once I cleared the passenger seat of newspapers, books, sketch pads, the tackle box of supplies I like to keep with me in the car because you never know what you might see that you later would wish you had taken the time to stop and admire and look at and put down on paper. Ever since Jack left, ever since Little Ted didn't come around anymore, ever since my parents moved, ever since my sister got way too busy, I found I had no need for spare seating. So things began to accumulate on the passenger side as much as they always had in my backseat and trunk.

Mary didn't seem fazed.

"A mess means you're not idle," is what she told me when I apologized for it. "Means you're a busy person."

What I didn't get into was my personal theory—that the status of both my car interior, as well as that of my pocketbook, said loads about how the rest of my life was going. And that only the week before, I'd taken to carrying only my wallet because my shoulder bag had gotten so heavy with the things I had the energy to collect along the way—books, clippings, film, coupons, free newspapers—but not to sort through once I got home. Even the wallet was getting out of hand. Receipts, business cards, scraps of paper napkins and envelope flaps with addresses and possible job information scrawled on them, photographs, a precious few dollar bills. Everything was shoved into it, and the wallet itself no longer even came into the house, night and day left jammed between the driver's seat and the emergency brake.

Mary and I rolled down the driveway road over which trees grew and interlaced themselves to create a tunnel. It had been beautiful in the fall, like passing through a kaleidoscope. But now the leaves were gone and we traveled through the grayness of ground and bark and sky. Winter was on the way and, as usual, there would be no stopping it. Heather, who knows that in an ordinary year I love snow and as much of it as can fall, had run upstairs the afternoon before to tell me she'd seen some fly past her TV-room window. But by the time she dragged me out onto the back porch, none was to be seen, not even the smallest flake, not even when you stood still and stared at something dark like an eave so the white would show up better against that background if it truly was out there. I told Heather I was disappointed, but I really wasn't, as this was not an ordinary year and the things I once held dear and close had lost much of their attraction for me.

"I'm sorry," was what Heather had said. "Maybe tomorrow."

Next to me, Mary held the bag that held Michal, each bottom corner secured between a thumb and forefinger. She was looking not just straight, as most passengers do, but to the side and up, in a way that made her put her head close to the window. I was expecting her to come out with some related fact about Michal. Like she had on the days she gave me the other people. Something about how maybe he liked snow. Or maybe how he didn't. Maybe he was like most people, who prefer warmth. Who wish to go to Florida, where, according to my parents in their first summer there, some days you need to take a minimum of three showers due to all the constant sweating. But Mary Ziemba didn't tell me anything at all, and I didn't bait or ask.

I just announced, "Here we are," like she couldn't see the printing place right there. There was one single, angled parking spot vacant in front of the door and I had snagged it.

"Good," Mary said, and she opened the door and got out.

Inside, the front-desk lady, who always wears a very nice dress even though she is surrounded by printing presses and probably ink flying everywhere, listened intently to my request, especially because I repeated several times how important a photo this was. She took the bag from Mary and walked the several steps to the fancy copier, then unsealed the opening and carefully slid the photo onto a large glass. A whirring sound and lights could be seen flashing, and at our end of the machine, a blank piece of white paper slid slowly into a plastic tray.

The front-desk lady went over and picked up the paper and turned it to look at the image. She examined it for a second or two before walking back to the counter and letting us see Michal, who now was twice the size of what he'd been when I'd first met him. A bit fuzzier, but darker, and, for my purposes, a lot better.

Mary took the copy from the woman, and it was noticeable how she drew in one small and sharp breath, like the sight of

Michal that much closer to life-size was something that grabbed the whole of her. A man in a brown UPS uniform interrupted, walking through the door and waving a small square box and calling out, "Hey, your part's finally here!"

The woman ran around the counter to grab it.

"You are a lifesaver," she told him slowly as she signed her name on his electronic pad. "Did anybody ever tell you that?"

Back in the car, Mary held both the bagged photo and the extra enlargement that the woman, seeing how the first one had affected her, had run off for her at no cost but that Mary had insisted on paying for with some change from her coat pocket. She said she never in her life had asked anybody for something for nothing, and she wasn't about to start now. Here I was thinking surely she'll come out with a story about Michal. How he was the same way. Never wanting what wasn't his, or anything he didn't rightfully acquire. That's what he was doing on the road that day . . . But, no, none of that. What I got was stories about the things we passed, as if this was Sunday afternoon and Unc and Phyllis were in the front seat and I was in the back with the pan of leftovers from Marinara Madness Days at Pasta Aplenty.

I kept on our track, heading east on Route 20, passing the mountain of old tires neatly corralled by a stockade fence, coming up onto the divided highway out of town, taking that first turnoff before the state park road, proceeding slowly like the small sign planted next to the beginning of the driveway requested, and spotting the heavy wooden arch ahead of me over the road. In our rush to enlarge Michal, we'd left the gate open.

When I asked her if she minded that, Mary said it was no big deal. "It's nice to have it shut at night, to not have strange cars coming up, thinking they're on a regular road," she told me. "Or kids parking. I don't mind them parking, understand, but they block my way if I'm coming in late. Not that I do that often, but it's nice to have the road clear."

About as clear as the road that was in front of and in back of Michal and his sack of stuff as he and it posed for the photo. I saw that as a natural lead-in, but Mary apparently didn't. She said nothing for the duration of the ride through the forest—except for did I see something running past the big oak?—nothing until we pulled up to her front walk and she let herself out and stuck her head back into the car to thank me for not minding her great concern about the photo.

"I understand," I said, trying not to sound like Wally Wazocha.

"Then you have everything you need from me."

"I do."

"And you have your deadline."

"I do."

"Then you get to work."

"I will," I told her.

11

I don't remember my first sin.

I remember preparing to confess it, reciting "Bless me, Father" in Polish as Sister Lugoria had us do, leading our third-grade class with an accent as thick as the glasses of buttermilk she drank during lunch in her little corner hideout behind the piano. But I don't remember committing it—the sin. If I had to guess its category, I'd say it was a lie. The easiest kind.

Grades three through eight, I used to confess everything, just before Mass on the first Friday of every month, at six A.M., an hour at which I could hardly recall my own name, never mind exactly the number of times I easily had peeked over during mathematics tests at Peter Karcz's clearly marked and always correct answers. Now I reveal those secrets only once a year, during the big special confession night held a couple evenings before Christmas, when Father Krotki invites all the priests he can dig up to come to the church and stake out a pew and lean with an elbow on the back of the seat and a hand to the forehead, signaling that they are ready to connect you and your misdeeds to the divine mercy of God. I don't mind telling my sins to a complete stranger priest I'll probably never ever see again, some guy who drove all the way from East Brookfield or Athol or Turners Falls to assist Father Krotki, and to partake in the big buffet Alice Pilch always puts together beforehand at the rectory. These guys from far away I can tell my darkest deeds to without blinking an eye—they don't know me. But there is no way I would spill my envy and sloth and impure thoughts to Father Krotki, who regularly calls me up for little jobs like freshening the hair color on the Saint Peter statue, or giving my opinion on which tone of flocked wallpaper will be best in his study, or lettering first, middle, and last names on the certificates to be given to the students who have perfect attendance at CCD. This year, I will have to kneel in back of somebody I've never seen before and confess that I lied each and every time somebody asked me how I was coming along with Mary Ziemba's painting.

Unc: "How's it going?"

Me: "Almost done."

Phyllis: "You must be so excited."

Me: "Oh, of course."

Wally: "How's the painting?"

Me: "Nearly done."

Alice: "What are you doing today?"

Me: "Working on the commission."

Heather: "Can I see it?"

Me: "If you can just wait another week."

Leo: "Almost finished, I hear."

Me: "Right."

Claire O'Hare: "Don't make yourself sick with all that work."

Me: "Never."

To each of them I said yes or thanks or how nice of you to ask. To each of them I said things were going fabulously, that I didn't know if I was prouder of the painting or of the discipline I was using in devoting all the time I could to getting it finished.

To each of them I lied.

Reality was, I was scared.

The sketches had been one thing. Easy, no problem. I would come home from Mary Ziemba's and lay out the newest photos across the top of the drawing board and keep them there, passing them by, studying, figuring out for myself which would be the best look to use in an eye, the set of the jaw, which was the better tilt of the head, the particular and unique ways the subjects stood in their bones. I filled page after page of my sketchbook with Davy and Aleksander and Flossie and Tim and Michal, so many that I eventually could draw them from memory: The curl of Flossie's hair right where it hit her temple, Michal's three circles under his left eye and only one under the right. How Davy's ramrod posture was evident even if you were only working on his face. Aleksander's sloping shoulders, Tim's that went straight out like you could serve a meal on them.

"I do tend to work fast once I get everything I need." This is what I had told Mary early on. And usually it's the truth—I can. Like how Claire says she can divine some career options for a client only after learning all she can about the path that brought the person to her doorway. Like how Alice always sets out all the ingredients for a recipe in one long line across her kitchen counter, in the order in which they will be used, progressing from left to right, using a teaspoon of this or a pinch of something else, and by the time she gets all the way to the counter's end, everything is all ready to mix or knead or simmer or bake. Like how Unc starts planting his garden the night before the actual digging takes place every Memorial Day, emptying his envelope of bush bean seeds into a margarine container of water and letting them soak all night so they will be sprouted a bit by the time it's dawn and he can be out there poking his finger in the soil exactly up to the second knuckle, dropping a seed in and covering it over for the few days' wait until the first pale green shoot breaks the surface. Like how Little Ted would close his eyes to begin his dreams only if he had his left hand wrapped around what was left of the thin blue blanket he'd been brought home from the hospital in, and his right arm around the unnamed brown dog shape that was the first stuffed toy from Sylvia's trial line of them, and if he had set like a halo over his head the cloth xylophone hat I'd made him so he could look just like his father.

As it was with all of them, I had everything I needed to begin what I was supposed to be doing. But when I sat down at my table to start, all I ever did was stare so long at the blank paper that it began to move in a mirage. And that's when I'd see things: The grand dollar sign. The people down in Mexico. The monks with their fancy paper. The freedom. The exhibit. The time, if that is something you can look at and see. I saw it there. All of it. Gliding past and up close and far away in undulating waves, from end to end of the paper like the wind-rippled American flag that fills the screen when the television stations are ending their broadcast day but I am still sitting up and awake and in need of more company.

"It's the fear of success," is what Claire O'Hare told me when I confessed, to an unordained person, that yes, I was indeed making myself sick over all this. I'd actually thrown into the trash the crinkle-cut crispy fries Heather had delivered the night before. I normally can't get enough, dousing them with Heinz 57 and pepper, and Leo always sends me up a basket from the first batch fried on Thursday, the ones made with the fresh new oil poured for the weekend. I wasn't sleeping, I also told Claire. It was amazing the number of things I could find to do at two in the morning, washing the fake crystal glassware I hadn't seen since I unwrapped it at my bridal shower. Flipping through phone books to see if old boyfriends are still in the area and whether or not they have a woman's name listed after theirs like some choose to do. Deciding to arrange my underpants in a flat and neat pile so I won't have to root through a sea of them when I open the drawer. Staring at the back of my head with a hand mirror because it all of a sudden occurred to me that this is a part of me everybody but me gets to see.

It was kind of like how I spent most of my free time right after Jack left. And when I said this, Claire said she knew some of what I was talking about.

"I had that same feeling when I started my business," she told me on the Friday that we were finishing up the ceiling and getting ready to do the floor, working on half of the room at a time because the bed—a big, creaking, iron-canopied deal she'd picked out from a tractor-trailer full of them at the flea markets in Brimfield—would be too much of a pain to dismantle. So we planned to move it to one side, paint the cleared section, and then carry the bed over to that half and complete the project.

"I'd rented the office, decorated it, stocked it right down to the container of half-and-half in the little icebox, and the first morning I was going to be open, I couldn't put the key in the door. I don't mean that there was something wrong with the lock. I stood on the sidewalk and couldn't move my arm the few inches in front of me, to put the key in. It was only when my first customer arrived a couple minutes later that I actually went inside. He was only my cousin's neighbor, who I knew from some parties, so it wasn't too embarrassing. But here I was, supposed to be offering him my services as somebody who could give some direction, and I couldn't even unlock my own door. We spent the whole session talking about me. About what I really wanted, and how this was the start of it. And now that it was here, I was terrified."

Claire is up on a ladder telling me this. I'm down below in ratty clothes and a paper bag for a hat in case she splatters any of the fluorescent paint with which she's stenciling tiny stars onto the dark blue ceiling. Stars were what the sleeping pill lady had, and this is what Claire wants for herself.

"What did your cousin's neighbor want to do for a living?"

"I never found out," she said, not looking down. "He never came back for the second appointment."

The room is shaping up. Claire's outfit bears the proof that she has been working hard. Midnight blue, cerulean, silver, white, muddy brown, deep green, all represented on sleeves and legs and the bill of her baseball cap. Louisiana—or some-place close to it—surrounds us. After the stars, we'll roll the floor down with a warm blue. Then we'll add the waterlillies and the swan. Then a couple coats of polyurethane. Then Claire O'Hare can move her bed back into place and she can rest in peace.

"Well, is Mary Ziemba pestering you? Is that the problem?"

"She calls me, maybe once a week, but I don't consider that a bother. She just asks how's it going and do I need anything else from her? She'll always remind me that she wants the painting by Christmas, the latest. That gives me about a week and a month. The next thing I'm supposed to do is deliver it. Once it's done."

"Do you need more time than a week and a month?"

I gazed up at the stars. A single week would be plenty of time for me if I weren't feeling so squirrelly about it.

"No," I said.

Claire looked down at me from the cloudless sky.

"Then, well, I don't know—I sound like I'm selling sneakers—but just do it."

So I did.

That night I went home and I sat down in front of the big piece of white paper and I sketched the outlines of Davy, of Aleksander and Michal and Tim, of Flossie up front where she belongs. And Mary Ziemba in the middle of them all.

For her, I worked from the photo she slid at me the day I met Aleksander, a shot taken not that long ago, one requested by the editor of the company newsletter.

"She told me they needed a new picture of me, for some story they were writing, and she picked me up herself to go to the photographer, because she had heard that I am not keen on having my photo taken, and she didn't trust me to meet her down at Nadolski's like I said I would. She didn't tell me that, but I knew that was the reason. I just could tell."

The picture Mary gave me from that day was nothing really special. Mary just looking at you, pleasantly and happily. I had expected some fancy studio pose, maybe innovative lighting, a stab at the drama found in one of Flossie's glossies. There was nothing like that. So I said, "This is what you want." Neither a question nor a statement.

"I know, it's nothing great," Mary said, "but it's what I want. It's how I look now, and that's the important thing. To me at least. Now is when I am looking back and thinking of those people, and what could make me happier than to say that these here are my family? How lucky I have been, and am."

I nodded, because the way she said that, you just had to believe her. "Whatever you want," I said.

"Well, I know I could look around and I could find you a picture in which I look better, maybe more attractive, certainly much younger. Maybe an outfit you might find more suitable. But this is what I want. This is who I am. Who I've become. Because of them is why. They made me." Then she pointed to herself, though I already knew who she meant.

I took the picture from her, and I took the picture of Aleksander that she'd given me, and I brought them both home. I put them there along with the others, in the crowd along the top of my drawing table. And that's where they remained. Until more than a month later, when Claire O'Hare, up there in the stars, said what she did. And I went home and did what I did.

Which was to finally get going.

12

I was turning the radio dial a couple of months back when I heard it for the first time: Pammy Franklin's show.

And what was she doing but drawing and painting, which is what I had taught her back in my first and regretted teaching job.

Drawing and Painting with Pfranklin.

That was the name of her program.

Her radio program.

This is what she did now—taught art over the radio. That was what she called herself now—Pfranklin—pronounced like there was no *p*, which made you wonder why she bothered to leave it there in the first place. Maybe just so she could say, "Remember, it's Franklin with a P!"

Drawing and Painting with Pfranklin was a program broadcast from the little radio station in Ware that was the type that covered things big-city ones wouldn't care about. It set up microphones at the board of selectmen meetings, at high school plays, at dog officer hearings. It offered locals the chance to have their own programs, with the only cost being drumming up a sponsor to run commercials every fifteen minutes or so. One of my favorite programs was *Travel the Bay State,* an hour-long show in which a couple placed a tape recorder on their dashboard and left it running while they drove around on the weekends. You mostly heard their complaining engine and their descriptions of the turnpike and the backs of the vehicles they were following, but it was worth it to tune in because the couple, identified in the credits only as "the Happy Harrisons," often interrupted their occasional narrative to brew a fight about what a lousy driver the husband was and what a terrible navigator the wife was and who was supposed to be looking for that exit sign and what's it gonna take to get you to slow down and what's it gonna take to get you to shut up? It was great background noise for painting, and I tuned in each Tuesday and Thursday at nine P.M. to travel along with them to the Kennedy Compound in Hyannis Port or the new Norman Rockwell Museum out in the Berkshires or the plastic lawn flamingo factory up in Leominster. I had never, ever heard *Drawing and Painting with Pfranklin* until one night late this past summer when I tuned in early for my trip with the Harrisons and caught the tail end of her show, the final seconds that gave the credits: who'd been the producer, the director. Then a voice came on saying, "This has been D*rawing and Painting with Pfranklin*. Up next, *Travel the Bay State* ventures up to the Brattleboro Shopping Outlet, via Route Ninety-one."

I grabbed the *Pennysaver* and checked the listings for the repeat schedule. I had to stay up until 1:03 A.M., when the station replayed the program, an audio demonstration of "The Pfranklin Method," in which an artist could set herself free by throwing aside the usual brushes and painting instead with objects found at the scene that was to be the subject.

"And now I'm doing the sky," Pammy explained as she dipped into a can of blue paint with what she told us was the bottom of a Dunkin' Donuts cup and, with a series of little squishes, pressed it onto her canvas.

Then she picked up a flattened cigarette filter and mushed it around in what she said was black and we heard these little thumpings as she dabbed it around. "Now I'm doing the road." Then a piece of a branch. "I put it in the brown; I'm doing the bark." A faded scrap of newspaper, crushed. "It's kind of a whitey-bluey thing I mixed up with it. Now I'm doing the clouds." A snapped-off and bent antenna, *bap bap bap.* "I got red on it and I'm just stabbing little apples all over the branches." A sandal that had been run over many times. A beetle casing. A feather. All of these visited her palette, then her board, many times over until she stepped back and declared her painting finished. "Except . . ." There was only silence, and then, "There. Don't forget to sign your name!"

Of course I had to hunt down the program every week, often tuning in for in the reruns as well. That Pammy had her own show—and sponsors—to teach visual art over the airwaves, I couldn't believe. Nor could I keep away. It was like how, for the first few weeks after I signed the papers for the no-fault divorce that I secretly did feel was somebody's fault other than mine, I often would check my copies for Jack's full name there on the left-hand line. His regular signature and way of signing—thick blue Flair pen and all cartoony—did not look anything like how you should write your name on a document ending what was supposed to be a lifelong commitment. But it was there each and every time I looked. No matter the number of visits I made to the document I was storing in the pot-holder drawer, the fact was still true. I knew from my lawyer, who knew from Jack's lawyer, that he was long gone. ("Do I have any rights?" I asked him. "No," he said, "but I'd like to talk to you about lettering a sign for me.") He was also gone from this country: the SylJac line was doing well enough to be invited to expand overseas. So that's where they all were. The three of them. Overseas. Traveling from country to country, return date open. Overseas. The sea was big. Little Ted was, well, little. I missed him hugely.

As of the spring, as of the last time I saw him, Little Ted already was a better artist than I believed big Pammy ever could hope to be. He, not she, rightfully should have a radio show. He, not she, should be on the air, even if it was only so I could listen to him again and again as he rummaged through his treasure box for the correct materials, and if he couldn't find them, he wouldn't get all bothered. He'd just go ahead and use something else.

"Lily," he said to me on one of his last visits, when he needed a compass to make a half circle for a new solar system he was inventing but improvised with the bottom of a Hi-C can, "you know that anything can be anything you want, if you really want it to be."

What I wanted was to be listening to an hour of Little Ted at his drawing pad. Or him anywhere, doing anything, just so long as I could at least hear him. What I got was Pammy. I could have shut her off, or switched to the next station, but I had to listen to it all, right down to the end, when she thanked her sponsors—not surprisingly Franklin's Squash Club and Pro Shop, and Balicki Realty. "Please visit these fine businesses," she'd invite, "not only to patronize them, but to view my work up close and in person."

I took her up on that the very first night I listened. Even though it was past two in the morning, I went for a walk. Slowly past Balicki's. There on the wall behind Mrs. Balicki's desk lit up for the night by a crystal table lamp, hung a genuine Pfranklin. I recognized it from the name scratched into the right-hand bottom corner, a confident signature with a capital *P* and *F* joined and leading off the rest of the word. I was floored by what it lay claim to: a very nice acrylic of a big slice of blueberry pie on a green plate on an orange table. A silver fork leaning on the edge, a yellow napkin to the right. The colors were loud but pleasing. I couldn't get close enough to the window to make out the intricacies of how she'd achieved the bright shine on the rim of the plate, or along the handle of the fork, or on the berries that had slowly spilled from beneath the top crust. I could only guess. And at two-thirty in the morning that's what I did, sitting on the front steps, that big piece of pie hanging there behind me never once letting on whether or not I'd come up with the right answer.

That was the last time I was jealous. Something I said out loud at brunch at Wally Wazocha's a couple weeks later, when he brought out a book of 101 questions that are supposed to spark interesting discussions at parties. When it was my turn to answer, the question I got was, "What was the last time you were truly jealous?"

I had to check that this was indeed regarding the last time. Because most of the previous summer had been spent wishing I was Sylvia. Or wishing I was Jack. Only because they had what I wanted, which was Little Ted. I also had coveted what my parents have—each other, and in a place far from here where you never have to wear a jacket except for in air-conditioning. I also envied my sister, with her great focus on work and a whole city where she could be whoever she wanted to be. Sometimes, at my lowest, however odd and sick this sounds, I actually was jealous of Chuckie. Because think about it—if you were a person of faith, dead actually was the state you were shooting for, when you would see God and be able to relax finally and then maybe be given some kind of powers to do some good for all the people you'd left behind. Plus there's the whole attraction of having all your troubles mean nothing anymore because you are in heaven, and what could be better than that?

But if the question was about the exact last time I was jealous, and if I had to be honest, then I first had to ask if anybody playing the game knew Pammy Franklin. And nobody said they did, except for Alice, who asked wasn't that the girl she heard once on radio—or was it TV? So I went on to say that I last was jealous listening to Pammy on that program, which I described to them, and had to again because nobody believed there could be such a show.

"Not that I want it to be me doing that—but I could do the same, a program, you know. Maybe better." That was how I put it. And I could talk like that, openly, because everyone there was a friend—Wally and Claire and Leo and Alice playing the game, long after everyone else had left.

I was silent after that, and they all filled in the space. Claire said she could understand my feelings; Leo said it wasn't fair that she was getting attention—but why didn't I get some sponsors and do my own version? Alice said Pammy stunk, and Wally looked sad and said nothing at all, just put his hand on the back of my neck and made slow little soothing circles around the vertebrae that stuck out there.

"We're all sorry for you," Claire told me, and the rest of them nodded. I knew she was sincere and I settled into the warmth of feeling that I was loved by all these people. I was healthy and friends cared about me and I had work and a roof over my head. My jealousy was stupid. But I had to put my sadness somewhere. Down a long and unmarked side street in my heart lived the knowledge that things in my life wouldn't look that bad if I made a list of them. And when I took the time to do that, the good fortune of my general standing was clear. But the consolation of those around me at that moment was like a really fattening candy you just want one more of. So I took it.

Soon after that party, things changed. Mary Ziemba called, my first true commission was in the works, a solo show was on the horizon, along with a huge payment that I only needed to name. People up in Canada, and down in Mexico, and anywhere in between that mattered, soon would be looking. The feeling it gave was fantastic enough to be illegal.

It is a feeling multiplied by a zillion now, because I now am almost done with the painting.

Since Claire's pep talk a couple weeks ago, I have been working daily and for long stretches. I get up early and sometimes don't even change into real clothes or wash my face or brush my teeth or hair before sitting down at my drawing table and starting to work. It will be three o'clock and Heather will be back from school and running up with my mail, and I'll still have my nightgown on, maybe a sweatshirt thrown over it if the day is a particularly cold one, and an open box of cereal next to me from which I take a handful now and then to keep energized.

"I want to be an artist," Heather blurted out one day after standing there watching me for a whole minute, fifty-five seconds longer than she usually gave me. Early on in the first of her now thirteen years, I'd attempted to discover what creative things she might enjoy. But everything I gave her—clay, crayons, finger paints, thread and yarn and the appropriate needles, pre-mushed pails of papier-mâché, stamp sets, fabric, bead kits, spray paint even—got picked up one time maybe, if at all, then was never used again. The common ground I'd hoped to foster with her never materialized, and for gift-giving occasions I found myself eventually surrendering to the one interest she held then, and clings to even now, in eighth grade: Barbies.

"You? An artist?"

She nodded.

"You're kidding."

She shook her head.

"Where did this come from?"

She scratched. "Well . . ." She looked at the floor. "I like the uniform."

She was serious.

I pitched a sponge at her anyhow. It was dry, and bounced off the nearest of the two thick black ponytails that sprung from the sides of her head.

"Then go put on your own," I said.

After that day, Heather would come upstairs in the afternoon carrying the mail, and wearing a flannel nightgown—usually a pink-and-blue-striped thing with flouncy lace around the collar that stuck up from beneath the navy blue sweatshirt she wore on top of it—her hair out of its usual restraints and all messed up, on purpose, like mine. I would seat her in the phone chair with a drawing pad, and we would work silently together. Nothing was said, but some surprise connection was taking place. I'd get up for a cup of tea and I would stop by her chair to see what she was making, usually elaborate castles on which she'd draw every single brick, and knights on horses rescuing women who had big cones for hats. Better than making nothing at all is how I saw it, and I'd commend her for her imagination, something I'd honestly always questioned the existence of. If she took a break, she'd shoosh over to me in the big, pink, fake-fur slippers that weren't unlike the ones I had on my feet, and she'd say, *"Aaawwww"* and "That is just beautiful." Eventually, Alice would bang a spoon on the pipe to call her for dinner and homework, and that would be it until the next afternoon.

I didn't really have the time, but after a couple days of Heather coming by every afternoon, plus all day Saturday and what was left of Sunday once she'd gone to church and read the funnies and listened to *Freddie Brozek's Polka Explosion* and had her big meal, I made a few quick stops at the drugstore for some things I thought she would like to work with. Sure, I had supplies to lend or give, but there is something wonderful and fresh about getting a brand-new one for your very own. Because I'd tried this with her many times before, I didn't spend a million. Just got a small spiral-bound sketchbook, a couple of pieces of charcoal. I wrapped everything in pink tissue that I tied with a bow. Heather received them like they were bars of gold. When I gave her the first package, she hugged me longer than anybody had in my recent memory, or for reasons other than they felt sorry for me.

Alice told me not to get too excited. "It's just the age. She's looking for something new to latch onto. You're the big thing right now."

I know Alice didn't mean it, and I know she probably was correct because she has read practically every child-rearing book ever printed in the English language, but she hurt my feelings when she said the "right now" part. Like this is how it is right now, but tomorrow Heather was going to traipse across the street to Taffy's and ask to sit in the window with her all day because it was the new cool thing to do. Then I once again would be my former self: Cioci Lily. Upstairs, and weird, and alone.

But it didn't work that way. Heather continued to come upstairs. She even asked if she could stay over on a few Fridays. She helped me carry up from the cellar the soft little cot that folded for storage into a U shape and that for four and a half years' worth of two nights per month, in the space between the back of the couch and the wall, had opened up to hold the sleeping Little Ted and all his many necessities.

On my way back from the bathroom in the middle of the night I'd sit at the edge of the couch and, in the orange glow of the night-light, I'd look at Heather, something I really hadn't done since when she was so young she really didn't know what was going on around her. Back then, Heather had no choice but to sleep where Alice put her, to trust me to look after her if I were the one put in charge. Now, here, she was making her own decision about that sort of thing. And she had selected me. Even if it was a stage, it felt real and good. One time I got the nerve to reach out and pat her soft hair like mothers do on Robitussin commercials once the drug has kicked in and the child finally is down for the count. Heather moved slightly at my touch, and I took my hand away, not wanting to wake her, or bother her, or really give her any reason to want to go away.

The presence of Heather gave energy at a point in the afternoon that I normally would be flopping onto the couch and tuning in to *The Guiding Light,* then during commercials switching to *General Hospital,* and back again. Even though I long knew the boundaries of network and program, if I did too much clicking, the characters all kind of blended into a whole new show, and seemed related by deed or celebration or woe. But when Heather started showing up after school, there was nothing I could do but stay at my table and be a good example and keep working, since she now genuinely was paying attention to me.

I woke late the morning of the day I knew I was going to finish. But that's because I'd stayed up until after two working steadily and with focus, like a runner who can look ahead and finally see the tape stretched across the finish line. I've never run, for recreation at least, but I can imagine that it has to feel fantastic once you see that the end is near. I do watch the Boston Marathon televised every April, this big mass of athletes, first seen from a helicopter camera as the starter's gun goes off, in a couple of hours shrinks to a little thread of five or six guys who've come all the way from someplace like Africa to try to be the first to run down the center of the street into the heart of the city and through the tape. I like the end part. When the winners are wrapped in aluminumy space blankets and awarded little crowns of ivy. It's all very exciting and it can make me teary, even though I don't know any of the participants.

That morning I was running down the yellow line with the tape so close I could hear it fluttering. With any luck, and no interruptions, I maybe would be even delivering the painting that night, as I'd hinted to Mary when she'd called the morning before and asked the usual how was it going and was there anything I needed? and I answered, "Just for you to start banging a nail." On her end there was silence, with only the big clock interrupting it.

The she breathed more than said the word, "Done?"

"Except for just a few picky things."

"Everybody? Everybody's there?"

"Everybody.'"

"Everybody." I could see her nodding. "Everybody's what I wanted."

After that I turned off the phone ringer for that much less interruption. I kept it off for the rest of the day. If I looked over, I could see some form of a red number telling me how many calls there were awaiting me on my answering machine, but I didn't go near. I had a job to do—at this point only the smallest of details, adding a bit of color or shadow, stepping back to check, like to see if that was too much pink on Tim's face.

That's when I heard footsteps. Quick ones. Up the back stairs. A knock, then, like that hadn't been necessary, the door pushed open. Alice was standing there. After all the commotion she'd made, just standing there.

"Lily," she panted.

"Alice," I said, not looking up. I was preoccupied—Tim was still too pale. He was a ballplayer. He had to have accumulated some amount of sun while on the field. I cautiously added another thin layer of peach to his cheeks, and brought him up to health and outdoorsiness in that one second. But maybe a little too much. "Come and tell me what you think—does this guy, does he look sunburned?"

"Lily," Alice was saying again.

"Alice," I replied again, and I dragged out the first syllable.

"Lily."

"What?"

Alice walked up to me. She looked kind of sickly, like she had a lot of the time when she was a kid and her parents made her wait tables when she should have been out in the fresh air. "Do you know?"

She held up a newspaper page that told me I had only ten shopping days left. She pointed to the first big article, what she'd come upstairs to make sure I knew: that Mary Ziemba was dead.

The photograph was what I saw first. Nothing Mary would have been pleased with. "File photo" were the tiny words printed beneath it, just above her name in all capital letters. MARY A. ZIEMBA. I never even gave a thought to what her middle name might have been. Or if she even had one. Agnes? Antonia? Alice?

Alice. I took the paper from her and went to the phone chair.

"I wasn't sure if you'd heard," is what she was saying.

I shook my head, both in answer, and in disbelief. I read to find out what had done it. An accident? Old age? What?

MARY A. ZIEMBA,
GRAND Z FOUNDER,
PHILANTHROPIST

The headline told me nothing I didn't know. I searched the little write-up that followed.

"Mary A. Ziemba, 83, of off Route 20, died Tuesday afternoon after a long illness. The funeral will be held Thursday at Wazocha's Funeral Home, with burial in the Saint Matthew and Michael Cemetery. Calling hours are tonight from 6 to 9. Born in Niebieska, Poland, she moved here in 1927 and became one of the area's first businesswomen, turning a door-to-door vegetable delivery service into the well-known Grand Z chain of grocery stores. She retired three years ago and since had been working closely with the various charities and related efforts she founded, including the Ziemba Library, Ziemba Park Recreation Site, Ziemba Volunteer Corps, Ziemba Grants, and Grand Z Food for All. She leaves no family."

I read it again. One more time, to make sure. But since my first time going over the words, nothing had changed. They were still telling me two things, one unbelievable—that she had been suffering for a long time—and one a thousand times more hard to understand—that she left nobody behind.

"This is wrong," I told Alice, who was standing there in an apron that we'd bought at a craft fair way back in the T-shirt summer. Some nervous little woman stood in a booth inking an actual flounder, then pushed it down onto cloth for a most authentic fish print. Alice bought an apron in each color available, and they were used in Rocky's until they got worn out and as bad looking as this one did now, with holes and stains of all sorts.

"This is wrong," I said again.

Alice just rubbed her arms. "I know," she said softly, and the person she reminded me of just then made me grab the phone. Wally Wazocha picked up on the second ring.

"It's Lily," I said, then ran out of words.

"I was wondering when I'd hear from you. I left a message, then another, another maybe, I'm not sure, everything's been happening. But I did try to call again, then there was no answer. I was going to come over, but I couldn't get away. It's really crazy here." He spoke quickly, in the manner of somebody who had too much going on that you, on your end of the line, could not see.

That's when I looked at the answering machine. Ten, ten, ten, it blinked, telling me I had more messages than that, but that's all the thing knew how to count. Ten, ten, ten. Ding-ding-ding. Only I'd won nothing.

"I didn't listen to the machine. Not yesterday. Not this morning. I was busy finishing. The painting. Alice just came up. With the paper."

"I'm sorry," Wally said, and he was as sincere as you'd want him to be. "I know this must be sad for you."

"Sad . . . Wally, it's like, it's different—I'm calling to . . ." I was making no sense, and I knew it. Alice was in front of me, crouching and giving me a coffee cup full of water. I pushed her away and sat on the edge of the chair.

"Wally. She has relatives. Family. Some of them have to be alive. There's a son; he's as old as me. She has family. I know this."

He was quiet for a few seconds, and in the background I

heard some papers being flipped. "I'm getting out the information, the sheet I faxed to the paper." He narrated for me as he did these things. "It was late at night when I took everything down and then made the call, but I know what I was told." Here he read silently to himself. Then he said, "Nope, no family. Under family members, a big *X*. Which means 'none.'"

"Who told you this?"

"Her lawyer called to let me know. He called to tell me about her, about Mary Ziemba. He met me at the hospital, where she'd driven herself yesterday afternoon. He drove in back of me, in back of the hearse, from the hospital to here. Filled out the forms himself. Handwriting like a typewriter. So there's no mistake—there was no family."

"Ask about the illness." Alice was whispering this. She was still squatting in front of me, elbows on her knees like there was something to watch other than my confusion. When she said "illness," she only mouthed the word, slowly.

"Illness," I said into the phone. "The paper said illness. What did she have? You might have that wrong too."

"I don't have anything wrong," Wally said kindly, probably a whole lot nicer than I would have been at this point. I heard more papers.

"Certificate says it was her heart, and the Latin on here translates to that she had problems for a long time. Heart trouble. The kind that doesn't get any better. That's why I wrote 'after a long illness.' I don't just make these things up, you know."

"I know, I know. It's just such a shock. She didn't look sick at all. Here I am painting her face, and bang. That's it. I just talked with her yesterday morning."

"That's great, Lily." You could tell he wasn't listening, and then he asked me to wait a second and he held a short conversation with somebody about picking up extra chairs at Taylor Rental. "Lily, I'm busy; flowers are already coming in, details—I have to call in everybody, Wendy and George. Moondog over at the crematorium, if I can get hold of him just to help in church. He's always looking for extra money. There's going to be a lot of mourners here, with all that she did for the town, and with the wake only being tonight. So I can't leave right now. But would you like to come over? Sit in the office with me? I wouldn't make you work, of course, just so you'll have some company? It might make you feel better."

The thought of seeing Mary flat dead in a box, like I would have to if I even for one second took my eyes off the green shag on my way from the delivery door to Wally's office, hadn't even crossed my mind. But there she would be, like that. "I don't know, Wally. I'll call you back." I hung up and said to Alice, "Heart stuff."

She grimaced, like she might know firsthand some of the pain involved, if in this case there even had been any.

I accepted the water from Alice. It was warm. I took a little even though I don't think I really needed it. People in distress are always being given water, so there must be something to it, though I can't say for sure if it made any difference to me other than being something to do. The number on the answering machine yelled at me silently. I pressed the button with my thumb, and Alice and I both listened.

I forwarded through the one from the guy who wanted a logo for the microbrewery he was starting up in his basement. I erased the hang-up, and the reminder about my dentist appointment. I kept the woman who wanted to know if I marbleized. Then I got to the important stuff.

"It's me," Wally was saying in a message the machine's

halting baritone told me had been recorded at 10:17 the night before. "I need to talk to you."

"Lily, call me." It was Wally again, half an hour later, sounding urgent.

"It's me again, Lily," he was saying, this time at almost midnight. "It's nearly midnight. I won't try again. But call me whenever you get in."

"It's me," Unc was saying this very day, a little after six A.M., midmorning for him. "Are you awake? Did you hear about your friend? Call me."

"Lily, Phyllis calling. I know it's early, but you must telephone me the minute you hear this. Or call your uncle."

"Lily, this is me," Claire O'Hare was saying in a jittery voice. "I'm just calling to see if you're okay. I can come over if you'd like. I can cancel my appointments for the day; just say the word and I'll be there in a second."

"Lily, I'm just checking if you're there," Unc said.

"Me again, Lily." Wally again. "Pick up if you're there. It's important."

"Lily, are you up?" Alice's voice. "Stomp on the floor if you're up . . ."

"I couldn't take it anymore, I had to come up," Alice was saying in person. There was a whimper to her that annoyed me though I couldn't put my finger on the reason.

"Thanks," I said. I didn't need anything more from her, but I couldn't say that. She could tell, though, because she knows me, so she said, "Stomp on the floor if you need me. You know that."

Even so, five minutes later, I was still sitting in the chair and Alice was still in front of me. Only now we were listening to Leo's take on the whole thing.

"She had to have been crazy."

That was how he saw it. He'd come up to fetch Alice for something, and to give me a typical guy's condolence, a mumbled "I'm sorry" with head down and one foot scraping the floor.

"Leo," Alice said in a scolding tone. "That was Lily's friend."

"Yeah, but you said she never saw anybody at the house. That's because there was nobody to see." He said this to her, though he was talking to me and pointing at me. "I don't want to sound mean, but that has to explain it. She was old. Old people get crazy. Don't tell me I'm wrong there."

"Then I guess you must be old," Alice told him, and she sounded angrier now. She and Leo rarely fought. Not at least so loudly that I could hear them. The times that Alice got really mad at Leo, she struck out creatively, pulling something like washing his favorite clothes in the hottest water, so the next time he put them on, he'd get all upset thinking he'd gained a bunch of weight.

"Enough," I said. "Go and do what you were going to do today." I wanted them out of my place. I didn't need the extra confusion. "Thanks, Alice. Thanks for telling me." I stayed there in my chair. She bent down and hugged my neck. I smelled the toilet water Heather had bought her, a putrid mix that reminded me of lilacs and church incense coming at you at the same time.

"You sure you're okay?" Alice was still bending down, but had released me into fresh air.

I nodded.

"You want a ride to Wally's?"

"No thanks."

"You're not walking, are you? Want me to walk with you?"

"No."

"Well, call me if you do. You shouldn't be walking or driving if you're upset."

"I'm not upset," I said. "I'm confused."

Now Alice was nodding. Leo was holding the door for her. He said to me, "Stomp if you need us. You know that."

"Okay." I sat in my chair and listened to their feet make it down the stairs like they were one big four-legged animal. I heard their storm door open, the kitchen one beyond that, then the sound of both of those closing solidly. The month before, anticipating winter, Leo had stuck long, modern, high-tech self-adhesive strips of insulation around all our entrances and exits, and ever since we all had been marveling at the difference, at the absence of the drafts that, before he sealed us in so well and efficiently, we had taken as part of everyday life.

I'd told that to Mary Ziemba. I'd told her my share of minutiae. But I'd never talked health with her. It was little stories, the handing over of pictures. The closest I remember coming to the topic was feeling punk one day and telling her I thought I'd make an appointment with Dr. Pluta.

"Pluta's nice for the flu," was what Mary had said. "But if you're real sick, go to a real doctor."

And I said, "Yeah, he has that on his sign out front: 'Dr. Pluta. Nice For the Flu.'"

Mary had laughed at that one—really laughed, all of her shaking like there was an earthquake going on under the chair she was sitting in. When she was able to talk again, she told me how that was a good one.

"A real good one," she said.

I'm pretty talented at sneaking my eyes around to gather information. Always have been. Looking at what's visible when somebody opens their pocketbook or wallet, what they have as a balance, how much they've spent, and on what when they are writing out a check and their transaction register is visible upside down. My eyes do inventory in the quick few seconds when somebody searches for something in one of their cabinets. They speed around a room I'm seated in—checking out what's on the shelves, how someone chose to place this big shell over here on the mantel and that little doggie statue there on the coffee table and not the other way around. I take in and I remember the things I've seen. And I couldn't picture ever spotting any little orange pill bottles at Mary's, no handy pocket container with seven little wells into which to drop the medications you need on specific days of the week, no thermometer in its sleek stand-up holder, no hot-water bottle draped over the sink and awaiting a refill. The books she stacked were titles on art criticism, the business world, gardening, fund-raising. Nothing on a particular disease or method of cure or ways to still think positive when all else fails and your expiration date is as sure as the one printed on your half gallon of milk. The calendar that hung in the kitchen, decorated with copies of drawings by twelve of the many students at Ziemba Public Library's summer program, was marked only with abbreviated handwritten reminders. "Lib. mtg.," "Vol.," "Rec. Dept.," "Whist," "FFA" (her food charity, I eventually figured out, not Future Farmers of America like I thought the first time).

Nothing at all like "Appt. w/ Real Dr.," "Get 2nd Opin.," "Bg Cty Hosp stay," "Pck Plot," "Call Wzoha."

And her face. I saw it enough—close up, too. Maybe she looked tired once in a while, or she walked slowly through a room, but, hey, she was eighty-three and I'd like to see how you're zooming along if and when you make it to that number.

I could go over every minute of our handful of visits, over every syllable that was said, over every scene I took in through my eyes. But none of it would mean a thing now. Mary Ziemba was dead and gone, and I was wasting my time wondering how I couldn't have seen it coming.

I got out of my chair and walked around to the other side of the easel. There in front of me, just as they had been when I'd last stood there not thirty minutes ago, were the members of Mary Ziemba's family: Flossie, Davy, Aleksander, Michal and Tim, all looking so pleased with where they were and who they were at that particular point in time. Tim's cheeks had dried since I'd been across the room, and they now looked appropriately ruddy, so it turned out there had been no reason for concern. Which was the same look I right then realized I had accomplished on the face of the woman who sat in the center of them all: Mary Ziemba, looking pleased and finally among her loved ones, whoever they were, right where she had wanted to be.

13

The line leading to the framing window at The Craft Planet was surprisingly long, like the one that forms when Father Krotki ties together a couple of candles in an X-shape and invites everybody up to the altar so he can hold them against your neck to mark the feast of Saint Blais, who is supposed to shield you from all manner of throat ailments. This happens one Sunday each February, a particularly germy month, so you can imagine the number of people who stand and wait for their turn.

That week, The Craft Planet had a coupon in the paper for fifty percent off the custom-framing job of your choice. Everybody in front of me and in back of me was holding some sort of artwork and the pink-and-black coupon edged with the orbiting Saturns that were the trademark of the place that boasted an inventory of a million things to satisfy a million creative whims. As you walked in, a woman was demonstrating liquid needlepoint, paint in a tube that you squeezed to dot along the lines of a printed drawing, in this case a picture of a football.

"It couldn't be easier," she was assuring her audience. "Why take all that time to embroider, to try to thread a needle, to maybe injure yourself with something so sharp—or drop it on the rug and not find it and one day you're walking along and it sticks in your foot and breaks off halfway inside you and you have to drive yourself to the emergency room? Why go through all that when, to achieve the same look—or nearly the same—you can just blot, blot, blot?"

"Oooohh," was the answer from the pair of grandmotherly types that had stalled in front of her table.

The line I stood in was located behind the demonstration area and was further corralled by two walls of ready-made frames and precut mats, a good selection in case you didn't have the patience to wait for your time at the window. Some people did give up and head over there to pick something that might by chance match. "This is for the birds," the woman two people behind me said disgustedly, and she offered her coupon to anybody who wanted it, even though the fine print read "One per customer," and somebody quickly told her that out loud.

"You want a deal, you gotta be patient." This was what the lady in front of me said right after that, and she turned a little and winked at me at the same time. There was a color photo in her right hand, and she held it from underneath, with her fingertips around the edges so nothing would touch the surface. Like it was still fresh from being developed and was still drying from the chemicals.

After she looked back at me that once, the woman turned again, and she craned her head around the sides of the thing I'd taped between two huge sheets of cardboard.

"Got something special in there?"

"A painting."

"You make it?"

"Yeah."

"Of what?"

"Some people."

"People in general or somebody you know?"

"I don't know them."

"Maybe I'd know them then, if I could look . . ."

"Who's that?" I thought this might deflect her interrogation.

"Who? This?" She tilted her photo toward me.

"That." I pointed, to help her.

"Jillie? You don't know Jillie?"

She was facing me now, looking astounded. Though I am not usually good at guessing things like this, I estimated her to be in her fifties. Maybe closer to sixty. She dressed youthfully, as my mother would say. A stocking cap striped in rainbow colors, and a big long pink coat. On one lapel was a chocolate chip cookie for a pin. A real cookie that had been dipped in something shiny and hard that sealed it off from the rest of the world. Probably something shiny and hard that you could get in a spray can in the second half of the right-hand side of Aisle Seven—Preservation Materials and Methods.

I looked at the photograph, this woman, sweaty and teary-eyed and in a big green T-shirt on which the same cookie was pinned above rounded silver letters spelling out JILLIE! She stood arm-in-arm with a skinny, heavily made-up, pointy-busted redhead in a cropped white tank top that allowed an inverted belly button to wink at the world.

I pointed. "That's Jillie?"

"You have a radio? A TV? You never heard of Jillie?"

I shook my head. Meaning that I hadn't heard. Not that I didn't have the conveniences, though I don't know how they could have helped with this.

The person in back of me leaned in with her embroidered cornucopia that prayed "May We Always Be Blessed With

Plenty," and she whispered, "She's some kind of singer. Country."

"Excuse me, but she's been nominated for the Rising Star award four years in a row now," the fan said. "She's not just 'some kind.' She is the best. That's all there is to it." Then she was talking to me again. " 'Don't Take Those Pills Before You Hear Me Out'—you mean to tell me you don't know that one from the radio?"

I shook my head.

" 'When Nobody in the World Gives a Damn?' 'I'll Wait Two Life Sentences?' Those ring a bell?"

"Nope."

"You gotta get her CDs. No—wait—gimme me your address, I'll make you tapes. I got bootlegs. You won't believe it. It's like she's talking to you, like she knows exactly what you're going through. You going through anything?"

The man holding the yellowed certificate and the young couple who'd been sighing over their enlargement of them saying their vows, all were awaiting my answer.

"No," I lied because it wasn't their business. "Everything's fine."

"Then thank your lucky stars. I've seen my share, Lord knows. And Jillie, she knows too. She's half my age, but it's like she's been there right alongside me for every one of my trials. And she went and set them to music—stuff you can line-dance to." She pointed to the photograph. "This was the one time I met her. Last month. She played down in Providence. I waited one hour and twelve minutes to get her autograph, and to tell her what she has meant to me. I started to bawl when I was telling her how even though she's a stranger and we never crossed paths before, how I have kids but none of them mean as much to me or have done anything for me close to what she has done, that I consider her a daughter, one who, just from her songs on the radio, genuinely and really saved my life."

The cornucopia woman wanted to know what we all did: "So what did she say?"

Jillie's fan fell silent. Then she looked down at her rubber boots and said quietly, "Well, she interrupted me—politely. And then she said, 'Excuse me—but will the cookie get moldy after a while?'"

People want to know what I did when I found out about Mary. I give them this part of my day, that scene from my hour and a half in the line leading to the framing counter at The Craft Planet, a new and huge art-supply store that is open 24 hours a day, 364 days a year.

How I landed there wasn't direct. First Wally called me back and he asked me could I please come over because there was something we had to discuss? Not that he wanted me to just sit with him—"This is something else, Lily," he said. "Would you mind?" So of course, I went. Even though I didn't want to.

I drove myself over and later could tell Alice that I was fine the whole way. I parked out back like I always do, in the first space over from the big wide garage that houses all the oddly shaped vehicles in the shiny, black Wazocha fleet. I walked up the back ramp feeling greatly underdressed in my heels and long skirt and tunic, half my collection of beaded necklaces clacking against my chest with each step. The artistic gypsy look for that official funeral home visit is what I'd thrown on after he'd called. It wasn't all black, but it was a whole lot more dressy than what I usually wore when I came over to work on "The Eternal Serenity." Still, walking into what used to be the parlor's smoking room in the years before a woman whose brother had died of lung cancer made a scene at his wake, screaming at Wally for allowing people to light up right around the corner from the casket, I felt like I looked: out of place.

I stopped at the pair of ashtrays on their grand bronze stands. Retired, they now held several of the kind of bushy ferns that rarely need a splash of water or ray of sunlight. Wally came around and spotted me. He took me up in a big, slow hug that was a little more than just professional. All around us were flowers. Lining the room, tiers of them, set on the floor, propped up on stands, on a third row of shelving Wally later told me he had to invent just for the occasion out of some planks and bricks he had found out in the garage and then draped with old gold curtains he discovered down in the cellar. Never had there been so many flowers in the funeral home, Wally told me. It had to be some kind of record, and he was going to tally them up the first moment he had the chance. Some were arranged in the shapes of objects that pertained to Mary's life, the different colors of blossoms making up the darks and lights like this was the Rose Bowl Parade and the florists who created them were painters creating the soup can, the brown bag of groceries with flowers spilling from the top, the small replica of the rustic cart that you could imagine was like the one Mary once brought around town, the red-and-white Grand Z logo that just had to have been sent by shocked staff members who felt helpless to ignore the wishes that no flowers be sent because even though it's nice and all to give money to a charity, the people who come to the wake will never know the extent of your generosity unless they see your name written on a card paper-clipped to the stem of a basket of chrysanthemums. My eyes went from one arrangement and basket and vase to the next, each more fantastic, more beautiful as they led up to the front of the room and the simple oak casket with the lid left open to display what was left of Mary Ziemba. A dead person who, except for the supine position and the closed eyes, looked just like I had known her to be in real life.

"Do you want me to leave you alone?" Wally was asking this, and he had the point of my right elbow in his palm, gently, not pushing me, just to let me know he was there.

"No need to run off," I said. My eyes traveled around the room again, and that is when I noticed the empty easel to the left of the coffin. I pointed at it. "What's that?"

"That's where she wanted it," Wally said.

"What?"

"Your painting."

It took a second. "Mine? Hers?"

"Yeah." He nodded while saying this. "It was in her instructions. The ones she gave the lawyer. That he gave me this morning. She wanted the portrait put right there. Specifically. I had the easel already, because I was planning to begin a series of grief seminars next year. I thought it would be good for holding up a big notepad. You know, that I could write suggestions on, for people to feel better, that they might copy the ideas down for themselves to take home and study and try. Do you think it'll be strong enough, good enough for your painting?"

I didn't answer. I was looking for the first time at Mary, lying there, batteryless. She wasn't going to be answering any questions. I would have to give her the words. And the ones that came to my mind were those that had made up her request to me:

That she needed me to make a painting. That I could name my price. That she needed it completed by Christmas. At which time there would be an exhibition.

And this, I realized right then, was going to be it.

I stepped backwards, farther, then enough that the back of my knees hit one of the puffy green chairs in the front row, the sturdy and comfortable ones usually given to the surviving spouse or the eldest child to sit in during lulls or to collapse onto if the experience of receiving a line of mourners and their expressions of sympathy all gets to be too much. I sat down. Wally took the chair next to me.

"Will the easel be good enough, or should I think of something else?"

I nodded.

"I should think of something else?"

I shook my head.

"I shouldn't?"

I just said, "This is what she wanted," because it was the truth.

"She wanted a few certain things, but nothing that's too far out," Wally said. "The lawyer has them all in a notebook. Like how the flowers, I guess she knew they'd be sent anyhow, any that might arrive are later to be brought all around town—churches, the hospital, the nursing home, the housing for the elderly—not one arrangement is to be left at the gravesite. And the music. She wants Paderewski, Chopin— and I don't have that in the office. I'm gonna have to bring some albums from home."

Home. I thought of my stereo there, a small, black, plastic imported thing that gave you your choice of playing a compact disc, a tape, or Pammy's show on the radio. It was a splurge by Jack two summers before, a present for my great understanding, he said. He'd been away more than usual that season, always tacking one or two extra days onto whatever stretch he originally said he'd be gone for. Always when he was up north. Always when he was near where Sylvia and Little Ted lived. And wasn't it something how they'd manage to run into one another, at some fair or park or whatever? It's a small world, is how Jack put it. And I'd agree, because he was one hundred percent right. Even though I would point out how it was especially tiny when you found yourself in the same town as somebody else. "At least he tells you he ran into her," was what Alice pointed out. I'd nod and smile when she'd say this again after I'd tell her how Jack had phoned to say he'd be delayed for a few more days again. And when she was gone back downstairs, I'd turn the volume up loud.

The stereo sat on a little end table that was next to my bookshelf that was next to my supply cabinet that was next to my drawing table, on which there was a painting that had been commissioned by that dead lady over there. "I gotta go somewhere," I told Wally, and I got up and turned without looking any more at the front of the room.

When I returned from my errand, Wally answered the door in his shirt and tie, no jacket despite the cold that was outside and that I was letting in.

I'd had the painting matted and framed at The Craft Planet because it was the only place in the immediate area that would turn such work around in an hour. Guaranteed in that time or free of charge. For reasons of selection and price and control, I usually order my frames from a catalog, and I cut my own mats with a lethal-looking metal-and-wood gizmo Unc and my father built for me when I was in college. But this was a rush job if I'd ever known one. Originally, Mary was to have taken care of these things herself, probably would have had it finished off by the person who worked on her genuine masterpieces, maybe edging it with a gold frame that truly was finished with a coat of that substance. But suddenly the job was up to me. Whatever I finally decided to bill Mary's estate, the price was going to include a charge for the three hours I spent on it today, one and a half in line and the rest roaming the store while waiting for my order, finally locating the sixteen-ounce spray can of "Keepit" that Jillie's fan's cookie had to have been blasted with.

"Seals and protects any and all items," read the words above the can's name. Beneath it was this:

"Preserve the everyday things of every day—what you least expect will become the treasured things of tomorrow. Keep away from children, pets and open flames."

I dropped a can of Keepit into the previously empty little red-canvas shopping basket I'd been toting from aisle to aisle as I waited. Wandering the floor-to-ceiling maze of earring findings and antiquing kits and stamp pads and counted cross-stitch books was like a lungful of anesthesia against what was happening back home, forty minutes down the turnpike, a world away from the demonstration of organic vegetable dyes being applied with a brush to a row of simple white-cotton scarves at the foot of Aisle Eleven. I was just about to accept the invitation to try my hand when I heard over the intercom the words "Lily Wilk, your painting is ready."

From the window in his office, Wally had seen me pull into the driveway, and he walked me from the door back to my car. I unlocked the trunk and pulled my beach blankets from around the long cardboard box I'd carefully packed in there. I took the near end, and he followed up with holding the other one. Snow was flying, small and sharp pieces that hurt when they hit. We carried the box through that, squinting and hunching, hurrying up the Astro Turf ramp and through the door that was marked "Floral Deliveries Only."

We set the box down against a row of chairs just inside the door, next to four more newly delivered arrangements sitting and waiting to be brought into the parlor. One was little more than a thick spray of bird-of-paradises that shot into the air like pointed fingers. I read the card: "Condolences from National Can."

"I've had to start lining them up in the seating area, there are just so many," Wally said, brushing the snow from my shoulders and hair, then from his own. The cloying smell of carnations, the majority of the flowers present, was enough to knock you over. When I commented on this, Wally said he long ago stopped being able to smell carnations. To him, they were the same thing as regular everyday air.

I pulled the tape off the brown wrapping paper, and slid out the bubble wrap shroud. I opened the end of that and there was the golden oak I'd picked for the frame. Without any ceremony, Wally and I carried the painting over to the easel and set it in its place, making sure that it was steady, and that it was enough out of the way that it wouldn't be knocked over by mourners in line for their moment at the casket. I stepped back, then in again, to make an adjustment. Then I was satisfied, as much as I could be right then.

"Lily," was all Wally was saying. He brought his hands to his face and shook his head, appearing to be as astounded as you would want somebody to be right then.

I looked down his line of vision, and I saw what he did: beautiful Flossie and handsome Davy and proud Aleksander and mysterious Michal and youthful Tim, all of them prime and in their moment, encircling the contented Mary. The sun was shining and the garden was bursting and everything was just fine, nothing less than great.

Except if you looked a couple feet to the right.

"Pretty soon there won't even be wakes," my mother had said to me that morning, when she had called up here after Unc had called down there to tell her what had happened and mentioned that the calling hours would be only six to nine P.M.

"Down here, they have a drive-through funeral parlor," my father said from the extension in their spare room that I so far have seen only in photographs, decor pale yellow with the top of a palm tree big and bushy right outside the window. The painting I did of the impressive swath of daffodils that each spring works its way out of the ground at our end of the lot hangs over the queen-sized bed. On the pillow my mother, for the purposes of the pictures she took and I'm sure not for everyday sight, displays a big white piece of paper on which she has written "LILY'S BED."

"It's too hot—nobody wants to get out of their cars," my father is going on, probably sitting on my bed, certainly with his shoes off so he won't ruin the peach-and-yellow spread. "The coffin's in the window, like where the clerk stands when you pay for your order at McDonald's. A couple of little speakers play music. And if you want a prayer card with the person's name on it, you press a button and one comes down a chute. Like your money at the bank machine. But don't think I want to be shown off like that. Remember that."

"I will," I said. How could I not? Because you of course never know when your time is up, my mother and father didn't move to Florida without first leaving me with two sealed-up health-care proxy envelopes and another one in which their final wishes were listed. I was told not to open them until the correct time came, but I admit I peeked at the one containing their requests, which were pretty standard: wake at Wazocha's, Mass at church, the two left-hand spaces in the big plot where my long-dead *Babci* and *Dziadziu* Wilk lay, my father to be placed in the outside one because a man should be at the edge to guard his family (like he would have any energy left at that point), and, after everything, a buffet at Saint Stan's, complete with open bar. When the dust settled, we were to have their respective names and dates engraved on the back of the stone, beneath Chuckie's, as if the actual remains of him were under there even though we never received anything to bury, unless you count his personal belongings. But what kind of family would fill a casket with a toothpaste-smeared shaving kit, a messy briefcase, a carton of paperwork, a few pairs of shorts, and a stack of faded T-shirts?

At the bottom of her page of instructions, my mother had typed a line revealing that her and my father's respective burial outfits were hanging in their old closet at the old house. While visiting Unc shortly after reading that, I went upstairs and, sure enough, under the protection of recycled dry-cleaning bags, there was my father's better gray Anderson-Little suit, hung on top of a white shirt, black-and-red rep tie, and a plastic CVS bag that contained a red silk hanky, red knit socks, a pair of slip-on loafers, a black vinyl belt with a scratched gold W on the buckle, a sleeveless T-shirt, and a pair of white boxers with little blue diamonds all over them. Behind that was the red chiffon dress my mother had bought to attend the first play that Louise ever costumed, some long dragged-out story of a man trying to decide which of his three

sons should inherit his pathetic hovel on his small patch of rocky land. The man wasn't really sick—just faking so he could see the true colors of the boys he'd raised, how they might act toward him in his final days if they felt they'd soon be inheriting something. Then the father would reveal himself as being just fine and, while still in good health, could spend his remaining years concentrating on preparing the son who had shown himself to be the most worthy, without even knowing it at the time because that was just the kind of guy he was.

The play was set in some time before plumbing or soap, and Louise wanted her poor characters to really look authentic. So she made a special trip home just to go through the worst of the yard-work clothes that Unc doesn't even dare bring into the house, that haven't seen the inside of the Maytag for actual years, that are so disgusting with dirt and chemicals and paint and oil and who-knows-what that he just keeps them hung on nails banged into the far wall of the garage and changes into them there behind a tall piece of cardboard inside which a queen-sized mattress once was delivered. These were the clothes we saw on the three poor sons when the curtain went up, and my mother threw her hand up to cover her open mouth that was gasping because here an entire theater of maybe a thousand city people were looking at how terrible Unc's clothes were. Appearance is important to my mother, even though she didn't always have the finances to make ours the best. We got nothing if it wasn't on sale. So it was no surprise that even her wake dress was something from Steiger's Down From Up sale: fifty percent off, then twenty-five percent off that, and then fifteen percent off that, then another ten, so by the time you bought something it was like they were paying you. That's how my mother got her red dress. And as for the other things she'd be wearing for eternity, she kept the costs low as well. A big see-through plastic bag held a brassiere, panties and slip, all new with the tags from Kmart or Ames still on them, a pair of black pumps from a Payless two-for-one sale, and generic pantyhose in nude, with reinforced toe and control top, setting her back only a dollar according to the sticker on the package.

"FUNERAL CLOTHES MOM," "FUNERAL CLOTHES DAD," read my mother's all-capital handwriting on the pink pieces of paper that each hanger pierced. Then she'd put in smaller letters on the one marking her clothes: "Girls: Remember to take off us any jewelry before the lids are closed. Distribute fairly at a later date."

I wondered who'd picked out Mary Ziemba's final outfit, the soft pink knit turtleneck and the matching long-sleeved cardigan. There looked to be a matching skirt or slacks completing the whole thing, but you couldn't tell which of those it was as you could only see to her waist, where Wally had gathered and folded her hands, lacing her strong fingers and intertwining a string of old silver rosary beads. Wally had done nice work on her makeup, not overdoing it, just patting on enough so she didn't look too dead. She had on little silver studs for earrings, and she wore the plain silver watch on her left wrist, like always. Its second hand swept faithfully, bringing a bit of life to the scene. I shivered to think how long after they buried her would the watch be still ticking away, glowing in the dark, giving the hour even though nobody would be checking for it.

I knelt at the casket and blessed myself. I said an Our Father and a Hail Mary, in Polish, which I figured she'd appreciate if she were listening, and then, I couldn't help it, I rushed on to ask my questions, talking from inside my head.

"I don't understand," I said to her face.

What she said back is what they always do. Which is nothing. But thank you very much for asking.

It seemed like seconds later I heard people arriving. Many car doors slamming one after the other, the series of bangs like a muffled gun salute. It was only five, an hour before the wake was to begin, but people were out there, ready and waiting. Lining up at the door and deciding to snake the formation to the left and up the side street that ends at the river. From inside, through the thick walls that normally kept the inside of Wazocha's fittingly tomb-silent, you could hear the great numbers of them, murmuring at first, then louder as more of them gathered. Then some laughter, growing, then all kinds of crowd noise like they were going into the World Series or something.

Wally was in his office, poring over details with his helpful friends, a troop of black-clad men and women who happened to be free that night to leave their own funeral homes in neighboring towns and help here with crowd control, with opening the door, closing the door, pointing to the coat rack, turning the page on the condolence book, refilling the rack of prayer cards, checking on rolls of toilet paper and stacks of towels and boxes of aloe-infused facial tissue in the Powder Room and the Gent's Lounge. Out in the parlor, I moved aside one of the thick golden curtains and checked out the wide line of people jammed on the sidewalk. The snow was still coming down, lightly, frosting with crystals the many who hadn't come early enough to claim a dry space beneath the blue canopy that shielded the front stairs. A plow went past, too early in the storm to really be necessary. Sparks shot from beneath as its blade made contact with the mostly bare pavement. A sander followed, coating the street while making a swishing salt-shaker noise. That's when I also heard a voice.

"I'm Kip Black," said the person who was holding out his hand to me. I shook it while trying to remember where I'd heard his name. That was solved when next he added, "I was Mary Ziemba's attorney."

I told him, "Well, I'm sorry about your friend," and he thanked me and said they actually were more business acquaintances than anything really friendly. "I've actually only known her for about a year," he said. "I took over for one of the partners. He'd known her for about thirty years longer. But he died a couple of Augusts ago, and I sort of inherited Ms. Ziemba. I'm the 'next of kin' the hospital called. I didn't know her well, but I really liked her—what I did know. We didn't have too many dealings outside of a few things, one of which I need to talk to you about. Mr. Wazocha told me you were out here. I don't mean to intrude, but before it gets busy . . ."

Kip Black had to be the money man, ready to cut me my check. It didn't feel right to be discussing such things in this place, but he was the one who'd brought it up. I just said, "You want to talk about the painting."

"Yes, the painting," he said back, and he turned to look at it from across the room. I noticed that in profile he resembled Tweety Bird, a little sprout of a nose, tiny beaklike lips, a forehead big enough to project a movie on. He was about my age, but he had only the smallest tufts of featherlike red-blond hair at the tops of his ears and around the back of his head.

"The painting," is what I replied, because I was nervous and didn't know what else to say.

Kip turned to me. "It's simply beautiful."

I lowered my head and said, "Thanks."

"Take it home at the end of the night."

"What?"

"You're to take it home at the end of the night."

"And do what with it?"

His mouth tightened. "I don't know," he said. He was shaking his head slightly, and I could tell he was confused as I was. "All I know are my instructions. That the painting is to be yours at the end of the night."

I looked toward the coffin. Doing that had gotten easier the longer I stayed in the room. I wondered about this—if I spent a week here, would Mary Ziemba just fade into the decor, another end table or settee to pass by each day? I brought my voice down to a loud whisper. "You know what?" I asked Kip. "It already is mine. Because I was never paid. I was to be paid when I was finished. And I finished this morning."

"I know nothing about such an agreement," he said plainly.

I heard Leo, back that first night at The Happy Tap, telling me to get everything in writing even though that was not my style. He had advised me the same thing regarding my interest in Little Ted, if I ever wanted an on-paper connection to him in case anything bad ever happened. Both times I told him I didn't need to, both times I said nothing bad was coming. Both times I was wrong.

"There was no agreement," I admitted to Kip. "No contract on paper."

He looked like he was feeling sorry for me. "I really can't help you; I don't know anything about this except that you're supposed to take the painting. I had instructions from Ms. Ziemba. Several pertained to you and your work." Here he counted them off on a couple of his matchstick fingers. "The painting was to be obtained from you to be displayed at her wake. After that, it was to be returned to you."

"And then what?"

"Then, then you can do what you want. That's what she said. That you can do with it what you want. She gave me the impression that she had confidence in your knowing what that would be."

"I don't get any of this."

"I'm sorry I can't be more helpful," Kip answered. "Here's my card, anyhow."

I took it. The gray lettering that made up his name and degrees and firm and address and telephone and fax and E-mail was raised and plasticky. I ran my fingers over it as I parted the curtain and looked out again at the crowd. I thought of the sightless people who have to read by Braille, how their touch tells them the story. I followed the forms of Kip Black's letters with the end of my pinky and paid full attention to the shapes. But I learned nothing.

"This, this 'event' is what she wanted the painting for, obviously." Kip was talking. I hadn't realized he was still here. "She knew she would never see it. She trusted you to do this for her. Why, I don't know. But she wanted this painting made. And she wanted it exhibited here tonight."

Exhibited.

I looked up at him, high in his tree, ready to fly away. He had used that word. I heard it, I did. I could feel it on the tips of all of my fingers.

Outside, a lot of well-dressed strangers crowded near the front of the line, mostly men, and most likely businesspeople with some connection to the Grand Z or its suppliers or some business or group that had benefited greatly from the chain's success over the years. A couple of them had to be from the board of directors that had been running the stores since Mary's retirement. A little farther back in the line stood some of the regulars—town noseys, mostly older and misery-loving people with nothing better to do, the ones who were known to dress up and attend the wake of anybody short of an ax murderer.

Under a small blue umbrella was Dorcas Byc, like the pen, who'd landed the rectory job after my mother left town and who loved to boast how she got paid under the table so her earnings didn't affect her Social Security check in the least. She was always looking for the easy, the free, the steal. Though in perfect health, she usually parked in the choicest handicapped spot, then got out of her car and dragged a leg until she got inside whatever building she was visiting.

Next to her, unfolding a plastic rain bonnet, was Mina from the big black house with white shutters up the river and next to the boat launch. Behind her back, probably just like those down the line were doing right then, her friends called her Mona. Because she was always moaning, always complaining about something. As a new bride she had wanted kids more than anything, and was heartbroken when Dr. Pluta took a glance at her inner workings and informed her that motherhood would be impossible. Mona wouldn't listen. She and her husband didn't have this kind of money, but they ran around anyhow to all the closest hospitals until they finally found somebody who figured out that a stitch here and a slice over there would be the answer. Mona went on to have eight children—and to never shut up about what a pain and a chore and a disappointment they were. Even once they were grown and gone far from home, like all of them were that night. I was listening to her talking loudly enough to be heard through Wally's soundproofing double-paned window: "So she calls that she's sick with a bronchial thing and she feels so lousy she's sobbing, 'Ma! Ma!' and then she asks me what I think she should do because she feels like she's gonna die. This is the vegetarian one I'm talking about. So I just say to her what I always say: 'Other than a steak, I don't know what to tell you.'"

Behind her, clutch purse held over her head, was Mrs. Joe Dull, who, in a monotone, always introduced herself as that, as if she had no first name. And whose life, as far as anybody could tell, pretty much lived up to the last name she liked to use. A few years ago some lady from my mother's class returned to town for a visit and ran into Mrs. Dull outside church and exclaimed, "I haven't seen you since the sixties! What's new?" And Mrs. Dull replied, "Nothing."

Next to Mrs. Joe Dull was Martha LaDue, her head bravely exposed to the elements. She loved to watch the home shopping programs but never bought a single thing from them because everybody knows they only sell junk, despite that all of it does come with a thirty-day money-back guarantee. She just liked to listen to the banter and could quote extensively from the conversations callers had with their favorite hosts. Even if she hardly knew you, except that it's your uncle who every late fall pulls all the wet leaves and other rotting stuff out of her ancient wooden gutters, she would have no problem pulling you aside after Mass to tell you how just this morning during the Silver Savings jewelry showcase, a woman phoned to order a pair of brushed-sterling hoops and to say this: "I'm trapped in the house twenty-four hours a day, seven days a week, with a dying husband and the only pleasure I get out of life is shopping with you people."

On the other side of Martha was Adella Murray, the only woman in my line of vision who had the sense to wear a genuine winter hat that night, and the person whose house I painted last year not for her but for her son who recently was transferred down to someplace in Kentucky and maybe the sweet sight every day of the place where his mother still was alive and on this earth would get him to consider coming back if there ever was an opening in the region. Unlike Martha, Adella Murray hasn't watched television since soon after her son bought her a modern one, the kind that flashes on the screen the number of the channel you happen to be tuned in to. She says that the numbers that advanced so quickly as she was clicking the stations reminded her how fast the years of life go by, and it really disturbed her how they stopped at sixty-five, because she was fast nearing that age, and after that, according to her new television, there seemed to be nothing.

In a black woolen cap with earmuffs down, Tony Borwaski stood in back of the women and in the center of his own small circle of people who no doubt were dying to hear more details of the terrible ordeal that had landed him in the paper and temporarily out on the street the week before. "KISHKA CAUSE OF APARTMENT FIRE" had been the headline of the news brief that told how somebody identified only as "a resident" of the new elderly housing complex across from the Irish cemetery had fallen asleep as his blood sausage fried in a pan one afternoon around four. "The victim refused medical treatment," the paper said, "but did request something to eat."

Whoever they were, whatever the reason they were there, the first of the mourners were let inside Wazocha's around five-twenty, when the snow picked up and Wally felt it was only fair that the crowd be spared from the elements. He had no one's permission to ask—it was all up to him, there being no family to consult, nobody seated in the big first-row chairs, nobody flopped inconsolable on the couch in his office or locked in the bathroom sneaking a nervous smoke that was the only thing short of a drink that would get them through this night. The doors unlocked and people stomped and filed into the entryway, and the first of the names were signed in the book. They got in line, one behind the other even if they had come in as part of a couple standing side by side, or in a threesome with arms linked for the warmth the night called for or the courage that going into such a place often entails. They gasped audibly at the flowers, floor to ceiling like wallpaper. They all stopped just short of their final destination. They all stopped to look at my painting.

The businessmen did. Dorcas Byc did. Adella Murray did. Mrs. Joe Dull and Tony Borwaski too. So did the nuns from school. The kid from the gas station. The lady who drives the bookmobile. The retarded man with the one ear higher than the other. The guy who lifeguards at the lake. The woman from the copy center, in a nice dress. The police chief from Warren. The lady from out near the Belchertown line who year-round keeps her plastic nativity set lit up on her front porch. The man who makes birdhouses cut from dried-out bulby squashes. The couple from the trailer park whose son is some kind of a military guard everybody says often is assigned to stand as close as five feet away from the president. The selectman who voted against the town providing insurance to the domestic partners of municipal employees.

Every one of them stalled, some having to be tapped or gently pushed forward. It was their turn at the kneeler but even while praying some of them stared at my painting. The farmer who uses one of his milk tankers in a side business filling new swimming pools with water. The Boy Scout who got his Eagle credentials by going around town and warning everybody not to put their gas grills right next to their houses like his father did, not once thinking that the tank would explode and burn the whole place down on the Fourth of July. The hairdresser from North Street who ages ago was the one who put the French braids into the Lopata girl's hair, at her home, before her brother's wedding, in the manner that I never got to enjoy.

All eventually walked back to one of the many chairs, but saying none of the usual things you hear at this point. Like didn't they do a horrible job on her? Or don't you hate the hair? Did you check out the jewelry—does she think she's going to a ball? She looks just like she's sleeping, so why do they always leave the glasses on?

None of that. Instead, what they were talking about was my painting.

I was still sitting all the way in the back, in my chair by the window, idly staring out at the slowly shuffling line, and this was all seeping in. Slowly, the realization accumulating on my brain like the snow on the curled-up leaves of the rhododendrons planted outside Wazocha's front windows. Little frozen grains coming to rest upon other little frozen grains, making up the fact that everything I was hearing was some comment on what I had done: Did you see that? Wasn't it beautiful? Doesn't it make her look, well, alive? Who are they? Who painted it? Who? What did you say? Lily Wilk? Did you see her signature? I thought she only did signs. "Or ugly things," was what one person snorted, and he went on to give his examples: "The egg-box factory. The fish market. The canal."

He asked, "Who wants to look at things like that hanging on their wall when they have to pass them every morning and every afternoon?" Then he went on to say, "But this I could look at all day. And I don't even know those people who are in there with Mary Ziemba. But I could look at them all day."

It was a wake. Everyone there to acknowledge a good life lived without a scrap of it wasted. You could stand most places in town, turn in a complete circle, and you'd need two whole hands to count the things around here that are better or nicer or more hopeful or more palatable because of Mary Ziemba. There she was, over at that end of the room, and here was everybody, suddenly in front of me, saying Lily, Lily, Miss Wilk, Lily, did you paint that?

"It was her idea. To have it here. Her idea." I made this clear. This wasn't a new way to advertise, I wanted to assure them. I stood up to retrieve my coat from Wally's office and go home. It was getting way too crowded in my corner of the parlor, and way too strange, people seeking me out and standing there in my way as they were now, telling me don't go anywhere, we have to ask you something.

And the first question was, how did I know how to capture Flossie?

I stopped trying to move forward. "You know her?"

The woman who'd asked me, the one who every Saturday at three-thirty walked from her farmhouse up behind the common to our church down at Four Corners in all weather, and who refused offers of rides in every condition except glare ice, nodded yes.

"Flossie," I repeated, just to make sure. "You know Mary's sister. Flossie."

"I didn't know her sister, dear," the woman corrected. "But Flossie, yes."

I ran her words over in my mind. "Flossie, her sister," I repeated.

"Flossie wasn't her sister." The woman's head moved back and forth smoothly like it was on a stick. And two or three of the people standing in the crescent assembled there echoed no no no. She wasn't.

"They were close as you please, I think because both of them came here with nobody else," said the woman whose name was coming back to me. Kielbasa. Chuckie's favorite meat. Anna Kielbasa. "But Flossie was her sister like I'm her sister. You know, when you say 'sister' regarding Mary, you must hook your fingers into quotation marks." And here she did that, in the same manner as the guidance counselor who had come to parochial school hoping to ease our transition from private eighth grade to public ninth. He used to crook his fingers when he'd unveil strange new words like "home room" or "study hall" or "detention" or the "moment of silence" into which we were supposed to jam the prayers we would no longer be able to say out loud at the beginning of our school day. He also for some reason told us that if we ever burned our fingers we should automatically grab our earlobes and transfer the heat into them. I've done it, and it works. As does putting cold water on your inner wrists to cool off when you are real hot—another thing he told us. Those are the only three things I remember about that guy. About Flossie, whom I'd never once met, I knew a ton more. But obviously not the most crucial part—that she was not Flossie Ziemba but Flossie Pirelli.

"She changed it, to Flo Parker, once she got to Holly-wood," Anna was saying. "She found a room to live in; it was near a park. Park, Parker, get it? Did Mary tell you she moved out there?"

In my head I saw the picture—the train station, the two young women, the one sister who was leaving, the other who couldn't go. I said slowly, and I could feel myself squinting, "You sure—they weren't sisters?"

"I knew them both at the rooming house. They lived behind Saint Stan's, a large place that is now a private home, now just one family for all that space. Flossie's name was Pirelli. It was definitely pizza, not *pierogi.*" When she said that last part, a couple people chuckled.

I thought of the chorus line shot, the tiny Flossie Pirelli among so many other Flossie Pirellis who had to have felt it necessary to shed the most easily cast-off part of their ethnic identities. The generic Flo Parker rolled over in my mind. I tried to imagine it printed on the fancy closing credits of old late-night movies, where the names of characters and their portrayers sometimes are presented on scrolls, with maybe a drawing of a pen and ink bottle at the bottom like somebody's just finished writing the whole thing out by hand. I asked Anna a question that, if I'd posed it to Mary Ziemba, considering the way she was in her own world when she was presenting these people to me, would have seemed to me like prying. "Well, what was she in?"

"Oh, a couple of those movies where they'd have one hundred dancing girls coming down a staircase at one time," she said, and she waved her hand as if to emphasize that it was really not the big deal it sounded like because there was no enormous talent involved. "One time you could see her in a crowd of people waiting at a train station. Another was a living room party scene, with Katharine Hepburn on a couch, talking with an actor, out in front of everybody else. Katharine Hepburn talking, not Flossie. Flossie never got to talk, because then they'd have to pay her more. That's how I understood it. It was really a silent career. Not silent movies, that was farther back. Just silent Flossie."

She lasted about six years in the business, said the woman in back of Anna, another whose name escaped me, but who I knew for what I always thought was a nice and humane gesture of putting her parakeet's cage out on her side porch in good weather so the bird could have a change of scenery and imagine it was out in the wild for a time, not just living in a kitchen all its life with the refrigerator's humming maybe making him nuts. She is one of those people I always am meaning to commend, with a few words in person or maybe just with a line on a note card, to let them know that these nice things are noticed by somebody. But I never get around to many things like that.

"Then Flossie ran out of energy after those six years, having been turned down so many times for actual acting work." The bird woman was telling me this. "Mary many times offered to pay her way home, but Flossie first said she could never return until she became a star, and then once she figured out that was not going to happen, she said she could never return home a failure. She stayed out there. It saddened Mary. She'd always wanted a sister. She had one, in Flossie, a perfect one. But once she moved, the distance between them was too much. Their best times were when they lived here, both in Aleksander's house, in the same room. Nice like that, I imagine."

I knew a family of Pirellis, pleasant ones who lived out by the old dump. They had concrete mushrooms decorating their front yard—big enough to sit on. I couldn't imagine them criticizing anybody—especially a relative—for not making a dream come true. But maybe Flossie had the bad fortune to be related to some other ones who would.

"She became a beautician." Anna was continuing the story. "She always liked creams and preparations and such like that. So she got a job where she could have her hands in them all day. Sometimes she worked on the faces of famous people—but she never would reveal their names out of respect for their privacy. I met her once, maybe a dozen years ago. I was in Los Angeles for my grandson's wedding and his fiancée helped me look her up, which is good because you never in your life saw so many streets. In a little apartment building filled with dozens of other elderly ladies who'd once worked in some kind of showbiz, that's where she was living. There was an outline of a movie camera on the sign out front. I remember her skin looked as good as it did the day she left here. When I complimented her on that, she gave me a little pill bottle of some lotion she mixed up in her kitchen to keep herself looking so good. It smelled like lemons and I was supposed to keep it under refrigeration or it might spoil. I was traveling—we were staying in a Holiday Inn with only a coffeemaker. I was going to keep it on ice, but instead I used it once and then threw it out. I tell you, though, for the one day—the wedding—I looked really good."

I asked, "Does she know?"

"About how I threw it out?"

"About Mary. You know." I nodded toward the casket.

"Probably," the bird woman said. "She's probably showing Mary around by now. Introducing her to Cecil B. DeMille and Clark Gable and those kinds."

"Like five years ago," is what Anna calculated fast, quicker than I could follow the story and the news that Flossie, too, was gone. "Just keeled over. Mary got all the details, how Flossie was giving a facial to a neighbor at the time. She got to the part where she put on the mask that hardens, and she left the room while that was happening. The poor woman she was working on—her face got hard as cement because Flossie was in the kitchen getting water to clean it off, but then she died and just left the lady there to dry. The EMTs had to work on Flossie. Then on the lady, but only to get the stuff off, finally."

I brought my hand to my face. My apartment had a forced hot-air heating system that blasted warmth into the rooms like the exhaling of a big monster. My skin always got dry this time of year because of that, and it stayed that way until May. I worked my way from one product on the drugstore shelf to the next one over, looking for the answer that probably had gone to the grave with Flossie. I didn't want to look fifty years younger, as that wouldn't be possible. But five wouldn't be too much to ask. I felt ashamed thinking of my beauty problems after such a sad story, but I was only being honest.

"So how did you know how to capture her?" Anna was asking again.

"Photographs. Mary gave me photographs. Of everybody there. She wanted this portrait; she wanted it shown here. It wasn't my idea."

A little voice came from somewhere behind the round white-haired man with his hand on the bird lady's shoulder. It said, "What a beautiful idea."

She was much taller than most of the few who had gathered, all of whom were being joined by others coming to listen in. "As a child," said the woman, "I knew Davy."

"The serviceman," somebody whispered.

"The carpenter," another added.

"We were in a wedding together," the tall woman said, and I took a look at her—red-tailored suit, ivory blouse with a chic scrunched-up neck, one pearl dangling from each of the gold ropes falling from the earlobes above, two thin, gray, braided buns of hair growing from either side of her head. And I saw her suddenly at the top of my drawing board, decades before, to the left of Davy in a shot of them alone. She was out of focus and what you could make out about her was that she looked uncomfortable. Maybe it was the weight of her huge bouquet, a big upside-down teardrop packed with white flowers and then, if that weren't enough, ribbons falling from that, their knots holding soft ferns. Around their feet, new petals made a carpet.

"I know you," I said. "Mary gave me some of those pictures. There's one of just the two of you. From the wedding weekend. When everybody was getting married. She said everybody wanted her brother at their wedding."

The bridesmaid frowned. "Who was her brother?"

Davy was somebody else Mary had found.

And where he was discovered was the rooming house— fertile ground for such things, it seemed.

The bridesmaid and I were sitting knee-to-knee now. All conversation was whispered. The line kept moving toward the front of the room, and those who didn't leave and could squeeze through came to the back where we were. "A wonderful guy," she told me. She was wearing a silver charm bracelet and I saw the cutout shapes of boys' and girls' heads flashing on it. Like a grandmother would ever forget such information, their birthdays were engraved on the profiles with the neat, rounded, Palmer-method penmanship that Phyllis used. "Mary had several brothers in the old country, but they never —how shall I say?—they never had the ambition she did. A life of poverty, that seemed fine with them. Over here, Davy became them for her."

I could have told the woman how Mary recounted the stories, of Davy being so nice and everybody loving him and his helping when she started her business going door to door. But I had to ask what was hanging over everything right then in my mind: "So, is he going to be here?"

The bridesmaid gave the same look that she had in the photograph, only now in focus.

"Davy made it fine to the last day of the war," she said, picking her words. "Coming home, well . . ."

The transport carrying Davy went down in the Atlantic. The news nearly did Mary in. She had to interpret the telegram to his father, who didn't speak English that well, never mind read it. She had to tell him that the boy had lived through the war, but had gotten killed on his way back home.

"Imagine that," the bridesmaid suggested.

I couldn't. I felt horrible for Mary, and along came a whole wave of the amazement I get when I've found out something similar about somebody who seems fine and dandy with life. Like when my mother told me, forty years after it happened, that the shiny-headed bald man who sang so beautifully in the choir, who was so cheerful when you'd pass his house in the summer and he was out working and he'd interrupt his car waxing or whatever to run inside and get you a Popsicle in your choice of flavors, well back during the flood of fifty-five he had watched his eight-month-old baby get sucked out of his wife's arms when they were on the roof of their house trying to get into a boat and to higher ground. It's always baffled me how these kinds of people can go on to put one foot in front of the other, never mind crack a smile. Mary Ziemba had lost her beloved Davy, but somehow was able to draw a breath afterwards. It was too much to comprehend.

"Well, I won't expect her father here," I said to nobody in particular. "I mean he has to be gone now."

The bridesmaid shrugged. Anna did the same. The bird lady and the guy in back of her said nothing. From in back of me there was a tap on my shoulder.

"Mary's father never came over, over to this country—I know that much," said an older man I saw on many summer days collecting blueberries from the wild bushes at the edge of the woods upriver from the wastewater treatment plant.

I was going to correct him, but I realized that by this point in the night I should know better. And the blueberry guy told me as much:

"You're thinking Aleksander. Right? Okay. You know he was the landlord. A widower. Right?"

It was like taking a quiz and getting every answer wrong. After I thought I'd studied enough and without a smarty boy sitting next to me to steal from in case I needed it.

"Mary's parents stayed behind," he said. So many other people in her village were leaving to come here once they got the money, but everybody in Mary's family—except for Mary—they all were a bunch of scaredy-cats. They had no relatives here. Nobody here, on this side, ready to welcome them, help them. They couldn't imagine leaving the life they knew, as hard as that was, for the unknown. Mary said she was afraid too, at the idea of it—but she asked what good was that?"

So she left, without her mother, her father, her four brothers. On a tip, she landed at Aleksander's place, and all he had to do was to be his usual nice self and she latched onto him like he was blood. Which I guess is what she turned him into. And he had no complaints. Himself, he'd come here with a daughter and a son, but they moved on. Ohio, the blueberry man thinks it was. Where there was more work. "They didn't want to make beds. They wanted to make money." That was how Aleksander told it to this man. The daughter and the son left the boardinghouse first chance, but Mary and Davy came to stay.

"I don't mean to make a pun, at a time like this, but it's like there were vacancies in Aleksander's life," the man said. He tilted his head. "You know, a big sign hanging out on the porch, saying that. And only the right person is able to spot it. Mary filled at least one of the spaces for Aleksander. Maybe that's how it happens. Even if you don't know you have these holes, somebody comes along to fill them. And you wonder how you ever got along before."

The talk stopped. The women nodded, and Anna Kielbasa said, "Yes, yes, you are right."

I thought of what Aleksander had done for Mary Ziemba. Taking her in. Giving her a roof and walls and a floor and a door. Waving the big radish, unknowingly pointing it in the direction of what would turn out to be an unbelievable future.

"I know he was 'Pa' to her," the man said, "but her first father was back in the old country, never seen by her again, except after he died and they sent Mary this little photograph of him laid out in his coffin. She showed it to me once. They used to do that, you know, for the benefit of family members who are far away."

I was aware this still went on. In this country. Wally kept a Polaroid camera in his desk just for this purpose, all loaded and ready to snap in case anybody ever drew him aside and whispered how it would be nice to have something to show the folks back home, especially with all these expensive and impressive flowers here. Sometimes people wanted just the casket photographed, with the arrangements. Sometimes they wanted the living family members in it too, and everybody would gather around with their black clothes and baggy eyes and balled-up Kleenexes and somber expressions, making sure to leave a space and not block the view of the dead person, who, after all, let's not forget, was the reason for the shot.

Father Krotki was up in the front now, near Mary, and everybody there had parted to give him a little stage from which to say the beginnings of a few prayers. We couldn't hear well way back in our corner, and Father had a cold, so he wasn't speaking loud. My new friends and I just joined in on the responses once we could tell he was done with a line:

"Amen," we'd say. "Amen."

"Tim," I whispered to the blueberry guy.

"Who's that?"

"Tim."

"Amen."

"Another brother?"

"Her son."

"Son?"

"Amen."

"I don't know nothing about a son," he said. "Anna? Son?"

"Son?" Here Anna stopped, and I thought maybe she was praying, but she was actually thinking because next she shook her head and gave her answer: "No, no. She came from another age. Not like today. No son for Mary. Because there was no husband. You didn't go and have a child back then if you did not have a husband."

"Amen."

Skip one question, move to the last.

"Michal," I said.

"Amen."

"Who?" Anna asked.

"The husband. His name was Michal."

"I told you she didn't have one."

"She told me she did." I said that, and Anna just rolled her eyes.

"Amen."

Father Krotki had on his black, boxy pompon-topped hat and his woolen vampire cape, the same things he wears when he drives to your house on Holy Saturday to bless all the ingredients of the Easter dinner you have arranged so beautifully on your dining room table. Anna had worked her way over to him as he was making his exit, and she was pulling him into our group.

"Well, hello, Lily," he said. "What a painting." Here he clutched at his chest and closed his eyes for dramatic effect. *"Aaaahhhhh!"* That was sweet. Father Krotki was a good guy and always pretty comical. Up to when he lovingly and without one bit of preaching blessed the marriage that a plain old justice of the peace had made legal for Jack and me on a sand spit in Truro, he never stopped campaigning for my becoming a nun, never missing an opportunity to tell me, "You know, you'd look good in black."

"Father," Anna said, "say how Mary Ziemba wasn't married."

Father looked at her. "Well, I don't have much on that. That's the problem. Nobody really knows the whole story."

"The story of how she and a Michal got married?" Though I was feeling that the odds were bad, I still was hopeful for something real in Mary's life.

"They never got married, no," he said. Then he put up a pointer finger and added, "Though he was Mary's fiancé as I understand it. And there was a great love between them, she told me this. They were supposed to be married, in this country. She left for America first, because that was the way things fell. She had saved the fare ahead of him; he told her to go. To prepare a place for them is what he said. He told her he'd be there a couple months later, with extra money, like a man should have. Then they'd be married. Together. Over here. It was supposed to be wonderful."

But Michal never showed up. People saw him pack to leave; they saw him hug his mother and shake his father's hand and say some words to his siblings that they might remember long after he was gone that day, down the road that led to the town in which the train out to the coast stopped once a week.

"Nobody ever laid eyes on him again," Father said. "Nobody knew if he ever went straight to the train and left the country, or if he did come over here and just took a wrong turn once he arrived. Nobody knows if he got attacked, if he backed out, what. He just never came to town. Mary never ever saw him. But a few years later, she came to own her only photo of him. Somebody who was related to the family that had a candy shop on Main Street came over from Michal's village, and that woman brought this little photo of him, taken on the day he left, standing in the middle of the road out of town. Proof that he was leaving, for wherever he was going. Maybe the first picture ever taken of him. Maybe the last. Mary treasured it. Once in a while when I was visiting up there at her house and we'd be talking about the old days, she'd get out the photograph from somewhere in another room and she'd show it to me and say, 'See, Father, that's my husband. Right there.' Because to her, he was."

Anna patted Father Krotki's cape. "Thank you, Father," she said, like he was done giving testimony in a courtroom.

He asked me, "Is that all?"

I didn't need to think about my answer. "It's more than enough."

I never went outside during the wake, but people tell me that the line stretched four whole streets over, almost up to the parking lot for Pathfinder, all the way down to old Agnes Dojka's, who came out onto her porch with a sweater around her shoulders to see what was going on with everybody standing there in the snow, and that is something to make note of because once it's like the end of September, she won't leave her house until the spring. It's not that she's got anything wrong with her—she's as old as the hills yet she cuts her own lawn and throughout the fall splits wood to heat the house all winter. She just doesn't want to take the chance of catching anything. Every Sunday after *Freddie Brozek's Polka Explosion* she calls up Deacon Tenczar to drive over to her house with her weekly Holy Communion, like he's delivering pizza. He has true sick people to console and comfort in the hospitals and nursing homes, and there Agnes Dojka is, taking up his time, all because she's afraid of catching a little sore throat.

She had to be the only person in the immediate world who did not come to Wazocha's that evening. It was nine when Wally went out onto the street, and between the combination of the dark and the snow, he couldn't see the end of the line waiting to come in. He did the same thing at ten, with the same lousy results. The mourners already had filled three condolence books, and Moondog had been sent to the cellar to print up a few more stacks of prayer cards on the ancient little press down there that personalizes with the name, age, and death date the blank space between the line "In Loving

Memory of" and the prayer of Saint Francis of Assisi that asks God to make you a channel of his peace.

When he walked by with a box full of the new cards and distracted my corner, I slipped into the office to get my coat and I left through the floral door and walked toward home, leaving my car to gather snow. It was lousy out, but I didn't care. I needed the air and I had a hat and I'd done my job. I'd been entrusted to string together line and circle and square to make somebody's world as no one before had ever viewed it— apparently not even the person who'd requested it of me. Mary Ziemba had asked me to paint things that weren't really there. She'd wanted them to look so real that you might walk right into them and knock yourself silly in the process, having believed they were just part of how things truly are. I knew well that I'd accomplished that, because I could look at the painting and see the family I'd made. And because my head was hurting from the collision with it.

14

Claire O'Hare, not that she is any kind of doctor even good for the flu, has determined that I am depressed. She insists that this should not alarm me. "It's the common cold of mental illness," is how she puts it. If you were going to be sick in the head to any degree, she says, this is the kind you would want.

I didn't want any of it. I just wanted to get back to work—something that, previous to Mary Ziemba's death three weeks before, I didn't think I'd ever have to do. Her portrait was supposed to have changed all that, was to have cleared the decks of my work future, taken one big arm and swept from my table all the police-car lettering and the maple sugar signs and the kitty portraits and the brochure line drawings on how to do the Heimlich maneuver even on infants if you can imagine having to attempt that. The only thing left on the plate would have been time. For nothing but painting and drawing the things that I alone wanted to. Without a single worry as to would they ever sell or was I just wasting another day. The great desire of anybody who correctly or incorrectly calls themselves an artist: to make something just for the pleasure and the challenge and the heartache involved. The reality that this now wasn't going to be the case had slid me into this funk first verbalized as I sat in the doorway of Claire O'Hare's bedroom and aimed a window fan at her so she wouldn't pass out while applying to her floor something like the eighth coat of polyurethane.

It was done. The whole swamp was completed, except for this final protective coating that would allow her to walk on water, even in her pointiest heels, without a chance of nicking the paint.

"It's a big letdown," Claire said loudly but still sounding like she had a pillow over her face, speaking beneath the mask worn to protect her lungs from fumes. "It's normal to feel lost right now. You need a break. A change of routine. Do something different. Take a trip. Get some new clothes. Rearrange your furniture. Start an exercise program."

I picked the last suggestion. I couldn't afford a trip or clothes, so those were out. I tried the furniture idea. I asked Unc to come over and we moved the phone chair to the other wall and the couch on an angle where the chair had been, and maybe it didn't look great but it was at least getting me thinking about something else. So all that was fine until Unc picked up the big, thin cardboard box that had been behind the couch and he asked me, "Where do you want this?" and I had no answer for him. That was when I decided maybe it was silly to change things. "Let's just put it back where we found it," I told him. We slid the couch over to its original place, and I gave it an extra shove against the wall so there was no chance of noticing that it was hiding the box that contained Mary Ziemba's painting.

After that I tried walking. I went out for a string of days first thing in the morning, even if it was lousy out. I'd get as far as Phyllis' by myself, then I'd pick up the little smoke-colored rat dog that Unc had impulsively given her the Easter before, when he fell for its overexposed little picture in the corner of the page the *Pennysaver* gives to the animals being caged up at the pound.

Phyllis named the dog Albert, bowing to any Parisian heritage he carried, therefore you had to drop the *t* when you called him. For somebody who even got nervous when we used to bring out our stuffed animals, Phyllis was surprisingly crazy about him. She took him to a series of obedience lessons held on the enormous lawn of a Protestant church in East Longmeadow, and he systematically beat out the most pure of the purebreds for top dog in the class. And that's why I didn't mind taking him along on my walk, because, with Albert, even though you were with a dog, it was just like walking alone. I'd bundle him up in his little tartan jacket and I'd take him up Main Street and down Route 181, onto the path cut through the woods so you can walk for a length without fear of cars, across the watershed field, over the bridge, past the farmstand where all the Christmas trees were gone from their posts set in a measured grid of six down and six across, and then we'd turn down the road to the cemetery.

There's a square drive edging the part where the stones are, and we'd walk on that, sometimes making a detour to where my mother's parents are buried and Chuckie's name is engraved. The few times I went through, I thought about who else was planted there, in a solitary plot beneath one of the common flat stones. What else could I do? She had no one else to do this for her, so I'd trudge over there, to the last row right up next to the road, the one with the newest people and markers, to the stone that said only her name and her dates and nothing else about who she was or what she'd done, and I'd bless myself and say an Our Father and a Hail Mary, in Polish, which I figured she'd appreciate if she was listening. Then, in English, which is all he understood, I'd say to Albert, "Heel." And he would bounce up from his good-dog seated position and we'd head back home.

• • •

According to Phyllis, the times Albert and I made that walk, he would be lazy the rest of the day and then in midafternoon would fall asleep on the living room rug, staying in the same place and position right through his dinner and into the morning. I reacted pretty much the same way. Except when Heather came home from school and demanded to sit in the chair and fill up another page in her sketchbook.

"Show me how to do something," is what she'd whine to me down there on the floor. "Come on!"

I'd moan and open my eyes, and I'd see her in the phone chair and my family portrait on the wall, everything upside down. I'd do nothing more than order her to use her imagination, which, for the time being, would have to be enough for both of us. I'd hear her pencil working on the paper, and the soggy sound of the cars rolling through the slush outside, and once in a while the phone would ring, calls from people who obviously didn't know I had no ambition left. No clue that it was sapped. Gone. Vanished. As good as overseas. I let the machine pick up.

Somebody I never heard of, who got my name from somebody else, was calling to ask if I did repairs, because she had opened her moving cartons to find a small rip in a painting her grandmother had done back in nineteen hundred something. It was only of a vase of begonias, or some such flower, and she didn't know what my professional opinion of it would be—of the picture itself—but she really only cared could it be fixed? She was really upset by the damage, she said, and even though I had never heard her voice before, I could tell she sincerely was.

The hospital auxiliary's vice president wanted to know if I would once again calligraphize—her word—the addresses on the envelopes holding the invitations to the annual fund-raising auction. Get back to her at the gift shop, or at home, but not after nine because she goes to bed early. I was in her kitchen one time, at her request, to give her my professional opinion on the best shade from the several floor tile samples she had brought home. I remember she had a small metal cabinet on the counter, the kind Unc keeps his various nails and screws organized in. Only this one was used for all her vitamins, every little drawer labeled neatly with stickers. On her icebox door was a magnet in the shape of a cake with the words "Diet Tomorrow" written on it in thin frosting, the whole thing coated by what had to be a couple sprayings of Keepit. She referred to her husband as "the husband," and when he came in, he referred to her as "the wife." It was only two weeks after Jack took off and I remember looking at them and wondering if they ever had troubles. Whether anything bad ever went on between them. Without being shown any of the other choices, I hastily pointed to the square of linoleum on the top of the stack—something blue is all I remember it being; I'm not even sure it went with their decor—and I told them that would look the best and that I had to go because I remembered I had to be somewhere else. I drove far enough down their street that they couldn't have seen my car if they went out on the lawn to look, then I pulled over next to a stubby cornfield and wept out my abandonment into two whole hankies.

I didn't care what she wanted this time. Sick of looking at Heather, I rolled onto my side and peered under the couch. Because I'd vacuumed beneath it when Unc and I had moved it a couple weeks before, there was nothing blocking my line of vision, no junk or shoes or papers or dust bunnies. I could see clear through, across the darkened carpet to the bottom of the brown cardboard box that leaned against the wall. It didn't move. I didn't move. But something in me wanted to—to just up and go and shed everything that was dragging me down. I thought about doing that, then decided it sounded like too much work.

"We should both go outside, once it's nice out again, and set our drawings up on stands, like you see in commercials, people painting outside; that would be fun, don't you think?"

Heather was saying this, doing what I knew Alice had asked her to—try and cheer me. Alice knew I wouldn't snap at a kid like I had at her when she sat down next to me on the carpet and confided that whenever she was feeling sorry for herself, all she had to do was think of the kids flat on their backs down at the Shriner's Hospital and she would instantly realize that she truly didn't have any problems at all when you looked at it like that, how you weren't in a body cast or traction or having a limb amputated or your face reassembled from the flesh and cartilage harvested from other areas of yourself. I didn't want to think about those kids. I wanted to think about myself. And I told her as much, in about as terse a tone as I'd ever used on her. She left after that, giving up on getting me to turn on a light, shutting the door behind her in slow motion. It was only Tuesday, but the next thing I knew she had Leo fire up the oil and make me my own extra-large serving of crinkle-cut crispy fries. He knocked and opened the door and put the tray on the rug, his hand sliding it in like how you feed something in a zoo. He closed me back up in the solitude changed only by the smell of the potatoes cooling there in their happy red basket.

After that, they left any contact to Heather, who hadn't missed a day of coming upstairs to work on her art. She did so without help or encouragement or invitation, some days without even a sound from me. Like it was normal to let yourself into a quiet apartment and spend an hour or two there in silence while the so-called grown-up who lives there lies on the floor a couple feet away, awake but saying nothing. Like I am doing right now, in a moment that surprised me, the kind I now think maybe was what Jack experienced that morning eight months before. When he realized this was not the way he wanted it, and that something had to be done, and that he had to be the one to do it. Fast, without thinking. Because otherwise you might keep on doing nothing.

In what seemed like a second later, I was driving east on Route 20. Just past the snow-frosted mountain of old tires neatly corralled by a stockade fence was a sign and a big red arrow inviting people to cross-country ski. Coming up onto the divided highway out of town, I slowed just in case the cars making their way down the icy-looking street to my right weren't able to stop when they came to the crest near the road. Taking that first turnoff before the state park, I felt sorry for the backpackers with their big tall boots trudging along at the edge of the highway where there were no sidewalks that might offer some safety. Proceeding slowly like the small sign planted next to the beginning of the driveway requested, I wondered why I was doing that—I knew nobody else would be coming along. Spotting the heavy wooden arch ahead of me over the road, I wasn't surprised to see that the gate was closed.

I put the car in park and got out. I was grateful that the driveway had been plowed, probably by Mary's lawn guy, to give a lived-in look that would fool passing thieves. It was an easy walk over to the metal loop that held the fence closed. I flipped it up and swung the gate over to the side to allow myself room to pass.

The oak forest was bare now, except for the bunches of brown leaves that clung to some of the branches as they do on that kind of tree, sometimes all winter, and you wonder if you were as fragile, how would you ever have it in you to hang on? I was thinking about things like that right then, so the sight of the house as I came out of the woods was jarring. But maybe only because I knew there was nobody inside. I left the car in the space on the driveway where I had parked it the few times I'd visited. I got out and stretched myself like I'd traveled ten hours, because that's just about what it felt like. Then I walked around the back of the car and unlocked the trunk. I pulled my beach blankets from around the long cardboard box I'd carefully packed in there just a few minutes before. I took the near end and pulled. There was nobody to follow up with holding the other one, so I had to do the job myself.

I made the only sound I was aware of, walking through the wet snow nobody had removed from the path that snaked through the two front gardens and up to the big front door and over to the right front of the house and around the side and up to the kitchen, where I opened the storm door and set the box down against the inner one and closed it in tight. It wasn't easy to do. Like at our place, Mary Ziemba had similar modern, high-tech, self-adhesive strips of insulation stuck around the doorframe. I had to push but good against the door to get it to latch, and it did so only after letting out a relieved-sounding sigh of air that spoke for me. I walked back down to the front of the house, went into the garden, shoveled off the wicker chair with my hands and took a seat.

The sloping meadow was just begging for somebody to come by with a sled. Or an easel and some paints. The view from here into the valley where I lived, the one that I'd left minutes before, belonged on one of those 1,500-piece jigsaw puzzles that Phyllis and Unc spend all those hours on, only to crumble the scene back into the box after a week or so of admiring it. From up in Mary Ziemba's garden, the wide bowl of white was pierced only by the spikes of gray trees, wide patches of evergreens, three tiny steeples, and the water tower that now had to contain one big ice cube.

The seat of the rickety chair creaked beneath my long coat. The snow at my feet was punctuated by the stems Mary had been cutting back that first day I'd met her. I stared at one next to my right foot. A thick trunk of a thing that probably had held up one of her sunflowers. You could tell how sharp had been the blade with which she'd clipped it down, the straight and severe cut now dotted with black spores of mildew. But she hadn't taken care of everything—still standing was one row of giant sunflowers down by the driveway. The heads had been left up for the birds, Mary Ziemba told me the time she walked me out to the car after I'd come over to meet Davy. She said winter was a rough time for everybody, not just people. And people were what I saw when I looked down at that row—two figures, in something dark or black, moving up the driveway and out of the trees. Whoever they were slowed their pace, like they didn't expect there to be a house up here, or, if they did, they didn't think anybody would be seated out in front of it, on a chair stuck in the middle of a snowy garden. I worked to make them out. I squinted through the thick stems. That's when they spotted me as a stranger, I could tell. I stood up fully and saw they were the two backpackers I'd passed earlier walking on the side of the road. The taller one followed my tracks up the gravel path and to the big front door. He took the right and came up to me in the wicker chair, like he knew where he was going. Which I found out he did.

• • •

When you are a member of a family, a living and breathing member who does indeed exist even though nobody—even legal representation—is aware that you are on the planet, these are the type of things you know: That even rich bigshots hide keys to the back door. That this particular one had kept hers on a small hook behind the first shutter on the third window over. That the alarm code is a sequence of numbers that takes four star-shaped taps to the keyboard and then one to the square marked "ENTER." That any mail or packages or big flat boxes you find inside the door you place on the dining room table for checking out later. That the thermostat for the kitchen is over near the pantry. That a guest you stumble across sitting on a rotting chair in the front yard should be welcomed inside and shown to the little table at the far end of the small and narrow kitchen. That the Taster's Choice instant and the Salada box are in the white cabinet to the right of the white stove. That the green teapot is under the quilted cozy next to them. That it's chipped, so when you fill it, turn the damage to your own side of the table.

With the fascination that the first audiences of moving pictures must have known, I stared during all this, the opening and closing of doors and packets and lids and taps, the removal of the knapsack with Greyhound check tags dangling from it like blossoms. My host dropped his big blue jacket on the floor next to the pack, and he sat on a stepstool to unlace and pull off the mukluks that had carried him this far. He opened a small closet door that revealed several brooms and hooks hung with aprons, and he stuck his hand in the bottom of it and came out with a pair of old running shoes that were already laced and that he pulled on easily like they were bedroom slippers. "Okay," is what he then said as he gave each foot a shake. It was the only word he'd spoken since he'd come up to the garden and asked if he could help me and I'd answered that I'd visited Mary Ziemba a couple of times here. "My name is Tim," is what he had answered. "Come on in."

Lots of people you meet after not seeing them for forever, you might tell them how they still look the same. Even if they don't. But with Tim it was true. I know I'd only seen him in photos, but he was pretty much the Tim that Mary Ziemba had been glowing about. Still short, though I shouldn't make too much of that because he was actually just my height—maybe just a little less—and I don't think of myself as smaller than most people. But for a guy, I guess he was. He wore a version of the same haircut he had in the pictures, but now the bangs were different—straighter—and the whole style was fitted closer to his head, so he looked more like Caesar than like the kid on the paint can. Even though he was in the middle of his thirties, he appeared to be still able to fit into the high school number six uniform, if the reason ever arose.

Tim stood at the stove watching the water boil. I felt the awkwardness of being strangers alone together, even though I knew a lot more about him than he could have guessed right then. I had to say something. I wanted so badly to ask where he had been when his mother died a month back. But it was too early in all this, so I only stated the obvious: "You're just coming home."

He pressed down on the handle of the kettle and the water inside roared from the contact with the coils. Letting it go, he said, "That's right," just a notch above the level at which I would have had to ask him to repeat himself. He got a couple of mugs from the little tree of them and brought over the kettle and the pot and the tea and the coffee and then took what I knew as Mary's seat. He leaned back to zero in on the exact drawer where he could find a pair of spoons. Then he was across from me. Not in a stack of photos. But in the flesh. Tim lived. I wasn't crazy. And neither had been Mary Ziemba.

We stirred our cups in unison. I'd noticed how he put two heaping teaspoons of the coffee crystals into his cup, one more than I think the instructions say is necessary. He'd skipped the sugar and didn't touch the brand-new bottle of Cremora that he'd pulled from the spice drawer and put on the center of the table, which was when I noticed the watch on his left wrist, a black plastic thing with all sorts of buttons and dials that gave the impression he had a lot more than just the hour to keep track of. After the spoon noise stopped, there was no sound at all in the room. I wanted to move the big clock in from the dining room just to fill up some of the vacant space. I heard myself saying, "I was very sorry to hear about your mother."

And Tim looked up and asked quickly, "What about her?"

He didn't know. My heart began to tap out all sorts of SOS codes at the prospect of breaking the news. Not since the phone call about Chuckie had I been in that position, to be able to completely devastate somebody by saying just three or four little words. From the man who'd phoned about my brother, and from TV hospital shows, where people expired on a regular basis, I knew that it was best to first ask the survivors to sit down before announcing any bad stuff. Tim was already in a chair, so there would be no more stalling. But then he spared me the chore, pushing out his hand and saying politely, "Hey, no, don't tell me. I don't care. It's none of my concern."

I was sure he would feel differently if he knew the truth. Wasn't he wondering where Mary Ziemba was, why everything was locked up and dark, why the icebox was empty and turned off and wiped spotless inside and its doors were swung open like it was on sale back in the showroom?

"But . . ."

"But I'm sorry. I hope I didn't sound rude. You don't know me. Maybe you know my mother, and her problems. But they're her problems, and I've pretty much distanced myself from her since I was a teenager. It was either do that, or end up just like her."

I looked out at the pool, its blue cover now hidden under the snow. I could sooner dive through it than I could make sense of what was being said here. What problems did Mary have? Except for the sick—then dead—part, why would you not want to end up like her, big success and a nice person loved by so many that attendance records had been set at Wazocha's? Were the problems the reason why Mary had focused on Tim's high school years in the photos she'd shown me—not because she was proud of his accomplishments then, but because it was the last time they'd really gotten on well? Across from me, her son was watching me think all this.

"I have to tell you," I said, and was starting on my next word when he ran it over.

"The only thing I want anybody telling me right now," Tim said, leaning toward me, and he was all intense like somebody who has a lot churning inside, "is how I can someday do for somebody else what Mary did for me."

"And that is . . ."

"Save a life."

"Your mother saved your life?"

Tim looked at me like I had fine print on my face and he was caught without the glasses he needed to make it out. He shook his head.

"No, no," he said. "My mother screwed up my life. Mary Ziemba came along and saved it."

They were two different people. The woman who had given birth, and little more, to Tim Roque. And the woman who had given him a chance to make it beyond age thirteen, which was about the expected lifespan for somebody existing as he was at that time, having run from an abusive household right into the blackest circles he was able to find. Drinking and drugs and sex and crime and violence, behavior that at that age I was only mildly aware of from watching the stories of troubled teens on the ABC Afterschool Specials. Tim's mother told the cops they had the wrong number when they called to say that her son, never reported by anyone as missing even though he'd run off half a week before, had been discovered beaten and positioned perfectly across the railroad tracks behind the Basketball Hall of Fame. When he recovered and became a ward of the state, Tim officially was branded a CHIN, a child in need of services. Luckily, he was awful enough a kid to fit exactly into the high-risk youth rehabilitation program that Mary Ziemba and Grand Z were funding down at the jail simply because nobody in the public sector was interested.

"I wouldn't want to have met me back then," Tim said. "That's the long and short of it. I work with really tough kids now, and the times when I suddenly see my old self in them, it chills me. I got a chance when nobody else cared if I lived or died. Nobody except this lady old enough to have been my grandmother."

Mary Ziemba had done this. On a press tour of the high-risk program she spotted Tim slumped at a desk and staring out the window with eyes that had next to nothing left in them. She asked him what he wanted, and in an answer crawling with profanities he told her he wanted out. "Okay," Mary answered, and that's where she took him when she left that afternoon. Out, and into produce, where he'd go on to work three hours a day, wearing a light green polyester blazer with his name embroidered on the breast pocket. A supervisor supervised, and Mary watched both of them from the mirror window upstairs. She went downstairs and thanked Tim for his help and his good work every afternoon just before the van came to take him back to the center. At every turn, she pried more conversation out of him. She pestered him about his homework. When he graduated from the program and was enrolled in high school, she sent him a congratulatory card he still keeps on his person, folded thin and worn. "I am proud of you," she wrote, making herself the first person ever to say such a thing to him. She encouraged his baseball ambitions. When he made the team and brought her the uniform to show off, she cried right there in the office, in front of her secretary and some man from advertising, and she embarrassed Tim but good even though there was something about the whole scene that very much pleased him when he later reflected on it.

He became part of a foster family located near the woods on Route 9 where the hermit used to live, but he spent a lot of time at Mary Ziemba's, on the weekends biking a good fifteen miles to work in the garden with her. Sometimes she would tell him her stories, something harmless about being a kid back then in the old country, and he would give one of his, something disturbing about being one in the here and now. A good part of the time there would be no words as, over the seasons, they turned the soil, planted, tended, weeded, watered, harvested, pulled out the dead plants, and covered the beds for the well-deserved sleep of winter.

They clicked. "I'm not exaggerating," Tim told me. "First time I saw Mary, I could tell she knew what it was like to have nobody. Don't know why, I just did."

I said I'd seen the picture. Of the jersey. The day he got it.

"She told me," I said, happy to have something to contribute. "She told me about Roy White. The statistics. He was little, you were little. She only cared about him because you did. She could stand like he did when he batted; it was only a couple of months ago that she showed me. Right in there [I pointed to the dining room]. Knock-kneed. Bat on the hip, nearly. Whoosh."

Tim smiled at the table like it contained a screen showing him a film of what I was narrating.

"It was nice," I said, "how I could see what she thought of you, from telling me all that. She called you son, you know. A lot. She called you her son. So much that I thought you were. For real, I mean. I don't mean that, I mean, you know—biological." I looked to see if I'd offended him, but I couldn't tell.

All he said was, "What I've come to see is, biological doesn't have anything to do with it. It didn't with us. It doesn't with him." Here he pointed to the figure out the window, his walking companion, the smaller, slighter one who'd disappeared when Tim had come over to me in the garden. At the top of the rise above the pool, this person was forming large snowballs to push down the hill and watch grow in size during the trip. "That's my son," Tim said, underlining the middle word. "As much as he'll ever be. But I didn't meet him until last February. Everything goes right, it'll be legal by this February. But the papers don't matter. He's my son."

Tim lived in Arizona, tending to really bad end-of-the-line kids in a program that dragged groups of them out into the desert for weeks at a time, which is where he had been when

Mary died. He took them whether they wanted to go or not, and taught them life-or-death teamwork and self-reliance and confidence. Kind of like the adventure vacation Claire O'Hare once took up in Maine, paying a thousand dollars to be dumped on a deserted island for five days and four nights with only something like a length of fishing line and a hook and a blanket and a gallon of fresh water. She was finishing her bedroom floor when she told me about this. Working on the middle of it reminded her how she'd stayed on that island in the middle of the ocean—or at least that's how it had seemed to her way out there, even though at night she could see the lights from a generator-powered cottage on the next island, and after that the Portland Headlight beaming and its low hum of a warning timed as sure and expected as your heartbeat. "I'd never been so cold or lonely or scared," Claire said, and then she stood up tall to add, "or proud of myself." But the participants on Tim's trips weren't there willingly. Santo hadn't saved his money and vacation time for years just to be tested like that. He was just another lost boy that nobody was going to bother to go looking for.

"He's never seen snow close up," Tim said. "In pictures, on the tops of the mountains far away. But not in his hand. When we got off the bus, it was snowing. He couldn't wait to touch it."

Now on the hill, Santo was running and laughing loud. He threw snowballs at the trees, and as the reward, the boughs gave up their layers of snow when he hit his target. Tim enjoyed watching all of it. It was Heather grabbing for things all over again. Tim was Alice and he could have sat there for hours.

"I'm sorry about Mary," I said. "That's what I meant, that I was sorry about your mother. Meaning I thought that was Mary. The way she talked, when I saw the obituary, and it said there was no family, I thought there had to be a mistake. She always made it sound like she had loads of family. Well, certainly a lot more than none at all—again, biological, of course."

The sun had gone down during our talking. I felt like somebody coming out of a movie matinee, having gone in while it was still light, emerging afterwards into the dark. Tim seemed to have had enough talking. He was up and flipping on lights, looking in the cupboards. "Mary had a family, all right," he said without turning to me. "Just maybe not the kind everybody is used to."

I watched how he navigated the shelves, knowing the homes of the different kinds of canned goods. His back left pocket had suffered a rip and somebody had sewn it back up, with blue thread that almost, but not exactly, matched the color of the denim. I wondered if Tim sewed. I think they now teach it to boys in home ec, but not in my day. Tim was pretty much from my day, only now that I'd been told how he'd grown up out by the hermit, I knew he'd gone to school in Ware, one town over. Which is why our paths had never crossed except for maybe walking through the same gate for the annual football rivalry, if he ever attended that. Now he was bringing down a bunch of ingredients and then bending to get out a large pot from behind a stack of smaller ones, which was where he just knew it would be.

"You're staying here," I said more than asked. "Tonight you're staying here?"

"We're staying here," Tim said. "For good." He turned from the utensil drawer, ladle in one hand. "Mary. Her lawyer finally tracked me down. She left me the house."

A big happiness fired up in me on his behalf. It made sense, that this place would go to somebody who loved it and would care for it. And I told him that much. That it was good that it was him, not just some status-seeking person who wanted to lay claim, asking the realtor, "Just show me the best place in town. Skip all the others. Because I'm not interested in anything less."

"That's perfect," I said.

He nodded and smiled a little. "I sometimes feel funny about it, but then other times I don't. I never really had what I considered a home—before I met Mary. After that when I thought of the word, this place was the picture I had in my head. Not so much what it looked like, the style or its size, but what I found here."

He slowly listed those things: safety, food, quiet, nature, harmless ways to pass the time, somebody who cared. None of them were too much to ask for, as I saw it.

"He's only now getting used to having those things on some sort of regular basis," Tim said, pointing out the window. "There's no guarantee how anybody's life will go, but I'm thinking that here, this place, would be good. For both of us."

I watched him get out three bowls and open a drawer for spoons. I stood up.

"Thanks, but you don't need to fix me anything—I'm not staying. I just came to return something."

I walked over to the dining room door and found the light switch. Tim followed. I pointed to the box, the big cardboard one with the small indigo stampings of planets. The one Wally had handed me the day after that long night last month when I was told I was supposed to take the painting back home, that I would know what to do with it. Until now, I hadn't. Sure, I'd come up here to dump it off, but back then—back an hour or so ago—I didn't care where it was going to end up. Now I knew exactly where I wanted it to go. And I was confident about that. I said to Tim, "Here. It's for you."

He pointed at the box to make sure that's what I was talking about. "From who?"

"It's, well, I guess it's from Mary."

Tim touched the cardboard with a finger.

"Mary—she commissioned me to paint it. I'm an artist. She wanted this done, but she never got to see it. The lawyer, he said I was to do with it what I saw fit. Right now, I see that this is where it fits best."

I took my car keys out and ran one along to slit the masking tape Wally'd secured the box with. I opened the flap and slid out the bubble-wrapped portrait. I pulled the tape off that, and revealed Mary's family, as I knew it.

Tim stood as still as he was depicted there in his place seated on the ground below Mary and Michal. Then he put his hands on the edge of the table and leaned in close to get a good look. At his aunt. At his uncle. At his grandfather. At his father. At his mother.

I could tell he was one of those many guys undecided about how to exactly dispose of their feelings. He ran them through his hair. He breathed them out loudly through his nose. He tapped them into the floor with the toe of his sneaker. He held them tight across his chest with folded arms. He squinted to keep them from pouring out of his eyes and down onto the glass. I wanted to pat him on the shoulder to comfort him regarding whatever was bothering him, but I didn't know him except for that one hour or two. So I turned away and let him do his looking on his own.

When I did speak, I explained what Mary had wanted me to do. It was never going to happen in reality, so she had to ask somebody like me for help. To show everybody happy, and around her, for this one time. For everybody to see.

I told him of the many others who had gotten the opportunity. The crowds who lined up to pay their final respects and, in doing that, also got to view Mary with her family. The one nobody thought she had. Because most people consider there must be a certain type of a ceremony to make two people spouses. That a sibling is somebody with whom you share a father or mother, a bedroom, a childhood. That a son is yours if you raise him from the first day, or if not that, then it's best that you get custody of him from when he is so young you might be able to get away with never explaining the circumstances that brought him to you. I now was seeing more clearly than ever that Mary wasn't most people. She hadn't gone to school, but if she had, hers would have been the one that said if you don't have anybody to call your own, you can get somebody— maybe somebody who once had their own people and lost them, or got tossed out by them, or simply and plainly didn't like them, and who is more than willing to be taken on by another. What makes up a family, Mary was asking anybody who looked at the painted content of her life. Genetics? Shared housing? Paperwork? Or the love, understanding, support, laughter, and presence of someone you know for the rest of your life after one long afternoon getting stuck in line with them at the Registry of Motor Vehicles? Sure it's confusing, like a ball you've grown by tying together different lengths of string, yarn, rope, or the pieces of thread that you pick off the arm of your coat. You can unwind it and in that way find the ties that connect, the places where everything is joined. But why bother? Does it really matter? It's still one, continuous thing.

"You have a family?" Tim was asking this in a quiet voice. He didn't look at me when he spoke. The painting still held him.

I nodded, even though he couldn't see me. "I have a family," I said. I called them up in my head. Those with the same last name, and the rest that I'd picked up along the way. And I heard Little Ted saying that anything can be anything you want, if you really want it to be. To him over there overseas, I answered with this one word: "Bullseye."

The back door opened. Soaking wet, another boy, one as dark-skinned as Little Ted was light, entered and smiled so wide you could have counted his entire set of teeth.

"Dad!" was what he shouted. "Did you see me out there? Dad?"

15

A few nights later, the one of the day I turned forty, we all went out to supper at a new place that every week inserted a fluorescent green sheet of specials into the paper and invited diners to stop by on their birthdays for a free meal complete with beverage and dessert. Once I produced my driver's license and my eligibility was confirmed and I finished my entire eggplant parmesan and tossed salad and the rolls covered by a napkin to keep them warm, and after I blew out the fat white question mark–shaped candle jammed into the fudge-covered brownie with the glob of vanilla ice cream melting into the side of it, I was led by our waitress over to a big golden throne where against my quiet protests I was forced to have my picture snapped with a crown on my head and a red cape around my shoulders. All this so they could later tack me up on a wall meant to show diners just how many people chose to mark their big day at this very restaurant.

"Hang on a second," said the waitress, a woman who cocked her head to the left the entire time we were there so maybe it was a physical ailment rather than the annoying habit I first thought it to be. "What kind of place would this be if we let you leave without giving you a birthday present?"

She brought out a small stack of flat gold boxes and confided they contained gift certificates offered only on special occasions like the one I was marking. She fanned them out neatly in her hand, the seven or eight of them all unmarked and mysterious at that point. I closed my eyes and brought my finger down on one, pulled it away from her and went back to the table to show off the contents.

"Ahhh," everyone there said. And, "You'll make great use of that," and, "It's perfect for you."

Then they said to me, "What do you want to do now?"

I took the moment to think, and to look. Straight ahead, and to my left, and to my right.

And I, the birthday person, who this night could have anything she desired, said, "I want to go home and paint."

So I did.

I opened the door and flipped on the light and went over and pushed up the thermostat. I threw my bag on the phone chair, then stood there to unbutton my coat. On the wall in front of me, my family as they looked and were thirty years before stared back at me, just as they'd been doing since my father banged the nail and hung the painting there to remind me of who I have. Some people are not as lucky as to have even one person who cares. I looked right then, as I had that first day, at the portrait that had started out as a picture of my mother and that had gone on to become more. My father's head to the right of hers, Louise's and Chuckie's above. Me down below, next to the house that once contained all of us. The essential wreath of people who were my family, who made each of us who we were now. Now most of them gone off to one place or another.

I can make anything you want. Or anything that I want. So for my fortieth birthday, I make myself a painting. Of what I saw at the restaurant table that very night. Not anything near a replacement for what is already on that wall, but maybe some kind of update. The people who were around the table tonight, singing to me the birthday song and asking me to tell them the wish I made even though they knew good and well that I wouldn't because then there would be was no chance it would come true. The faces of those who, in the here and the now, make me feel at home.

I start the circle. I draw Unc in his one suit coat that I think he also wore on the day I made my First Communion. I put Phyllis' head to the right of his, the little spiraling ringlet curls hanging in front of each ear like Christmas ornaments. Below that, Alice in the red turtleneck I gave her for her birthday two days before, leaning into Leo, his hair even combed for the night, their heads tilted in together like they did a lot, as if their bodies were joined at that point. Then Heather, proud of the beaded choker she made one afternoon in the phone chair, out of the kit I got her years back, when she didn't realize or care that she might have the ability to make cool things. Then I draw Claire O'Hare, all in black, who spent the night telling Heather of the many great opportunities that might lie ahead for her, even though to someone at such a young age she can't give too many specifics. But if it's art she's got any interest in, the options are practically limitless. Just ask Lily, is what she tells her. Next I draw Wally in a white shirt with no collar like back in the Wild West, enjoying a night off with his phone on forward to Moondog and his words sincere as I tell him I am happy and he says that he knows how I feel. Then I draw Tim, who was on the other side of me, Santo to his left, the two of them still in their overcoats because even though its nice to goof around outside, truth is they have been freezing since they got here. Both are shyly friendly and appearing generally grateful to be invited out to meet some people in the town that will be their new home. I fill up the paper. White space must be left for the sake of balance, but it also must be left to acknowledge those I don't include. Who might have made it into this scene, but for whatever reason, aren't here. In Florida, in showbiz, in Europe, in heaven. One space I fill in last, in the center, where I draw myself. I am Mary, who knows and appreciates the people around her. I am Flossie, starting out my life's adventure. I am Davy, tall and proud to be next to the rest of these people. I am Tim, who makes mistakes but gets things in order. I am Michal, with the choices of where I can go, backwards or forwards. I am Alexsander, just happy to be here. Whoever I am, I am tired of feeling stuck.

What I know, if Heather asks me as Claire O'Hare suggested she do, is that my life itself has been a box. One thing to most people who saw it, something else to me, who got the best look inside, who got to shake it, to open it, to guess that all the many pieces inside might connect together to make something way beyond any imaginings.

Something you'd want to seal and protect. So another trip to The Craft Planet is in order.

I arrived there on the midnight of my birthday day, to use the gift certificate the restaurant gave me for twenty-five dollars off anything there—the paints you can apply to your windows to simulate stained glass, the blocks of wax waiting to be taken home and melted into scented votives, the kind of clay you can fire in a kitchen oven and the accompanying glazes that the label swears are guaranteed not to poison.

If you, rather than me, had opened the box that night thirty years before, it would be your name, not mine, that would come so joltingly from the public address system, as it did when somebody from framing spoke into the microphone and told the world:

"Lily Wilk, your painting is ready."

That is it, the all of it, the whole entire thing, the longest and the most detailed version of the reply I give people when they ask me when and why and how I got started in all this.

The short answer is that I am an artist.

Because that is what the instructions told me. "Artist" is the title under the line of lily of the valley flowers under my name on the pale-green business cards that I hand out. It is what that same card, enlarged fifty percent, tells readers who spot the ad I run every other week. It is what my friends and relations go around telling everybody I am. It is what I tell myself, out loud, when this morning I take the time to realize and appreciate the things I can do. And now, thanks to Mary Ziemba, and to Tim Roque's kindly pointing out that he was now the one paying the bills and was there anything I was owed, that is whatever I want.

I have to say I resisted at first. I even said the words "No charge" when he asked me if the painting was paid for. There are some jobs you feel odd taking money for. The ones that, when you sit down and are very honest, you know you shouldn't be getting a red cent for: those you did not give as much attention or spirit to as you should have, the ones you made ten attempts to do perfectly and still ended up with nothing you wanted to put your name on, the pieces that were for someone else but that ended up meaning almost more to you because of what you got out of the whole experience of creating them. When I sat down and was honest, I knew that my part in making the family that Mary had put together in the first place fell into that last category. But Tim once sewed moccasins

271

to sell to tourists, because it is true that people on vacation have money to burn and they'll buy anything you can come up with, and he knows what it's like to try to earn a living making things most people don't see as vital. He said Mary had been a generous woman, and in her memory he insisted on giving me a check. A good-sized one. He even went ahead and estimated my expenses for one entire year so that I could enjoy a good long stretch with nothing to do but paint and draw the things that I alone want to paint and draw. Without a single worry as to will they ever sell or am I just wasting my time. And that's why this morning, the first real one of a new year for me, Heather and I, our work up on easels like you see in commercials, we are people painting outside, in front of Tim and Santo Roque's house.

From here, the valley I just left minutes ago, the one where I live somewhere to the left of the stone steeple, is begging to become my subject. My favorite part of painting is how the colors run into one another. And ones you'd never imagine would look good together pool and blend and flow and create whole new shades. It's always a surprise and it's always amazing. You never know what something can do until you put something else next to it, how they might turn out to look like they were made for each other. Sometimes things you stumble across end up being just that.

Behind me are the artists in Mary Ziemba's careful collection, the one I got to see the night I met Tim and Santo. Just before I left them, we all went into the long, white-walled room just beyond the one for dining, and we stood on the receiving end of Cassatt's sun-dappled children, and the calm, golden sea of Homer, and the rounded lines in the elder Wyeth's pencil sketch of the big man's head, and the exact brushstrokes in the barn roof by his son, and the rain that further darkened the black-and-white city street Stieglitz exposed for one sixtieth of a second, and the staggering wealth of colors O'Keeffe managed to find in the tiny overlapping of one pinkish white petal shading another. And, in its own space under a perfectly positioned pair of spotlights, my painting of the six relatives all in their prime, whenever that was. For one of them, that is right now.

I hear all their voices as I look out onto the valley and pick up my brush, and they encourage me as proudly if we were related.

"Go on," they say. "It's your turn. Make whatever you want."

So I do.

Lily of the Valley

Suzanne Strempek Shea

A Readers Club Guide

ABOUT THIS GUIDE

The following questions and author interview are intended
to help you find interesting and rewarding approaches to
your reading of Suzanne Strempek Shea's *Lily of the Valley*.
We hope this guide enriches your enjoyment and
appreciation of the book.

Many fine books from Washington Square Press
feature Readers Club Guides. For a complete listing,
or to read the Guides online, visit

http://www.simonsays.com/reading/guides

An interview with Suzanne Strempek Shea

Q: As a novelist, how did you prepare to write in the voice of a painter? Are you a painter as well? What parallels and differences do you see between writing and painting?

A: I have an art background, so there was no great research necessary. I was raised in a very creative family, and always was encouraged to try my hand at whatever craft or art that interested me. I have a bachelor's degree in photography from the Portland School of Art (now the Maine College of Art), but always have enjoyed painting, especially watercolors. I think that studying visual art had a great effect on my writing skills. The questions you ask when preparing to make a photograph, or a drawing, or a sculpture are the same you ask when you write a short story or newspaper article or novel: What's the point here? What's important? What caught my interest in the subject, and what do I want to say about it? How do I make this thing the best I can?

Q: You write very powerfully about family in all of your novels. What is the role of family in *Lily of the Valley*?

A: In this story, family doesn't so much have a role as it is the story itself: Mary's family, and the importance of each member as she looks back on her life; Lily's family, still a work in progress. Two women, 40 years apart in age, asking and answering the questions of who we consider "family," and how do they earn that honored term?

Q: Lily's great dream is to have the luxury of making art for art's sake, without having to worry about money. In your own life as a writer, have you ever had to contend with the conflict between the work that's important to you and the work that pays the bills?

A: I always loved being a reporter—every day was something new, a real education, a public service that could also be a living. In the 15 years I worked for newspapers, I always felt I had the coolest job. So it wasn't like I was doing that work, and in my spare time doing what I really loved. It was only after the publication of my first novel, *Selling the Lite of Heaven*, and all the thrilling experiences that followed, that I got the bug to try to write fiction for a living. I began to write my second novel and to hope for an advance that would allow me to devote my workday to fiction, to give that writing the best try that I could, and to see where it would lead. I'm happy to say that all that has and is taking place, and I'm making the most of my time and my good fortune.

Q: Were you influenced by any specific literary works when writing *Lily of the Valley*?

A: Not so much by a specific book, but by a collection of artists whose great creativity, and the huge part that plays in their lives, fueled me as I wrote *Lily of the Valley*. These include writers, my husband Tommy Shea, my mentor Elinor Lipman, and my friend Tanya Barrientos, as well as a painter, New England watercolorist Susan Tilton Pecora, and a rock band, The Saw Doctors of County Galway, Ireland. Read, look at, and listen to their work, and you can't help but want to see what you yourself are able to do—and to try to do that the best you can.

For Discussion

1. In *Lily of the Valley*, Suzanne Strempek Shea invites us to see the world through the eyes of Lily Wilk, a painter. In what ways does Shea, a literary artist, reflect her narrator's unique perspective as a visual artist?

2. What methods does Shea use to 'paint' the novel's big picture? Consider the manner in which Lily slowly unpacks her story through separate scenes—her attention to detail, her eye for color, and her tendency to present each scene as a distinct, fully realized portrait.

3. In a sense, people pay Lily to use her art to create illusions—illusions of happiness, illusions of security and, of course, illusions of family. What are some specific examples of Lily's role as illusionist in *Lily of the Valley*? Does Lily harbor any illusions about her own life?

4. Beginning with Lily's early portrait of the Holy Family for her mother's kitchen, Catholicism plays a significant role in Lily's life. How does Lily's sense of spirituality inform her work? Her sense of family? Her relationships?

5. Each of Mary Ziemba's photographs triggers in Lily an extended memory of someone in her own life. Through this unique structure, Shea allows us to gradually piece together Lily's personal history one memory at a time. Just as Lily paints Mary's family portrait from individual photographs, the reader comes to perceive Lily's entire life through a series of distinct memories. Why do you suppose Shea wrote her novel this way? Identify each of the members in Mary's "family," and then discuss their counterparts in Lily's life.

6. Discuss Lily's relationship with her sister, Louise. On one hand, Lily seems bewildered by her sister's elaborately conceived new life as "Lu Wi." On the other, Lily intimates that in some ways she understands and even envies her sister's drive to escape her childhood identity. Compare and contrast the choices each sister has made. From what Lily tells us, how do you think Louise came to take this path in life? Who would you guess is the happier woman? Why?

7. By introducing us to Mary Ziemba strictly through Lily's perspective, *Lily of the Valley* encourages readers to consider and speculate about an elderly woman's life through the lens of a much younger woman. What parallels can be drawn between the two women's experiences?

8. Imagine if the novel were narrated by Mary instead of Lily. Reconstruct the narrative and quickly outline the plot of this alternate novel. What might we learn about Mary's ambiguous life, her surrogate family, and her decision to hire Lily?

9. Lily recalls how her father once protected the family from "the scary and uncontrollable world outside" by uprooting the "For Sale" sign in the lot next to the Wilks' home. How does this memory of her father as a fierce guardian against change inform Lily's reaction when her parents suddenly move to Florida? Does Lily fear change? What has change represented at various points in her life?

10. What is the nature of Lily's relationship with Claire O'Hare, "certified career counselor," as well as with Wally Wazocha, owner of the valley's funeral parlor?

11. Although he's already disappeared from Lily's life at the beginning of the story, Jack Murphy is perhaps the most powerful presence in *Lily of the Valley*. What do you think of Jack? Can his leaving Lily possibly be justified? Play the devil's advocate, and imagine how the novel would unfold differently if Jack and Little Ted had remained in Lily's life during her experiences with Mary Ziemba. Would Lily have made the same discoveries about her life? Explain.

12. At the end of the novel, Lily tells us, "There are some jobs you feel odd taking money for." What does she mean? In what ways is Lily richer from the experience of painting Mary's family portrait?

About the Author

Suzanne Strempek Shea, a former reporter for the *Springfield* (MA) *Union-News* and the *Providence* (RI) *Journal*, is the author of the highly acclaimed novels *Selling the Lite of Heaven* and *Hoopi Shoopi Donna*. A freelance writer whose work has appeared in *Yankee* magazine, *The Boston Globe Magazine*, and *The Philadelphia Inquirer*, she lives in Bondsville, Massachusetts, with her husband Tommy, a columnist for the *Union-News*.

Also by Suzanne Strempek Shea

Selling the Lite of Heaven	0-671-79865-0	$10.00/$14.75 Can.
Hoopi Shoopi Donna	0-671-53545-5	$14.00/$21.00 Can.
Lily of the Valley (hardcover edition)	0-671-02710-7	$22.00/$32.50 Can.

Available from Washington Square Press

Visit our website at: www.SimonSays.com/reading/guides/
E-mail Suzanne Strempek Shea at: Heavenmail@aol.com